SPIRIT OF THE DYING FLOWER

C.A. VARIAN

Contents

Content Warnings

Content Note:

This book contains explicit scenes, supernatural themes, & emotional subject matter including death and grief.

CHAPTER I

The Keeper

"Rent is due on the first of every month."

Anne, my realtor, delivered the line like she'd recited it a hundred times. Her tone was flat, practiced, every word carved down to its barest utility. She stirred her coffee once, then again, before letting the spoon fall with a soft clatter against the ceramic.

I tried to follow the rest of what she said—trash pick-up, lawn height, a list of cliffside expectations, but my mind drifted. Not from boredom. From something older. That quiet ache that comes after too many goodbyes. I'd grown used to silence, but it had never really fit.

I hadn't come to Crystal Peak searching for peace. I wasn't foolish enough for that. What I needed was stillness, a place where the noise in my head might loosen, come apart, and float away.

We sat tucked in a corner booth beneath a humming pendant lamp that cast more shadow than light. Outside, the windows were streaked with condensation, fogging the world beyond until it looked half-formed. Gulls cried into the mist, their voices warped and lonely. Somewhere past the haze, the sea waited. It didn't demand attention. It simply was vast and tireless.

Coffee and rain saturated the café air, soaked deep into old wood and sagging window frames. The scent had permanence, like it belonged more to memory than the present.

Creases hugged the elbows of Anne's blazer. Her bun was too tight—functional, not stylish. She tapped a line on the lease with her short and squared fingernail, slicing through the moment like a scalpel.

"Will the homeowner collect the rent from me directly, or is there somewhere I should leave it?" I asked, trying for casualness, though her brusqueness had started to unsettle something in me.

She glanced at the window, as if checking for something behind the fog. "She keeps to herself. You won't be interacting. Aside from the shared laundry, which she uses on a strict schedule, you shouldn't cross paths."

She took a sip of her coffee. A pause followed. Then the cup hit the table harder than necessary. "Rent should be dropped off at my office."

My brow lifted. "She owns the place… but I'm not supposed to speak to her?"

"She doesn't like strangers."

Her fingers hovered at the rim of her cup, like she wasn't sure whether to lift it again. "Just follow the rules, Mr. Hale. That house has its routines. Best not to disrupt them."

I waited, but she didn't meet my eyes. Something about the way she avoided my gaze stuck with me. It wasn't just disinterest. It felt like guilt, or fear, or maybe just a reluctance to speak the truth out loud. I didn't know *what* truth, but it pulsed there, quiet and insistent, just beneath the surface.

"I don't even know her name," she added after a moment, too lightly. Like it was supposed to be a throwaway comment. Like the words had been practiced, but still came out wrong.

That made me pause. "You don't know the property owner's name?"

"I've never met her," she said too quickly. "Everything was handled through a legal firm in Portland. I was hired to manage the place. It's all above board. If that's what you're worried about."

It wasn't. Or maybe it was. Ever since that flyer had drifted across the sidewalk and brushed my ankle like something sent by fate, I hadn't known what to make of it.

Crisp white paper. Typewritten font. Details that felt almost too precise, too exact to trust.

Studio apartment. Secluded estate. Ocean views. Rent low enough to raise suspicion.

Still, I called. Something in me needed to. Anne confirmed it was available.

And now, here I was. Pen in hand. Lease on the table. A tarnished skeleton key resting on a lace doily beside a chipped sugar jar.

The key didn't just look old. It felt aware in a way that unsettled me more. Not just heavy in my palm, but intentional, as if it had chosen me as much as I had chosen this place. Like it had seen every tenant come and go and had been waiting for me to arrive. Older than the town. Older than reason.

My name waited on the dotted line. I could walk away, go back to the overpriced inn with its rattling heater and a mattress shaped like regret, but I wouldn't. Even if it turned out to be a mistake, it would be mine, and I needed something to belong to again.

Maybe that was it. I wasn't chasing hope. Instead, I was fleeing emptiness.

Grief had hollowed me out six months ago. Since the funeral, I hadn't written. The cursor on the screen blinked like an open and pulsing wound. My father had never been gentle, but he believed in discipline. Show up. Sit down. Write, even if the words didn't come. I used to resent that. Now it felt like something to cling to.

My first novel had done better than expected. A small wildfire, enough to keep people watching. I didn't expect it to happen again. Lightning rarely struck in the same place twice. But still, editors waited. Readers too. Expectations piled quietly.

I tried to write. I opened the document and stared, willed something onto the page, but the voice I'd once trusted felt brittle, as if the story had drained from me completely. The words that used to flow like a river now felt like a dried-up streambed, and I was left with nothing but the echo of my own silence.

I called it grief, but whatever I buried ran deeper.

She had left before the funeral. Quietly. No big fight. Just a look across the kitchen in the dead of winter, and the shared understanding that whatever we had was no longer enough.

By the time I stood at my father's graveside, she was already gone, and I couldn't decide which loss cut deeper: the one I expected or the one that took me by surprise.

I needed quiet. Not isolation, just distance. A place where no one knew me, where no one asked about the next book, where survival didn't require performance. This house offered all three.

So, without further hesitation, I signed.

Anne didn't say thank you.

Without much more than a glance, she gathered the papers, slipped them into her leather folder, and then handed me the key. Her fingers brushed mine, cold like stone in winter, but she didn't so much as smile.

"Be sure to read the rules posted in the laundry room," she said, already rising. "And keep to your side of the property."

"Right," I muttered, sliding the key into my coat pocket. "Wouldn't want to bump into the resident ghost."

She didn't laugh.

The wind hit hard off the ocean as I stepped outside. It pulled at my coat, carrying the sharp bite of salt, pine, and something ancient, threaded with memory.

Leaving the café at my back, I got into the car and sat for a moment behind the wheel, the key heavy in my pocket now that the papers were signed. Fog pressed against the windshield, softening the world into silhouettes. The sea loomed close beyond the town, shaping everything with its silent pull.

It all felt strangely rehearsed, as if I had stepped into a life already lived, one waiting to repeat itself.

Above it all, the house waited. Cloaked in mist. Drenched in silence.

I hadn't seen it yet. Not in person. Just a few grainy photos. But even from a distance, it seemed to watch.

The road narrowed as I climbed, curving up the cliffs in deliberate spirals. No guardrails—just a strip of pavement clinging to stone. Fog threaded between the trees and stretched across the asphalt. Every few turns, the sea returned to view, steel gray and shifting, then vanished again behind pines.

I didn't need to see it. The sea was in everything here. It was under my skin, moving through the silence like blood in my veins.

The climb grew lonelier as the trees thinned, their silhouettes fading into a sky layered in deepening grays. The clouds pressed lower, uncertain, like they might break into sobs.

Then, without warning, the manor surfaced through the mist.

It didn't rise. It emerged, seemingly unearthed from the hillside. The roof was made of slate, and the stone was weathered. The beams framed it like a forgotten painting. It didn't welcome. It *loomed*—the kind of place that didn't ask permission to exist.

Gravel crunched under my tires as I pulled in, the sound echoing too clearly against the still air. The garden flanked the drive, overgrown, once tended, now surrendered.

Turning off the ignition, I stepped out into the chill of the night. Brittle stones shifted beneath my boots, and I got the feeling that there hadn't been many visitors there in years. My eyes followed the fog as it traced the steps as if to call me home.

And then I saw *her*.

High above, a window lit suddenly, its amber light shining behind sheer curtains. A pale and slight silhouette stood still, hair like moonlight falling around her shoulders. It caught the glow and shimmered like something half-imagined. She didn't move. Didn't reach for the window. Just stood there, quiet and present, a painting caught between breath and brushstroke.

Barely able to breathe, my pulse ticked faster, and a strange prickle touched the back of my neck. She was beautiful in a way that didn't feel safe. Not staged. Not artificial. Just quietly *wrong*.

Before I could make myself believe she was real, the curtain slipped shut, but the light stayed on. I didn't know who she was, but I knew she was the reason I had come.

The path to the apartment curved along the side of the manor, slipping beneath a low arch nearly choked with ivy, where moss softened the stones beneath my feet. The air had cooled further here, as if the shade of the house drew breath inward and held it. Above me, the main structure loomed. It was tall, but carried a weight to it, pressing against the sky instead of rising into it. Its windows were shuttered, its roof line jagged against the dimming light.

Tucked at the base of the house, the entrance was nearly hidden behind vines and stone. A plain wooden door was set low into the foundation, looking as though the earth itself had tried to reclaim it.

The entrance to my apartment offered no welcome, only secrecy. Perhaps a part of the manor it hadn't meant to keep, yet didn't know how to release.

This was where I would live, tucked beneath the house, inside its bones. The listing had called it a garden-level studio. In truth, it felt more like a crypt dressed in the trappings of a studio apartment, as if pretending to be something it had long forgotten how to be.

Shifting the box on my shoulder, I pulled the suitcase behind me. The key resisted in the lock, but then, with a click and a soft exhale of air, the door creaked open.

The scent met me first: cool stone, dry wood, and the faintest trace of lavender. It wasn't musty, just old. The kind of old that folds in on itself. Quiet, but not empty.

The stagnant air shifted, and in the absence of all other sound, I could almost hear the house thinking...*remembering*.

And I knew, with a chill that curled down my spine, it would not forget I had come.

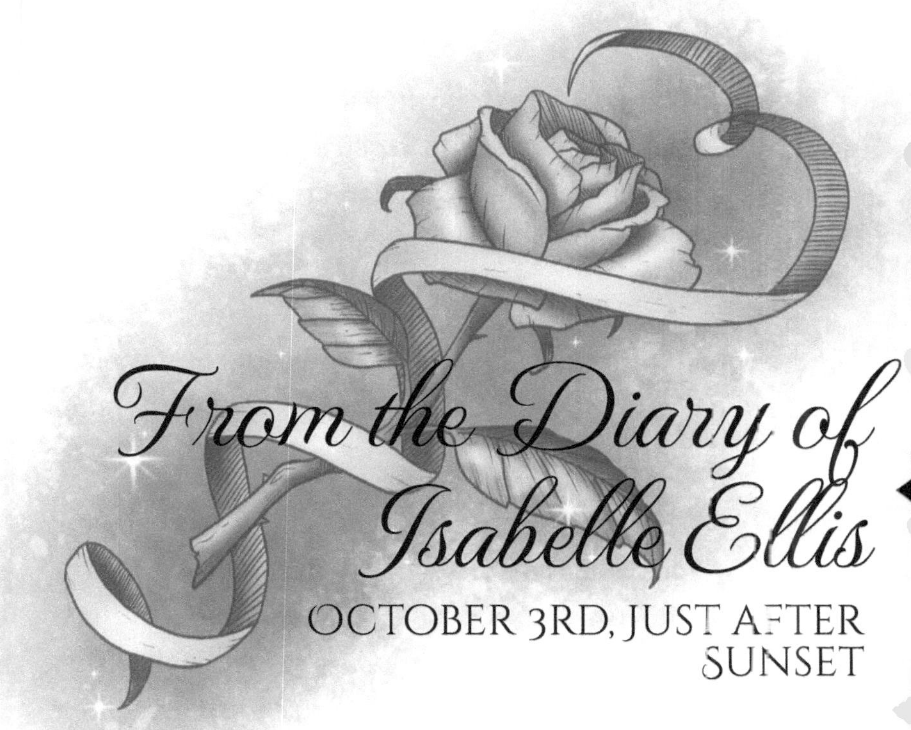

From the Diary of Isabelle Ellis

OCTOBER 3RD, JUST AFTER SUNSET

The wind sings through the cracks this evening, carrying the same hollow song it has held for decades. The curtains rise and fall like borrowed breaths. I have not lit the lamps. The house knows me better in the darkness.

My first breath clawed me back to life, raw and unwelcome. It always returns in that manner—a gasp, a shudder. Stillness lingers too deep to cast off. No warmth finds me until night fully settles in.

But tonight, the stillness broke.

Tires whispered against the gravel. A suitcase struck the earth. Through the parlor window, I glimpsed him, his shoulders hunched against the mist, his gaze lifted toward the house as though it might answer. I ought to have remained hidden, yet my hand stirred the curtain, just slightly, just enough. Whether he saw me, I cannot say. I pray he did not.

Yet, against all reason, something dangerous stirred within me—something the curse should have long since extinguished: hope.

I must not speak to him. The curse allows no second chances. It does not strike in fire or fury, but seeps, wears, erodes. All that draws near becomes undone. Kindness curdles into regret. Longing crumbles to ash. It punishes in silence, thinning its chosen threadbare until even hope forgets how to rise.

I have no freedom to offer. No life to share. Only disappointment. Only endings. And I have come to accept this.

He, too, will leave. He must.

And yet... I think I shall watch him for a while longer. Until the wind forgets his presence. Until I must forget it, too.

Love, Isabelle

CHAPTER 2

The Keeper

Morning unfolded across the sky in a washed-out slate, soft and heavy, indifferent in its quiet arrival. I woke slowly, uncertain about what had stirred me. The stillness in the apartment felt sharp and silent, almost expectant.

The bed creaked beneath me as I sat up. Sleep hadn't entirely left me. It lingered at the edges. I felt it in my shoulders, in the way my spine resisted motion. A hint of salt lingered in the linen, mixed with a faint trace of lavender, even though I didn't recall lighting anything scented. A chill hung in the corners of the room, subtle yet insistent.

Climbing out of bed, I moved through the space without urgency. It was the kind of morning where silence settled more as a presence than as a sound. Once the kettle clicked on, I measured and poured the coffee, but my new life had no rhythm yet. There was no comfort in the ritual, only motions repeated from memory.

Breakfast consisted of leftover noodles, eaten over the sink. The flavorless food lingered on my tongue, as if unsure it belonged.

No sound reached me from the house above. She hadn't paced. Only in its absence did I realize how much I had been listening for it. Last night, her footsteps had marked time. Now, only silence stretched above me, pregnant with the possibility of something or someone to give it shape.

For longer than I'd like to admit, I stood at the window with my coffee. The trees blurred into the fog. The sea and sky merged into a single smear of gray. Everything felt suspended.

I told myself to go into town, pick up groceries, walk through daylight, let the house breathe. But instead, I stood at the window and watched the sun drag its way up the sky, lost in contemplation.

Eventually, I rinsed the mug and found a pen. A grocery list formed on the back of a receipt: bread, eggs, fruit, something warm. I added tea, even though I had plenty of it, feeling a sense of connection to the routine.

With nothing else to anchor me, I pulled on my coat. It still held the stiffness of something unused, still unfamiliar with the shape of me. Outside, the path was laced with mist, and the wind carried fine threads of salt. Gravel shifted beneath my boots as I made my way to the car. I didn't look over my shoulder, but I still felt the house behind me, its gaze looming as I disappeared into the light of day.

The road into Crystal Peak curved downward in slow arcs. Trees enclosed the path on both sides, offering brief glimpses of the sea through narrow openings between them. The windshield wipers moved with the mist, making slow, resigned sweeps that cleared little, but I didn't need much. The road felt less like a route and more like instinct, a quiet descent from fog into fog.

In daylight, the town looked different. It was brighter, and the shadows softened. Buildings leaned into the wind, their paint dulled by decades of salty air. Storefronts appeared in soft succession: a hardware store, a bakery with its curtains drawn, and a florist spilling with pale blooms. A butcher shop and a shoe store shared a building; their signs tilted slightly from age. The street felt old in that particular way some places do—not forgotten, but content to be left alone.

A man swept the sidewalk while a woman unlocked a door, paper bags balanced against her hip. They moved like people who belonged here, quiet in their purpose, never once looking up.

I parked across from a narrow market, its windows fogged around the edges. Inside the market, warmth pooled around the floorboards. I filled a basket without speaking to anyone: bread, eggs, fruit, tea, honey, a jar of jam, and a pair of wool socks from a basket near the counter. They were simple, practical comforts.

The cashier didn't look at me. She handed me my change like she'd done it a hundred times already, her thoughts clearly somewhere else.

Outside, the wind caught the hem of my coat and nearly tugged me with it. I pulled it tighter around me, my eyes trailing down the length of the street, wondering if it would storm soon.

Not wanting to risk being caught in the rain, I climbed back into my car and drove toward the cliffs, returning to the house I'd left behind, the one that still felt more like a question than a home.

That evening, as the last light drained from a storm-stained sky, I returned to the cliffs behind the manor. The air was filled with the smell of sea grass and distant weather, a dampness that clung to the folds of my coat. The fire pit waited as I had left it, ringed with old ash and wind-swept leaves. I brought kindling, a few dry logs, a thermos of tea, and the notebook that continued to travel with me, unopened.

I built the fire slowly, more to feel the weight of it than to finish it. The match flared. After a few uncertain attempts, the flame caught and curled upward through the smoke, eventually stabilizing. It burned low and steady, casting a small circle of warmth around me. I sat with my back to the ocean, feeling its slow, unchanging breath push against the cliffs.

The house stood before me, quiet yet unmistakably present. I hadn't looked up at the window yet, and I was trying to avoid making it a ritual, even though that was what it had become. Instead, I stared into the fire, letting the warmth of the tea fill my hands and allowing the silence to swell until it shaped every thought I wasn't sure I wanted to complete. The notebook rested untouched in my lap.

I told myself I'd come to write. In truth, I was only waiting. It wasn't the answers I needed, or even her. It was something, anything, that might break the stillness and allow me to process it.

Eventually, I looked up. The window on the third floor remained dark, the curtains drawn, and the glass empty. Still, I stayed, unable to pull myself away from the possibility of her presence. The fire crackled beside me, and the stars scattered across the sky, halting as if testing the sky before claiming it. The tea cooled, the notebook remained closed, and then, from the bones of the house, a sound began to rise.

At first, I thought it was the wind, but it didn't move like that. *Music*—if it could even be called that—emerged in fragments. It was a loose melody, slow and uneven, more breath than rhythm. It sounded like someone trying to recall a song they hadn't sung in years: a handful of notes followed by silence, then another brief sequence.

I froze, listening intently. The sound didn't originate from speakers or the upstairs windows. It came from deeper within the house itself, beneath the very surface. It resonated through the night like an echo from long ago, drawing me toward the window without requiring a single step.

Light bloomed behind the curtain. A moment passed, and then she appeared. She didn't step forward. wave, or draw attention to herself. She simply stood there, her pale hair catching the faintest gleam. For a stilted moment, one hand rested near the glass. Her features were obscured by shadow, but she stood sentinel in the window. Watching me or watching the sea, I wasn't sure.

She didn't speak because she didn't need to, and I didn't dare move. I stayed where I was, not with hope nor expectation, but with the quiet recognition that whatever this was between us asked for nothing more than presence.

The fire had faded to coals by the time she slipped from view. The window returned to darkness, and the music fell away like fog thinning in a field. Yet I remained, caught in the pause she left behind—legs stiff and fingers cold—until the silence around me felt complete.

She had been there, and now she wasn't. I couldn't decide which haunted me more.

The notebook remained closed, yet the words came to me despite that. They drifted through my mind like fog on glass:

I did not see you,
But the air shifted,
And the dust began to stir.
The silence created space for your absence.
Something within me,
Something I believed was lost,
reached out anyway.

CHAPTER 3
The Keeper

The wind had changed the following day, louder now and edged with a colder bite. It no longer moved gently through the trees or whispered along the windows like breath through a sleeping house. Tonight, it pressed against the walls in bursts sharp enough to rattle the bones of the manor, testing the seams between structure and surrender.

The house held, but I didn't.

At the kitchen table, I sat with both hands wrapped around a mug of cooling tea. The candle near me struggled in the draft, its flame bending in the draft, then snapping back to center. The fire behind me had shrunk to embers. Not enough to comfort. Just enough to remind me I hadn't gone cold.

The sea was hidden behind fog and rain, and the sky had lowered until it pressed against the roof. On the laptop screen, the cursor blinked in rhythm, passing judgement without saying a word.

After several hours, I had written a single line: *The house had forgotten how to be quiet.*

I wasn't sure what I meant, but it settled into me like the truth anyway. This wasn't peaceful solitude anymore. It was pressure. A kind of watching.

She hadn't returned.

Three nights had passed, enough time for doubt to settle into the walls. The silence no longer felt like peace. It carried the weight of a decision I never realized I was making. Still, I kept looking up. I kept waiting. *Listening.*

But nothing came. Only wind, rising in her place.

Another gust hit the window hard, shaking the glass in its frame. I stood and crossed the room, pressing my palm to the cold pane. The trees bent in the wind, and rain streaked the glass like it had somewhere to be. It was the only thing that did.

Rubbing the chill from my arms, I moved to the narrow window that faced the cliffs and caught the third floor in reflection. And for just a second, something shifted—a flicker behind the glass.

Light, or only the storm? I lingered, searching the darkened glass for the shape of her, though I knew she wouldn't come.

Stepping away from the window, I added a log to the fireplace, and the flames responded slowly, reluctant but rising. The scent of cedar unfurled into the room.

The lights flickered once. Then again, just before the room went dark beneath a crash of thunder.

There was no hum from the fridge, nor warmth from the heater. Only the wind rising outside and the fire behind me, curling into itself.

Anne's voice returned from that first meeting. *The breaker is in the shared laundry. She keeps a schedule.*

I hadn't set foot in that hallway, but tonight, the house had decided for me. Duty called, and I had no choice but to answer.

The flashlight in my hand pushed an uneven beam into the dark. It trembled with each step, catching on furniture I knew too well, and making it unfamiliar. Corners distorted, retreating in and out of shape. Metal fixtures reflected the light in sudden flashes that unsettled more than they illuminated.

Outside, the storm had grown more restless. Wind clawed at the windows in sharp bursts, and rain battered the roof in relentless waves. The fire in the hearth had slumped into a dull glow, no longer strong enough to chase off the cold settling into the stone.

I stood for a moment in the center of the room, the beam of light tightening around me, the dark pressing in, tighter than before. I didn't want to go upstairs.

I wasn't afraid—at least not exactly. It was the uncertainty. What might be waiting on the other side of the stairwell?

Anne *had* said the breaker was in the shared laundry room. I hadn't thought much of it then. Now, the memory rang clear and absolute, sparking a curiosity that I couldn't ignore.

The apartment was dark. The heater was silent. The rules of the house were shifting.

Still, I didn't move. Not yet.

The shadows held no malice, only attention. As if the walls still remembered the weight of footsteps and routines that no longer belonged to anyone.

Eventually, I pulled on my coat, retrieved a stronger flashlight from the shelf near the kitchen, and stepped into the stairwell.

The door closed behind me with a gentle click that echoed too far. Beneath me, the stairs groaned, each creak traveling upward like a question the house hadn't yet decided how to answer. With every step, the air turned colder, sharper, edged with metal and salt.

At the landing, a narrow table sat tucked against the wall. The lace runner across its top fluttered ever so slightly, though no windows were open. A scent lingered there. Familiar, but not mine. Leather. Smoke. Something aged and intimate, just beyond recognition.

I paused, drawn to a familiarity I recognized but couldn't claim. Then I moved on.

Near the laundry room, I stopped again. The house had gone still.

Then came a shift, slight but unmistakable. Like the room had realigned around something I hadn't noticed. Weight moved across the floorboards. There were no footsteps, just the air adjusting, as if the space itself remembered someone who was no longer there.

Then the sound of a door closing. It wasn't slammed or hurried. Just...*closed.*

A breath later, the faint metallic slide of a lock fell into place somewhere down the hall.

The laundry room door creaked open under my hand. The hinges gave a quiet groan, softened by time and use. Blowing out a breath, I stepped inside, my light sweeping ahead into the narrow, timeworn room.

The space stretched long and close, paneled in dark wood smoothed by decades of sea air and touch. The crossbeams bowed low above me. Beneath my feet, pale tile dulled by endless steps held onto the cold.

Against the left wall sat an old washer and dryer, clean but aged. Shelves above them held folded cloths and antique jars of powdered soap labeled in fading script. Wire baskets hung overhead from iron hooks, some of which were rusted at the edges, but all were perfectly aligned.

At the far end, past the breaker box, another door stood closed.

The air in the laundry room carried the scent of soap and stone, but beneath that, a trace of warmth that didn't belong to the room itself. Her presence clung to the room like breath that hadn't yet faded. I moved slowly, aware of every footfall. The space held still, as if time had paused the moment she left.

My fingers grazed the surface of the folding table. The wood was smooth, but I could feel the ghost of motion, as if a weight had only just been removed. A basket. A hand. *Her.*

The beam of light swept past the breaker and landed on the other door. White, worn at the edges, the brass knob catching my light in a dim shimmer.

I didn't reach for it.

Instead, I stood still, the beam of the flashlight resting on its surface. I listened for the breath of a step, the soft shift of cloth, the ghost of movement that might reveal how close she'd been, but there was nothing. No creak. No whisper. Only the weight of presence already passed.

This wasn't imagined, nor was it simply longing or obsession. I knew she had been there. I knew she was real, even without proof. The kind of real that doesn't need to announce itself to be known.

Turning back to the breaker, my fingers moved over the faded pencil labels, flipping each switch in sequence.

The final one clicked into place, and a low hum stirred in the walls.

Before leaving, I cast one last glance toward the closed door. She hadn't fled. Hadn't hidden. She'd chosen to slip away without confrontation—to remain unseen, yet undeniably present. That quiet, deliberate choice said more than any explanation ever could.

The stairs creaked underfoot as I descended, but the house made no reply. No light flickered on. No door shifted. The quiet no longer felt passive. It was poised, almost listening.

Back in the apartment, the fire had dimmed to coals. I stirred it gently and added a few fresh logs. The heater began to murmur behind me, warmth returning to the air. And yet, the absence remained.

The room hadn't returned to normal. It had simply adapted. The sense of her hadn't vanished. It lingered in the corners, clung to the edges of the light.

For a long while, I sat at the table and watched the candle flicker in its jar, the flame bending to a draft I couldn't feel. I thought again of the door. Of how close she had been. How easily I could have spoken into the dark.

But I hadn't.

The house had gone quiet again. *Watchful.* Its stillness moved through the walls, settling back into waiting. And without meaning to, so had I.

Sleep came reluctantly.

I lay on the couch, one arm over my eyes, the other resting across my chest. The fire had settled into a low pulse. Shadows moved along the walls, dim and restless in the flicker of the candle I'd left burning. It didn't feel threatening. Only steady.

She had closed the door when she'd heard me coming. She had chosen not to be seen.

It was all I could think about, though it didn't feel like fear. More like quiet recognition—intimate in its restraint. As though she knew I was close but wasn't ready to be known.

And maybe...neither was I.

A faint trace of her scent still lingered: floral, edged with firewood.

Sitting up, I crossed the room and opened the notebook I hadn't touched in days. The pen felt awkward at first, foreign, like a tool I wasn't sure I still knew how to use.

The words weren't perfect, but they were mine.

She had been there.
Just beyond reach.
Just past knowing.
And when I slept that night,
I dreamed of breath brushing skin,
and the ache of love that could not wake.

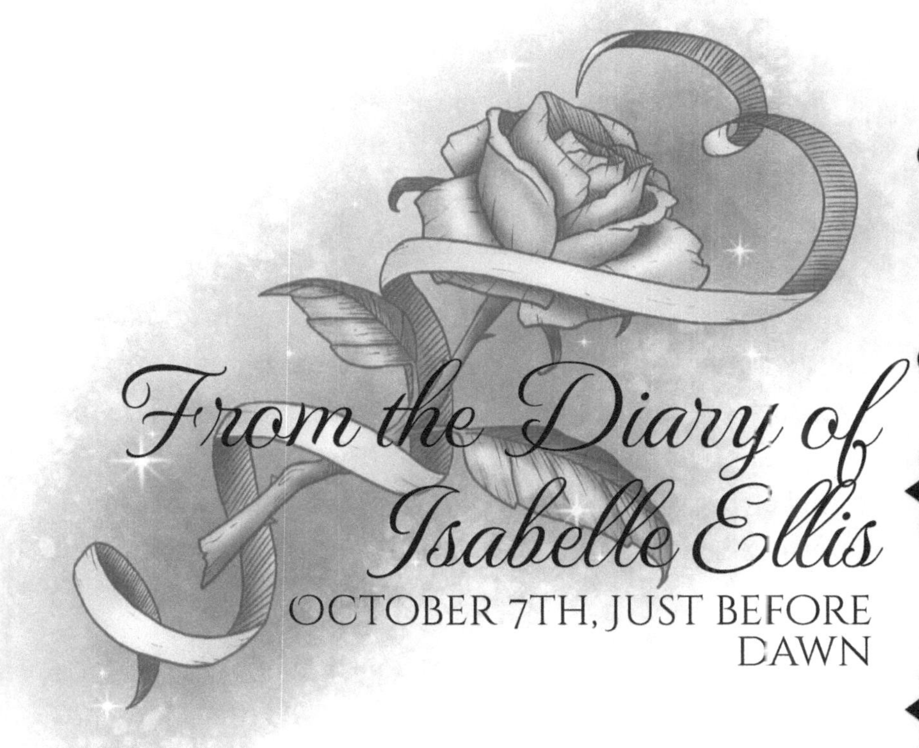

From the Diary of Isabelle Ellis

OCTOBER 7TH, JUST BEFORE DAWN

I ought not to have gone down there.

The power failed as the storm worsened, and I believed I could slip below unnoticed, swift and silent, but I was mistaken. He came sooner than I expected. His steps were quiet, not disruptive.

The house knew he was there. It held its breath with me.

I heard him enter the room just as I reached the door. My hand found the lock by instinct, though my fingers hesitated. The brass was cool to the touch, cool in the way that reminds one how long it has been since you last touched someone without consequence.

For a breath too long, I lingered.

Foolishly.

He did not speak. He did not knock. He simply waited.

For one perilous moment, I hovered on the threshold between habit and hope. We stood just a few feet apart, separated by nothing but wood and restraint. I thought, briefly, of opening the door. Of letting him see me not as a flicker behind a curtain, but as I am: pale, unchanged, unbeautiful in the quiet ways that render a person real to another.

But I couldn't. Not yet. I have touched no one in decades, and the curse grants no second chances. If I reach for what I cannot keep, I fear it will reach back and take more than I can afford to lose.

The house has always protected me from those who did not belong. But lately, I've begun to wonder if it also keeps me from those who do, leaving me in a solitary existence.

Because if he had seen me, if I had opened that door, I fear it would have undone something. In him. In me. In both of us.

There is a risk in being truly seen. Especially when you've forgotten whether your reflection belongs to a person or a curse. What if he had looked at me with pity? Or with kindness I had not earned?

Worse still, what if he had seen through it all and stayed?

The silence pressed between us, and I let it grow.

With my will holding firm, I stepped back into the dark and left the room as it was, though something of me remained. A hush. A trace. Perhaps he felt it. Perhaps he didn't.

But if he did, if he sensed how near I had been, I pray he would not mistake it for cruelty.

It was only fear, a raw and palpable emotion that gripped me, leaving me trembling in its wake.

And sometimes, fear softened by yearning doesn't close the door. It draws the curtain and dares the soul on the other side to pull it back, aching with the unspoken desire for connection.

Love, Isabelle

CHAPTER 4

The Keeper

By the time I put out the fire and returned to the basement apartment, the stars had scattered themselves across the sky like indifferent silver coins. The wind had quieted, but the cold remained, creeping into my coat and sinking into my skin in a way I hadn't expected. The kind of chill that clung to the weary.

Every window in the manor above remained dark. The place crouched against the skyline, a shape too stubborn to fade. That oppressive quiet pressed in like a closing fist, and for a moment, I stood outside the door, hesitant. The fire had kept away the chill. The wind had felt honest. It wasn't quiet. It was a tension stretched too thin, waiting to snap.

Inside, the apartment was warmer, but not in any way that mattered. Heat that came from wiring, not life. I microwaved a frozen dinner and ate it at the small table, the television droning on in the background. Something about war, or politics, or maybe a flood. The anchor's voice was all static to me—a lullaby of distant disasters.

My thoughts were still out on the cliffs, chasing that pale flicker in the third-story window. I replayed the moment in my mind like a scene from a film, frame by frame. Her hair caught the light. Her silence. The way she had vanished—less a retreat, more a folding into the dark.

I waited for her. For that quiet pacing that had become a kind of ritual. A strange comfort.

But tonight, there was nothing.

No sound of boards shifting underfoot. No faint pressure in the ceiling. Only the absence of her.

It unsettled me more than I wanted to admit.

Once I finished my meal, I poured more whiskey than I needed. I let it burn down my throat and spread warmth through my chest. A poor replacement for conversation. Or sleep.

It wasn't logic. It was gravity. Something about her, the way the house tilted toward her stillness, made everything else feel optional.

She had become an ache I couldn't ease. Even without sound, the question echoed.

Anne had said she liked her privacy. That she didn't want to be disturbed. But then why pace the floors so loudly? Why leave the curtain open, even for a moment? Why let me see her if she didn't want to be seen?

I thought about going upstairs. About knocking on that door steeped in secrecy and asking... what, exactly? Who are you? Why do you linger at the edge of every silence?

Instead, I rose and walked to the bathroom, needing a distraction.

The mirror remained fogged from the shower, my reflection blurred into softness. I wiped it with my palm, but the man looking back wasn't any clearer. Whatever I'd been carrying these past few months had changed me in ways I hadn't noticed until now. It had hollowed my cheeks, dulled the light behind my eyes. It had left me quiet, careful in ways I hadn't been before. I didn't look like the man I'd been six months ago, and I wasn't sure I knew how to be him anymore.

I brushed my teeth. Pulled on a clean shirt. Moved through the motions like they belonged to someone else.

Then I shut off the lights and climbed into bed.

The sheets were cool against my skin. The sharp scent of salt still clung faintly to me, like the air outside. I lay back, stared at the ceiling, and listened, straining for the sound of her.

But nothing came.

At some point, I must have slipped into sleep, or something like it, because when I opened my eyes, she was there, standing beside the bed.

Moonlight spilled through the narrow window and caught the silver in her hair. It glowed across her skin, turning her into something luminous and ethereal. She didn't move. Didn't speak. Her eyes met mine, steady, unblinking, filled with a sorrow I didn't understand.

For a moment, I couldn't breathe.

I opened my mouth, but no words came. What could I say? That I was losing my mind? That grief had grown limbs and learned how to stand beside me in the dark?

But then she reached out.

As I watched her, her fingers brushed against my cheek, light but certain. They didn't graze me like an accident.

They lingered. As if memorizing me. As if reminding themselves I was real.

I shivered beneath the touch. It was too much. And not enough. Intimate in a way that left no room for retreat, and even less room for doubt.

My chest tightened. This wasn't sleep paralysis. I knew what I was feeling.

Was I dreaming? Had the silence finally unstitched something in me?

Before I could ask her to ease my mind, I blinked, and she was gone.

The room was silent. There was no shape in the shadows. Just unoccupied space, but the air where she had stood still felt charged, like lightning had passed through it and left its trace behind. Like time had paused, just for a breath, and then kept going without her.

And my heart was racing.

When I woke the next morning with a pounding headache and a mouth as dry as sandpaper, I regretted every drop of whiskey from the night before. It dragged through my limbs like silt. For a long while, I lay still, staring at the ceiling, unsure if I could trust what had happened or if I wanted to.

Had she really been there?

I closed my eyes and tried to pull it back: the pale light filtering through the room, the warmth of her breath, the weightless pressure of her fingers against my cheek. There had been something sorrowful in her expression. A sadness that didn't belong to me. It felt like she hadn't come to meet me, but to say goodbye to something already slipping away.

It should have been impossible.

But the ache in my chest said otherwise.

The bed sheets whispered as I sat up. I rubbed the heels of my hands against my eyes and rested my elbows on my knees. The apartment held its silence. There were no footsteps overhead. No wind brushing against the windows. Just the slow, uneven drag of my own breath.

It would've been easy to explain it away. A dream. Sorrow, exhaustion, and whiskey colliding to conjure the woman I hadn't been able to stop thinking about, but it didn't feel imagined.

If she had come, then why?

She hadn't spoken. Hadn't lingered. Just looked at me. Touched me. Then vanished.

I considered going upstairs. Asking her directly.

Hi, I think you materialized beside my bed last night and touched my face like a mourning bride from a Brontë novel. Can we talk about that?

Yeah. That would go well.

Shaking off the thought, I made my way to the bathroom. Cold water. A clean shave. The quiet scrape of something ordinary. Familiar routines that didn't ask much of me.

The mirror offered no answers. Just the same tired face, drawn and hollow-eyed, as if my sleep had been borrowed and returned too late.

I dressed, ate cereal, and opened the blinds.

The world outside looked unchanged. It was still gray and distant, like it belonged in an old photograph. My laptop sat unopened on the kitchen table. *Again.*

I had come here to write. To lose myself in work, in distance, in silence, but the quiet here wasn't what I expected. It wasn't shelter. It was exposure. And the longer I stayed, the more it pressed into me.

The time I bought with my inheritance was supposed to feel like freedom. A second chance. Instead, it ticked in the background like a soft warning.

Some kinds of pain distort everything. Stillness starts to feel like safety. Silence becomes a kind of punishment. I thought I could write my way out of it. But now, the silence in this place had taken on a shape.

And all I could think about was *her*.

She haunted me, not with fear, but with contrast.

Everything else felt dulled in her absence, like she was the only part of the world still trying to mean something.

I *needed* to know who she was.

So, instead of heading to the cliffs, I grabbed my coat, laptop, and keys. If I couldn't go to her, maybe I could learn something from the town that surrounded her.

Crystal Peak was still rubbing the sleep from its eyes when I pulled into town. The streets were narrow, lined with weathered signage and wooden storefronts painted in fading pastels. It was the kind of place where everyone likely knew each other, and where newcomers didn't go unnoticed.

I returned to the café, the only one in Crystal Peak. The same table. The same scent of cinnamon and damp wood. A few days ago, I sat here with Anne and signed a lease I hadn't yet understood. Now I was back again, not seeking shelter this time, but answers.

I slid into the same booth, opened my laptop, and typed in the house's address.

The result came back almost at once.

Isabelle Ellis.

I stared at the name, reading it twice. Ellis, I'd heard before, but Isabelle meant nothing. At least, not yet. Still, the combination stirred something uneasy.

I looked at the birth year.

It could've been an older relative. A great-grandmother. Someone long gone whose name had lingered on paper longer than her presence had lasted. That would have made sense.

But it didn't feel like that.

The numbers stayed still on the screen, but something inside me shifted. A woman born in 1913 would be over a hundred. That kind of age didn't fit the figure I'd seen in the window, or the one who'd touched me like she belonged in the moment, not in the past.

I refreshed the page. Checked the address. Closed the browser and reopened it. The information didn't change.

The chill didn't either.

Swallowing the lump in my throat, I leaned back slowly. Around me, the café buzzed with quiet conversation and the hum of the espresso machine. Still, everything felt muffled, as if I were being spoken to from another room.

I'd come looking for facts.

What I found felt more like fiction.

Unable to make sense of my discovery, I closed the laptop and took a long sip of coffee. Outside, the cliffs loomed against the soft, shifting light. They looked unchanged, but I no longer trusted what I was seeing. I had no idea what Isabelle Ellis had to do with any of it, only that somehow, she did.

I left the café still repeating her name in my mind. *Isabelle Ellis.* The birth year. The impossibility of it.

I hadn't imagined her. Not the pale face in the window. Not the hand on my cheek. But the woman in those documents couldn't be the same one I'd seen.

Could she?

I walked for a while, looping the same few streets without realizing it. The sidewalks were cracked. Most of the shops were closed. A few wind chimes rang in the breeze, soft, metallic reminders of how still everything was.

Eventually, I ended up in front of a low stone building nestled near the edge of the cliff. The Bluff Bar. Weathered wood, slumped roof, a sign that creaked in the wind. It looked like it had grown there, settled into the bluff over time.

Inside, the lighting was low and amber-hued. The air held the familiar scent of fryer oil and old beer, with a faint citrus note reminiscent of a long-forgotten air freshener. A handful of patrons were scattered across the room, their postures shaped more by routine than conversation.

I slid onto a bar stool and ordered whatever was on tap. The beer arrived cloudy and cold, with a sharp edge that cut through the fog still sitting behind my eyes.

To my right, an older man nursed a glass of something amber. His skin was deeply tanned, his hands rough and calloused—*boatman*'s hands. Familiar in the way honest labor always was.

"You get out on the water much?" I asked, mostly to break the silence.

He turned to me, his expression open but unreadable. "Not today. Wind's too stubborn. The weekend was good, though. You?"

"Not yet," I said. "I'm new in town. Just getting my bearings."

He nodded, sipping from his glass. "Takes time. Crystal Peak doesn't show you what it's about all at once."

"Seems like the kind of place that prefers to be left alone."

Huffing a chuckle, he dipped his chin. "That, too."

He introduced himself as Howard. His voice had the rasp of salt air and the tales of old. We discussed tides, sailing, and the unpredictable nature of the sea. He spoke with the ease of someone who'd spent most of his life reading the water. Of disappearing coves, strange undercurrents, and weather that came without warning.

"You ever get out there," he said, "you'll see it for yourself. The ocean doesn't follow the rules here."

"I'd like that," I told him, and I meant it. *Eventually*.

He flagged the bartender for another drink, and I switched to coffee.

When the glass settled in front of him again, he asked, "Where are you staying?"

"Just outside town," I said. "Big Tudor place up on the cliffs."

Howard tilted his head. "Ellis Manor?"

I nodded. "That's the one."

Letting out a low breath, he looked into his glass like he'd been waiting to hear that. "It's strange. Always has been. Too still for a house that size."

I didn't respond right away. Instead, I let the quiet do the work.

After a moment, he continued. "You don't hear the name Ellis much anymore. The place used to be busy—staff, gardeners, and lights on. That was a long time ago."

"Someone still lives there," I said.

"Maybe... But nobody sees them. Has been that way for decades."

I hesitated. "The name on the deed is still Ellis."

Howard's expression didn't shift. "That name's been fading out of this town for a long time."

I took a sip of coffee. "You ever hear of a girl—*Isabelle*?"

He was quiet for a beat. "Isabelle Ellis? Stories," he said. "Always stories. Some say there was a girl, years ago. Beautiful. Young. But that was before my time."

"What kind of stories?"

Howard shrugged. "Nothing solid. Just the usual. That the house is cursed. That time moves differently up there. That the cliffs whisper if you listen long enough."

I studied him, trying to determine how hard I could push. "You believe that?"

"I believe places hold on," he said, tone pensive. "And that house? It's held too much for too long."

Outside, the light had shifted again. The windows had turned the color of deep water, the kind that holds its secrets until it's too late to pull away.

Trying to beat the storm, I finished my drink, thanked Howard, and stepped back into the wind.

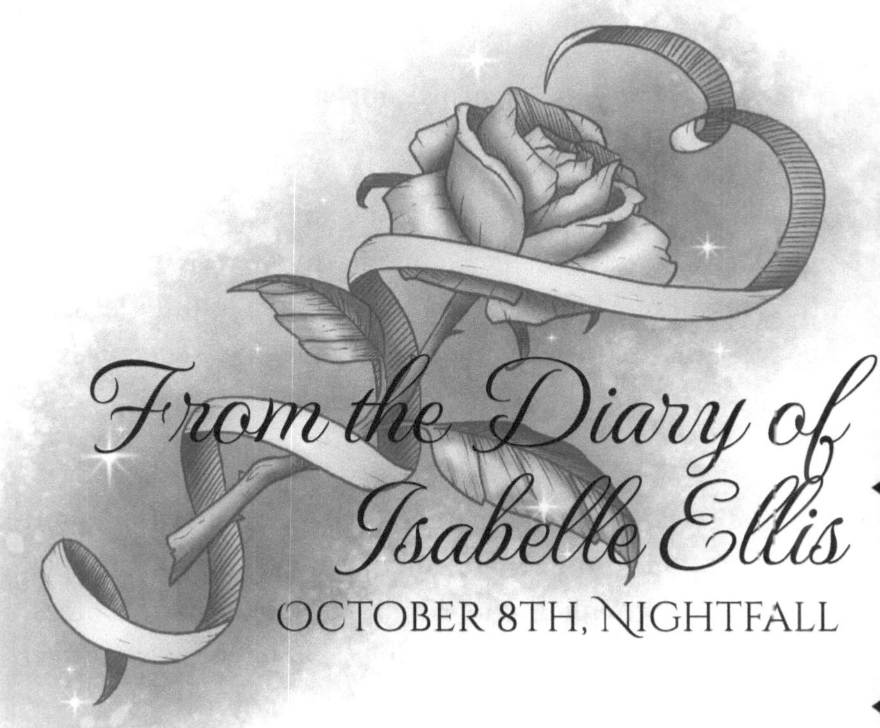

I used to count the days. One mark for every night I endured.

The first thousand are carved into the wall behind the linen closet, tucked beneath the shelf. After that, I moved on to the floorboards under my bed. When the wood began to splinter, I switched to the base of the cellar stairs. I still know how many there are, though I haven't looked in years.

Thirty-one thousand, give or take.

I told myself it was just a ritual, something to keep me sane, but I think it was always a kind of warning. A *graveyard of tallies. A record not of time passed, but of time stolen.*

My father left after the curse claimed me. He said he would find a way to fix it, but he never returned—not alive, anyway. Months passed before they found his body, but the cause of death remained a mystery. Regardless of the investigation's conclusion, I knew the witch was to blame.

My mother stayed. She watched me die night after night until something inside her gave way. When she stopped speaking, I thought I could bring her back with voices, with music. I read her stories, played old records, begged her to sit by the fire, but she faded anyway.

They buried her just after the winter turned, but I've never visited their graves. I couldn't.

I stopped carving for a while after that. It felt cruel to mark time she would never see. But when the silence became too deep, I started again.

Some nights, it's the only thing that reminds me I'm real.

Love, Isabelle

CHAPTER 5

The Keeper

By the time I reached the car, after visiting the market, a fine mist had begun to settle over Crystal Peak, the kind that softens outlines and distorts what you thought you understood. The town blurred at the edges, like it had slipped beneath sleep and didn't want to wake. It slid beneath my collar, dampened my hair, and settled between my thoughts.

I sat behind the wheel for several minutes with the engine off, keys in hand. The conversation with Howard replayed on a loop. *Isabelle Ellis.* He said the name as if it belonged to a different century. Like it had been whispered more often than spoken. Something passed down, not passed around.

He hadn't claimed to have seen her, nor did he know who lived there now. The whole thing was just... *strange.*

I turned the ignition, and the wipers swept the mist in half-hearted arcs. The sky had settled into a thick lid of clouds, heavy with a storm still gathering its strength. Branches swayed overhead like skeletal hands brushing the road. The house appeared slowly through the veil as I approached. It looked older than it had that morning. It hadn't crumbled. It hadn't fallen, but it wore its years like a wound refusing to close. A ruin that refused to fall to pieces. A monument to sorrow that had outlived its story.

Turning into the gravel drive, I let the car idle near the curve. My eyes lifted, without thinking, to the third-floor window.

When a light flickered on, my breath stilled.

She stood there, but only for a moment.

The curtain parted and her face appeared, pale and luminous, softened by mist and the sheen of glass. Her eyes met mine, or seemed to, and for a moment, we were held there together.

Then the light vanished, and the curtain fell.

For several minutes, I stayed where I was, the engine low and steady, my pulse louder than either. It didn't feel like fear or longing, just the constant pull of something I wasn't meant to resist.

I argued with myself. She had come to me once, if I hadn't dreamed it. I'd felt her hand. I saw her eyes. And now this. Another flicker. Another half-invitation.

Knocking on her door would break the rules. Anne had been clear, warning me about the consequences of disturbing the peace of the house. But what if those rules were meant to keep people away, not protect them?

Even then, I paused. I didn't want to be the thing she feared.

Pulling into the driveway beneath a sky heavy with rain, I cut the engine and reached for the groceries I had no real intention of eating. The first drops fell as I stepped out—soft, deliberate, soaking through my coat before I could shut the door.

Inside, the apartment held the weight of a mausoleum—air damp with neglect, the stillness too complete to feel accidental. I peeled off my soaked clothes and let them fall in a heap on the bathroom floor. The water took its time warming, but when the heat finally arrived, it struck like a wave breaking over stone.

I stood beneath it until I stopped shivering.

Steam clung to the mirror as I stepped out, a towel wrapped around my waist. My reflection looked half-formed in the fog. I wiped the glass, but the man behind it didn't look any more familiar.

Tired of reheated dinners and silence, I set a pot on the stove. It wasn't out of hunger, but to keep my hands moving.

I threw together penne pasta, cream, garlic, oil, and a pinch of red pepper. Vegetables softened in a pan, releasing their aroma into the air. Smooth jazz played low from the speaker, the kind that made the room feel less empty. I moved like I was expecting company. Like I was making something for *us*. For *her*. Even if she never crossed the threshold.

I didn't cook much. Not since my father passed. The kitchen had always belonged to someone else. But tonight, I wanted it to feel like ours, shared between me and the stunning woman in the house above.

When the food was ready, I poured a glass of wine and sat at the table. The apartment was lit warmly by lamplight and the amber glow of the stove top, while soft music played in the background.

It felt like waiting.

But the house remained still. No footsteps overhead. No creaking floorboards. Just the steady whisper of rain.

Later, I curled up in bed beneath a blanket, the sound of the rain rising and falling at the windows. My thoughts unraveled slowly. *What would I even say to her? That I felt her watching? That I wanted her to keep doing it?*

That I hadn't felt this alive since I buried my father?

I must have fallen asleep mid-thought, because I never noticed my eyes closing.

I woke to the sound of footsteps and a cool hand on my cheek.

For a moment, I was frozen, afraid that even the slightest movement might scatter her like mist. My heart thudded in my chest, louder than it should have been. When I opened my eyes, she stood beside the bed like something conjured from moonlight, silver hair spilling around her shoulders, the glow from the uncovered window tracing soft light along her skin.

Her eyes met mine with steady clarity, unblinking and luminous with a sorrow so quiet it stole the breath from my lungs. There was no fear in them. Only curiosity. Grief. A question she hadn't yet asked aloud.

Her hand remained where it was, cool and impossibly gentle, like it had always belonged there. It didn't fade. Didn't flicker. She stood rooted, not like a ghost, but like a woman who had stepped through silence to be seen.

I didn't know what I expected. That she'd vanish the second I blinked? That I'd pass through her like air? But she didn't move. She stayed.

Slowly, I lifted my hand and placed it over hers. My fingers trembled. Hers didn't.

She was real. Or real enough.

"Who are you?" I asked, my voice cracking under everything I didn't know how to say.

She hesitated. Her gaze drifted to the moonlight spilled across the floor, then returned to mine. "Isabelle," she said, so softly it might have been a dream.

The name struck like thunder behind my ribs. *Isabelle.* I'd read it on the deed, a name written in ink that had dried decades ago, but the woman before me hadn't aged a day. She looked untouched by time. Beautiful. *Impossible.*

And yet nothing about her felt wrong.

"My name is Kayden," I said, offering it like something that might anchor us both.

A small smile tugged up the side of her lips, only making her more stunning. "I know," she whispered.

My breath caught, tightening in my chest with a weight I hadn't expected.

Her fingers moved with slow intent, gliding from my cheek to the line of my jaw and pausing there, as if committing the shape of me to memory, one breath at a time. The space between us shifted.

Then, before thought could rise to meet it, she leaned in and kissed me.

Her lips were warm in a way that startled me, not just gentle, but seeking. She tasted of longing. Honeysuckle. Or maybe pure magic.

A low sound rose from my throat, pulled from instinct more than thought, and I drew her closer. My hand slid along the curve of her arm until it rested at her shoulder, holding her there—not to claim, but to answer.

She didn't vanish beneath the contact. Instead, she leaned into it, into me, like she'd been waiting to.

"Is this okay?" she asked, breathless, poised on the edge of everything.

I nodded. Words felt irrelevant.

With my permission, she moved with a grace that felt dreamed, not rehearsed. Like this was something she'd imagined more times than she dared admit. Her body settled beside mine, and I turned to meet her.

She kissed me again, slower this time, with a certainty that left no room for doubt. My hands moved to her back, then into her hair, drawn by the need to feel every part of this moment. A quiet, broken sound rose from her throat, unguarded and impossibly human.

We didn't speak. There was no need.

Together, we let the dark hold us, its quiet depth saying everything we could not.

When we were both breathless, she curled into my side, her head resting over my heart. Her breath was steady. Her presence was undeniable. The scent of her hair filled the room, a blend of lavender and age-old warmth, like candle smoke clinging to stone.

It was the happiest I'd been in a long time. Sleep took me slowly, with her warmth pressed against me like a vow.

But when I woke, the space beside me was empty.

No indent in the pillow. No heat in the sheets. No trace of her left in the air.

Only silence.

And the ache of something I'd only just begun to believe in.

You were there.
Pressed against my ribs like a second heartbeat.
And then you were gone.
Every breath since has felt like waiting to dream again.

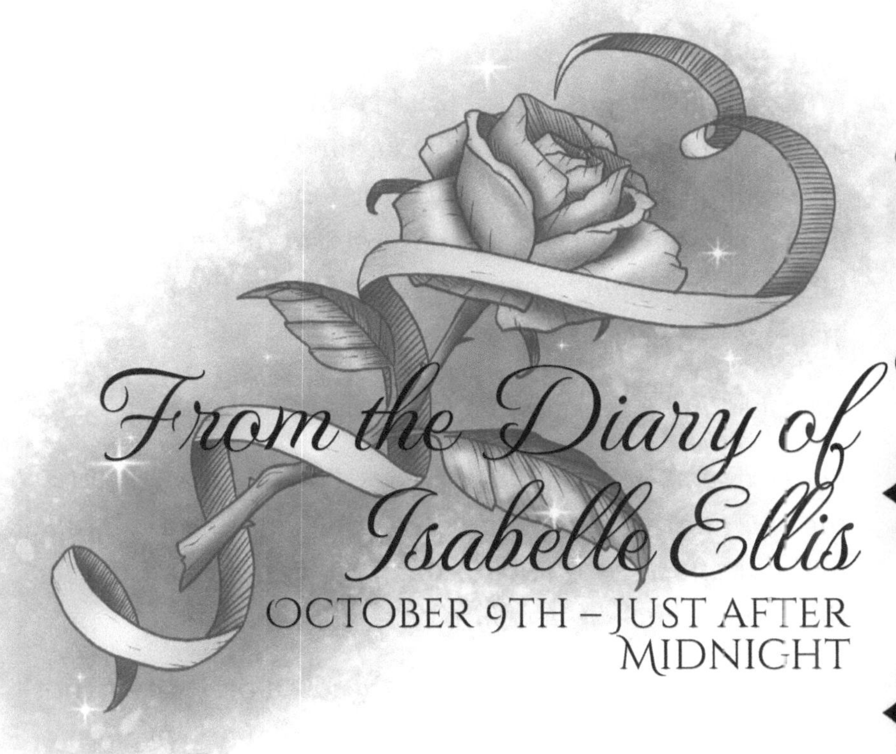

From the Diary of Isabelle Ellis

OCTOBER 9TH – JUST AFTER MIDNIGHT

Tonight, I kissed him.

I had no intention of going to him. I told myself I mustn't—that it was too dangerous, too soon. I meant only to see, to listen, to remain quietly at the margins of my own story, without trespassing upon someone else's. But in truth, I was vulnerable, my heart aching with longing and uncertainty.

But when I pictured him there, his body curled beneath the blanket, I found I could not remain still.

He looked so alive. So warm. And I—I have been dead for so very long.

I told myself I would only stand beside his bed. Just for a moment. Long enough to relearn the shape of closeness. The weight of being known. But when he opened his eyes and looked at me, not with alarm or fear, but with recognition I hadn't dared hope for, something within me yielded.

He asked my name, and I gave it to him.

I have not spoken it aloud in years. I had nearly forgotten the sound of it in my own voice. But with him, it came without effort. As though it had simply been waiting for the right silence in which to return.

I didn't plan to kiss him. My body acted on its own, not out of impulse, but because of a deep ache within me. It was the yearning I had kept pressed beneath my ribs, like dried flowers—brittle but still blooming—desperate to be felt.

His lips were warm and certain. When he drew me into his arms, I did not resist. I could not. I have never longed for anything so deeply, not even for the freedom I once dreamed of.

It was reckless. Impossible.

I have spent what amounts to lifetimes avoiding contact. I took in a tenant not for company, but for movement, for the sound of footsteps. To wake the stillness. To disturb the quiet that had begun to feel endless.

But tonight, I allowed myself to be held. And for the first time in decades, I did not feel like a ghost. I felt like a person transformed by the power of connection.

I do not know what the morning will bring. I never do.

But tonight, I kissed a man I barely knew, with a desperation that moved through me like a prayer.

And when I lay in his arms, I did not think of curses or rules or consequences. I thought only of his breath against my hair. I thought only of staying.

Love, Isabelle

CHAPTER 6

The Keeper

The next morning arrived draped in gray. Rain clung to the windows in silvery trails, and fog pressed low against the sea, cloaking the water in a serenity that belonged to some other world entirely. I hadn't slept well. Whether it was the echo of Isabelle's presence or because of it, I kept waking, convinced she would be there beside me.

But she wasn't.

The scent of her lingered faintly on the sheets, her kiss still warming my lips. The rational part of me stepped in, reminding me how little sense any of it made. She wasn't supposed to exist the way she did. But that voice, the one that clung to logic, was getting quieter. Less convincing.

The morning was a blur, a shadow of myself moving through the apartment. I brewed coffee out of habit, but my open notebook remained untouched. The silence wasn't just around me—it nested in my chest, heavier than before. The words I usually clung to now drifted at the edges of thought, like mist curling just out of reach.

It wasn't grief, not the kind I'd felt when my father died, but it filled the same hollow space, shaped differently, yet just as hard to carry. This wasn't the ache of losing someone I'd known. It was the ache of wanting someone I wasn't supposed to want.

I told myself it didn't matter. That it shouldn't matter. I didn't even know her, but the truth was harder to ignore: that kiss had undone something. The heat of her body against mine, the way her voice wrapped around my name. I know, she'd said, like she'd waited longer than I could understand.

By midday, the rain had softened to a mist. I pulled on my coat and walked the edge of the property, hoping the wind would help clear my head. The flower beds had collapsed under the weight of the season. Once-bright blooms now bowed and heavy with rain, their fragrance little more than a ghost of what it had been. I stopped by the fire pit, letting my hand trail along its cold stone rim. It no longer felt like a hearth. More like a threshold drawn between who I'd been and the man I was becoming, willing or not.

The cliffs were restless even in daylight. Waves slammed against the rocks below with sharp, uneven rhythm, as if trying to break the spell the house had cast. The manor behind me stood unmoved, untouched, still as a ruin.

When I returned to the apartment, I reached for my laptop without thinking, uncertain of what I meant to do with it. The blinking cursor continued, its rhythm steady, but it offered no guidance. I typed a few lines. Deleted them. Tried again. Still nothing. That relentless eye kept pulsing.

So, I opened a new document and typed her name.

Isabelle Ellis.

I stared at the letters until they fractured. Until they lost their shape, their sense of person hood. Her name dissolved into something vaster, something elemental. It wasn't just a name anymore. It was breath. It was warmth. It was her lips on mine, her body curled against me. It was what remained in her absence: the emptiness she left behind, threaded through every wall, clinging to the house and refusing to loosen its hold.

She didn't come that night.

Or the next.

Or the one after that.

Three days passed without a flicker of light in the window. The ceiling stayed silent. No distant creaks. No trace of her returning steps. I told myself I didn't care. That I had work to do. But each night, I ended up wrapped in a blanket by the fire pit, staring at the flames, waiting for something I couldn't put into words.

By the third night, the fire had burned down to faint, glowing coals. My laptop remained untouched. So did the whiskey. The sea pounded against the cliffs below like a beast gnawing at its chains. Overhead, the stars dimmed behind a thin curtain of clouds, flickering as if unsure they wanted to be seen at all.

When the cold finally made its way through my coat, I stood and gathered my things. I looked back once, toward the house and the rooms that still held her, and it took everything in me not to shred the rules she'd never invited me to break.

I lit the fire early the following evening.

The wood was still damp from the week's rain, and it took effort to bring the flames to life. I crouched near the pit in the fading light, coaxing sparks with cold fingers until they finally caught and steadied. Smoke drifted upward, carrying the scent of cedar and ash into the wind. With the air coming off the water being chilly, I pulled a thick blanket around my shoulders and sank into its warmth, if only for something to hold.

The silence hadn't changed. No footsteps above. No flicker of light behind the windows. Only absence, pulled tighter each day, stretched like fabric that might tear with the slightest weight.

I didn't know if I was still waiting for her.

I wasn't even sure what I hoped she might offer if she came. A reason? A truth? Some fragile explanation that could survive the moment it was spoken? I'd tried to make sense of it: her presence, her disappearances, the way she seemed stitched from sorrow, but none of it fit inside the world I knew.

And maybe that was the point.

Twilight settled in slow layers, and the fire painted orange light across the stones. My laptop rested beside me, unopened. The book I'd come here to finish had receded like a tide. Its characters had gone quiet. Its world now felt like scaffolding, thin and artificial. A story I no longer believed in.

I thought instead about her.

Isabelle.

Her name echoed between thoughts like a bell struck at a distance, soft but unrelenting. Every time I tried to write, I found her instead. Her voice. Her name. The shape of her absence.

The sun dropped below the cliffs, and the sky darkened to ink. I poured a small measure of whiskey into a ceramic mug and held it close, the glass giving me something to do with my hands. Above, dry branches rattled in the wind. Below, the sea moved in steady sighs. A foghorn called once from far out on the water, a long, low sound that seemed to mourn something forgotten by everything but the sea.

And when the air was silent again, I heard it.

Not footsteps.

Singing.

At first, I thought it was the wind catching in the beams of the house, but then it swelled, wordless and soft, threaded with grief. A lullaby sung to no one, too fragile to survive the world, and yet still trying. The kind of sound that shouldn't have lasted but did.

It came from the house.

From *her*.

I turned toward the third-story window, heart climbing into my throat. The curtain stirred, just slightly. A ripple across the fabric. Not enough to confirm anything, but enough to suggest it.

She had been there.

And then she was gone.

The fire behind me burned low, its warmth reaching only as far as my knees. I stayed in place, hands curled around the mug, the echo of her voice lodged somewhere in the space between breath and thought.

What pain had taught her to sing like that?

It hadn't been a sad song, though sadness lingered at the edges. Not mournful in the way funerals are. It had sounded like longing stretched across time. A voice that remembered being loved, even if it no longer expected to be.

When the cold finally settled in, I rose slowly and gathered my things. The wind tugged at my coat as I crossed the grass, and when I looked up one last time, the window was dark again.

But I no longer felt alone.

Somewhere above me, in that house that never seemed to sleep, Isabelle was awake.

And for now, that was enough.

You disappeared,
But the silence you left behind
never stopped whispering your name.
And when I heard your voice again,
It sounded like a memory
trying to live.

CHAPTER 7

The Keeper

I didn't expect to see her again that night.

The fire still smoldered outside, casting weak light through the fog. I returned to the apartment with my coat damp from sea spray, the cold clinging to me like an exhale on glass. My fingers ached from holding the mug too long, and my boots left shallow prints on the path as I stepped inside and shut the door behind me.

The manor groaned in the wind, its bones adjusting. No other sound followed. Silence returned the way it always did, settling in with the slow weight of something patient and waiting.

I moved through the motions. Stripped off wet clothes. Tossed them over the back of a chair. Changed into flannel pants and an old sweater. Heated a bowl of soup and ate it standing at the counter. The television murmured in the background, playing something about deep-sea currents or perhaps tectonic plates. I couldn't say. I wasn't really listening.

My thoughts circled her window. The melody. The silhouette. The way her hair had flickered in the dark.

By midnight, sleep still wouldn't come. Rain tapped gently against the windows, soft as a gentle touch. I turned off the lights and climbed into bed, one arm over my chest, staring at the ceiling until my eyes stung.

I told myself not to expect her. Not to hope.

But sometime after one, I heard it.

The faintest creak of a floorboard. Then a softer sound—the soft tread of bare feet brushing wood.

I sat up slowly, a jolt of something electric snapping through my chest. Every instinct in me screamed to move, to reach for her, to pull her close, but I stayed still, afraid that one wrong breath would scare her away.

In the faintest glimmer of moonlight, she stood in the doorway, her hair damp, the ends darkened and clinging to her shoulders. Her sleep dress hung from one shoulder like the night had tried to undress her. She didn't speak. Didn't move. Just stood there, silver-eyed and silent, as if unsure whether this space would still allow her.

"You're here," I said, my voice barely above a breath.

I didn't know whether to reach for her because I didn't want to startle her. Her lips parted like she might speak, but no sound came. Instead, she nodded. *Once.* A slow, careful gesture, like it cost her something.

"I didn't think..."

I trailed off. I didn't want her to explain. I didn't want her to owe me anything.

So, I pulled back the blanket. An invitation.

And to my quiet relief, she crossed the room slowly, her bare feet a whisper across the floor. When she slipped beneath the covers, she didn't reach for me. Didn't curl into my chest. She simply lay beside me, her head resting on the pillow, her body angled toward mine.

I reached out, hesitantly, and brushed a strand of hair behind her ear.

"You don't have to explain," I said. And I meant it, even with all the questions I hadn't yet dared to ask.

Her eyes closed, and there was a long pause between us. The kind that holds a thousand things unsaid.

Then, she tilted her face up to mine. Her eyes searched me, not for answers, but for permission. For reassurance.

"I'm sorry I stayed away," she finally whispered, her voice thin. *Raw*. Like it hadn't been used in years.

"You don't owe me anything." Reaching out, I dared to touch her cheek, needing the contact, needing to know she was still here. "I can be here for whatever you need... whatever you want."

She didn't reply, but her hand cupped mine, her fingers threading through mine as if relearning how to reach for someone.

Silence held us for a long time—our bodies unmoving, breath slow and shared, the quiet between us deep and unspoken.

A hesitant shift brought her closer, her body grazing mine in a way so vivid, so present, it made me fear I might only be imagining her come morning.

Without asking, without pause, she leaned in. And when her lips met mine, I felt the weight of every ache she had carried alone.

Her sleep dress slipped further down her shoulder, exposing a porcelain stretch of skin. I didn't speak. I didn't dare. I just looked at her, this impossibly soft, impossibly strong woman who kept appearing like moonlight through mist. And she was here. Wanting *me*.

"Anything?" she asked, her voice velvet and smoke.

I ran my fingers down her jaw, my pulse pounding beneath her touch. "What exactly are you asking for, Isabelle?"

She didn't answer. Instead, she kissed me.

Climbing onto my lap, she straddled me, her thighs warm around my hips. Her hands braced on my chest, her breath warm against my mouth. She moved against me slowly, the friction through our clothing enough to make me groan. I could already feel how wet she was.

"I want you," I whispered, lips brushing her throat. "But only if this isn't something you'll wish you hadn't given me."

The look in her eyes nearly destroyed me.

"I wouldn't be here if I didn't want you," she whispered, her cheek resting briefly against my chest. "I've never let anyone see me. Not like this. Only *you*."

As I threaded my fingers through her hair, I exhaled deeply. I could have asked her then about the name on the deed and the birth year that didn't add up, but I wasn't ready for the truth—not yet. What I had in that moment was her breathing, presence, and choosing me. For now, that was enough.

"There's no one else for me either," I said. "Just you."

When she looked up at me again, her eyes filled with endless need, she kissed me harder, tugging at the hem of her sleep dress. She pulled it over her head and let it fall to the floor.

I couldn't breathe.

She was like moonlight and flesh; everything I didn't know how to deserve.

"Maybe we should wait," I murmured, not because I didn't want her, but because I did. Because everything about her felt like a miracle I hadn't earned. Because I didn't know what would happen if I touched her and she vanished again.

But she guided my hand to her breast, her voice husky. "I've waited long enough. I want this. I want *you*."

I groaned, my mouth finding her nipple a heartbeat later. She moaned, arching into me, her fingers digging into my hair as she rocked against my cock, still trapped beneath my boxers.

"I need you," she breathed against my ear, her voice trembling with longing.

Not willing to deny her, I rolled her onto her back, kissing her like I wouldn't survive the space between us. My hips rocked into hers, her panties soaked against my length. I pushed the blanket down, trailing kisses across her stomach as I hooked her underwear with one finger and slowly slid them down her legs.

There was a kind of beauty in the way she opened for me, trusting me with more than just her body.

My lips traced the inside of her thighs, one and then the other, until she trembled beneath me and I gave her what she'd been waiting for. There were no words for the taste of her—only the quiet desperation it awakened in me, and the way I answered it with my mouth.

Her fingers twisted in the sheets as a gasp broke from her lips, raw with need and too real to hold back.

I licked her slowly, drawing soft circles over her clit before slipping one finger inside her, then another. She clenched around me, slick and warm, her hips bucking against my mouth as her cries grew louder with every flick of my tongue.

"Kayden," she moaned. "Oh god... don't stop..."

A cry tore from her as she came, thighs tightening around my head, her body trembling as she finally let go of whatever she'd been holding.

I kissed my way back up slowly, the taste of her still warm on my tongue.

"We don't have to go further," I said, even though every part of me wanted to.

Breathing heavily, she reached for me, pulling me against her. "I don't want to stop. I need to feel you."

I paused, only for a second.

Pushing my boxers down, I moved closer, guiding myself to her entrance but not pressing in—*not yet.* My hand returned to her hip, steadying both of us as I watched her face for even the faintest flicker of hesitation.

Her body met mine with warmth and softness, open but still tight. I eased into her slowly, carefully, giving her time to breathe, to adjust, to *decide.*

A gasp left her lips. One left mine, too.

That first moment of closeness held something I hadn't expected. The way her body held me—so new, so unfamiliar—stirred a quiet question in my chest. *Was I the first?*

Fingers slid up my back, her breath unsteady against my skin.

"I've never... let anyone touch me like this," she whispered, almost as if she'd drawn the thought right from my mind. "Not this way."

The words hit me all at once, and for a moment, my heart went still.

"Are you sure you want to do this?" I asked, my hips stilling, the tenderness of being inside her catching somewhere deep in my chest.

She nodded, her eyes locked on mine. "Yes. I want you. I want this. *Please...*"

At that moment, it felt as if I might break if I didn't give in. So, I kissed her deeply and began to move again.

Her body stretched to hold me, impossibly tight and soft, wrapping around me with a closeness that made me feel like I belonged to her. Once I was fully inside, I stalled, giving her space to breathe and giving myself the same grace.

There was something untouched in the way she held me. Not innocence. Not fear. Just a part of her that felt sealed off from the world until this very moment. Whatever she'd lived through, I didn't know, but this meant more than wanting. It was the kind of closeness people didn't give lightly, and she gave it to me.

"You have me," I whispered as I thrust deep, my muscles tightening with the effort it took not to lose myself too fast. "All of me."

She gasped and then her hips lifted to meet mine, the friction feeding a hunger that quickly burned through us both. She trembled beneath me, breath coming faster as I moved deeper, letting her feel every inch.

When she moaned my name, voice raw and cracking, her hands gripped my back like she couldn't hold on without it.

"Then don't hold back," she whispered, and she didn't need to say anything more.

Gripping her hips, I pulled her tighter, grounding her as she rode each wave. My rhythm grew harder, deeper, and her cries rose to fill the space around us.

Release took her all at once, her body rising to meet it with a hunger that undid me.

She arched beneath me, head thrown back, thighs shaking as her body closed around mine. I felt every pulse of her release, every tightening of her muscles as they tried to draw me in deeper.

I couldn't hold back any longer.

The pressure broke with a groan as I spilled into her, burying myself to the hilt.

Even then, I didn't stop moving. My body slowed, gentled, easing us both through the aftershocks until I collapsed over her, breathless and spent.

As we shared ragged breaths, she wrapped her arms around me and held on like she never wanted to let go.

And I knew, deep down, I didn't want her to, but one day, she would.

When I woke, the air in the room felt different.

The warmth between the sheets had faded. Her body, once curled around mine, was gone. Her side of the bed lay undisturbed, as if she'd never been there at all. Only the faint impression of her shape in the mattress remained, and the lingering trace of lavender.

I reached across the sheets, my fingers dragging through the cool indentation where she'd been, hoping I was wrong. That she'd just gone to the bathroom. Or to make tea. That she was still here, just quiet.

But the apartment was silent.

It wasn't peace. It was an absence. The kind of stillness that arrives after something beloved has left the room.

I sat up slowly, the ache rolling through me in waves: soreness in my limbs, tension gripping the back of my jaw. My mouth still tasted like her skin. My heart thudded with a steady, confused rhythm.

There was no note.

No message.

No explanation.

Only the echo of last night.

I didn't move at first. Just sat in the quiet, staring at the rumpled sheets and the space she'd left behind, trying to replay every moment. The way she looked at me when she undressed. The way she whispered not to hold back. The way she kissed me after, like I was something she hadn't meant to want but couldn't let go of.

It hadn't felt like a goodbye.

It felt like the beginning of something.

And maybe that was why her absence felt so devastating.

Eventually, I climbed out of bed, pulled on a sweatshirt, and moved through the apartment like someone re-learning how to inhabit their own skin. I boiled water. Burned my tongue on tea I barely tasted. Walked barefoot to the window.

Outside, the sea was quiet. The mist hung low over the cliffs, draping the world in a peace that felt too deliberate.

I looked up toward the third floor, half-expecting to see her in the window, curtain drawn back, eyes watching, but the window was still, and the curtain didn't move.

She was gone. *Again.*

But this time, it felt like she hadn't just left the room.

It felt like she had taken something with her.

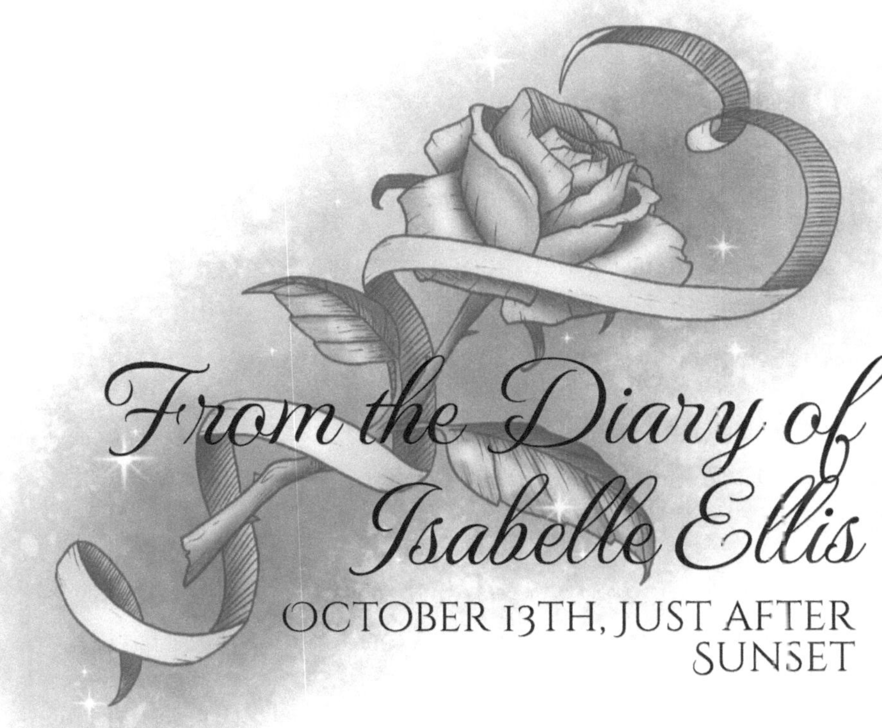

From the Diary of Isabelle Ellis

OCTOBER 13TH, JUST AFTER SUNSET

Last night, I returned. He looked at me like he hadn't drawn breath since I'd left. And when he reached for me, I didn't hesitate. I climbed into his bed, into his arms, and for the first time in nearly a century, I let myself be held as though I were real.

I let him touch me, and I touched him in return. Not with secrecy or shame, but with everything I had kept buried beneath a hundred years of silence. What I gave him wasn't just my body. It was longing. Trust. The quiet ache I had never dared to place in anyone's hands.

He worshiped me with more than words. With breathless reverence. With hands and mouth and eyes that never once looked through me.

I left before the light touched the windows. I always do. The shape of me remained in the sheets, along with the warmth I was never meant to carry.

And now, I am unraveling. Because I let him see me. Truly. And in that seeing, I gave him something I cannot give again.

I have invited him into a story that does not end gently. A story that punishes touch with loss, and love with ruin.

For what she took from me that night—my voice, my breath, the pause between heartbeats—was not just time. It was a sliver of soul, carved clean and hidden beyond my reach.

That is why I remain. I want to wake beside him. To live without vanishing. But as long as that missing part of me stays buried in shadow, the morning will always take me.

Still, I will return. Not because I deserve him, but because when he touches me, I remember how it feels to belong to the world.

Even if it's only for a single night. Even if dawn comes to claim me again.

Love, Isabelle

CHAPTER 8

The Keeper

The house held her, even in her absence.

I felt it in the way the air shifted at night, how the shadows pooled near the door like they were waiting for her shape to return. Some evenings, I swore I felt her breath at my neck, imagined the soft creak of floorboards above, but it was only the house settling. Only silence, stretching to fill the space she left behind, echoing in every corner.

I told myself not to panic. Not to imagine the worst. Maybe she needed space. Perhaps I had crossed some invisible threshold she regretted, but the emptiness felt different now. *Heavier.* Like a wound that couldn't heal without her.

Each evening, I went through the same motions. With no sign of her, I lit the fire anyway. I set out the blanket she had once curled beneath, smoothing it out, pretending I didn't notice the emptiness that lingered. I cooked meals I never touched, their steam curling toward the ceiling before fading into nothing. Sometimes I opened the window just a little wider, hoping the scent of fresh herbs, garlic, or simmering broth might tempt her down from the shadows.

And though I didn't admit it, not even to myself at first, I left the door unlocked for her.

I told myself it was a habit, but the truth sat quietly in my chest.

I tried to write, but the words came brittle and slow, like frost spreading across a once-clear window. When the rain eased, I wandered the cliffs with my notebook pressed to my chest, the wind tearing at the pages and leaving more of an impression than I did. Most days, I returned with no more than a single sentence.

She isn't a ghost, but she doesn't belong to the living either.

Even the sea, which had once been a balm, felt distant. *Muted.* The waves crashed endlessly, but they didn't speak to me anymore.

By the third day, the silence had curdled into grief.

That evening, I sat at the kitchen table, a half-empty glass of whiskey sweating onto the wood. My fingers still ached for the feel of her. The taste of her lingered on my lips.

I had held her like she was real, because nothing about her felt imagined. And now, she was gone without a word.

For a long time, I stared at the ceiling above me, willing it to creak. To shift. To give me some sign that she was still there. That the world I'd stepped into hadn't vanished with her.

But the house gave me nothing.

Eventually, I shoved the chair back, its legs screeching across the floor, and paced the apartment. The storm outside howled, rattling the windows, pushing against the walls as if trying to claim the silence for itself. The wind shrieked, drowning out my thoughts.

But she was louder.

Her absence filled every space. Every surface. Every breath. It was like her body had sunk into the walls and then vanished, leaving a weight where her warmth had been. A kind of reverent deadness I didn't know how to carry.

Had I done something wrong? Had I pushed too far? Or not far enough? Did it make her feel seen when she needed to remain hidden?

Or worse, had something happened to her?

The thought took hold and refused to loosen. I sat back down, my head in my hands, my breath shallow. My eyes were fixed on the narrow door that led to the laundry room. The one that stood like a boundary I wasn't meant to cross.

I didn't go to it. *Not yet.*

But I thought about it. Constantly, *helplessly.* My gaze kept returning to the knob, waiting for it to turn. Hoping it would.

And when the sky began to lighten, bruised with clouds and the pale colors of sunrise, I made up my mind.

If she didn't come back tonight, I would go looking for her.

Even if it meant stepping into a place I might never come back from.

I didn't sleep.

Instead, I lay on the sofa for hours, staring at the ceiling as the wind howled outside and silence deepened above me. I kept hoping the night would carry her back down the stairs. That I'd hear her footsteps on the landing. That she'd appear in the doorway with that look in her eyes, the one that made me feel like I wasn't completely alone.

But she didn't come.

And by the time the sun was making its descent, I couldn't take it anymore.

I rose, restless and wired. I made a cup of coffee I didn't want, and left it to cool, untouched, while I stared at the door. It loomed there, unassuming and quiet, like it had been waiting all along for me to decide whether I would obey or step into the unknown.

The thought of her lying alone in that silence, unreachable, *fading*. If she was even still... I couldn't let that thought finish. I wouldn't.

Before I could think better of it, I crossed the room and entered the corridor that took me to the laundry room, shoving open the door. The hinges let out a long, disapproving groan. The air on the other side was colder. *Heavier.* A breath not drawn in years.

"Isabelle?"

My voice echoed into the dark.

No answer.

The narrow hallway I stepped into was lined with foil wallpaper. Each footstep echoed sharper than it should have. Shadows hovered at the edges, alive with quiet intent. I ran my hand along the railing as I climbed the stairs. It was smooth and cool beneath my fingers, worn down by time.

"Isabelle," I said again, quieter this time. A whisper, hoping she would hear me, but afraid of what my intrusion would cause.

Still nothing.

At the top of the stairs, the dim corridor unfurled before me. Curtains hung like mourning veils. The only light came in slivers, fading sunlight pushing through gaps in the fabric. I walked slowly, passing one door, then another. Most were closed. The ones I dared open revealed unused guest rooms, covered in a fine layer of dust. Preserved. Waiting.

"Isabelle?"

No breath. There was no stir of air. Only stillness.

Then I reached the end of the hallway.

A pair of tall, ornate double doors stood before me. They were carved in delicate vines and roses, the kind of craftsmanship that spoke of another time. My heart pounded into a frenzy knowing she could be behind them, my hands trembling.

I had kissed her in this house. I had touched every part of her, and she had let me. She had given herself to me completely. And still, I had no idea what waited on the other side.

I raised my knuckles to knock, but stopped. Instead, I pressed my ear to the wood and listened, but I heard nothing, so I turned the knob.

The door opened on reluctant hinges, revealing a large bedroom swathed in shadow. Dim light slipped through the lace curtains, casting a spectral glow over everything. And in the middle of it all, on the four-poster bed, she lay.

Isabelle.

Unmoving.

Her skin was pale, her body motionless. Silver hair spilled across the pillow like snow that had never been disturbed. The room smelled faintly of lavender, layered with the quiet decay of air left stagnant by too many unchanging days.

Chest squeezing until I thought my ribs may crack, I stepped inside, the flashlight trembling in my grip. Its dim beam drifted across her face with hesitation, as if afraid to wake what it found.

She looked just as luminous as she had days ago.

But she wasn't breathing.

Panic thundered through my ears as I laced my fingers together and began compressions. Thirty. Hard and fast. My palms ached with the effort. My voice fractured into desperation, whispering against the silence.

"Please, Isabelle. Come back to me. *Please.*"

I pinched her nose, tilted her head, and breathed into her mouth. Again and again. Each cycle carved another piece from me. The air in the room felt wrong, as if it had forgotten how to hold oxygen. My hands kept moving, driven by instinct and the refusal to let go.

"I'm not losing you," I whispered, voice torn in two. "Not now. Not after I've found you."

Time unraveled around me, meaningless and merciless.

I saw her hands brushing mine in the dark. Her eyes looked at me like I was the answer to a question she hadn't meant to ask. Heard her voice saying my name like it had always been hers.

My muscles burned. My lungs screamed, but I didn't stop.

I wouldn't.

When my body finally gave out, I collapsed beside her, cheek against her collarbone, tears streaking down my face.

"I'm sorry, Isabelle," I whispered, voice raw. "Please forgive me. Please come back."

The room pressed in. Candle wax. Stone. Lavender and rain. I felt her stillness in my arms like a weight I couldn't carry. With nothing left to give, my body curled around hers, trying to shield her from the world, from whatever had taken her away.

Sleep didn't come as rest. It came as a surrender.

A gentle touch brushed my cheek.

I stirred, not fully awake yet. The weight of grief lingered in my limbs. My eyes opened slowly, as if surfacing from a long and heavy dream, and she was there.

Isabelle.

Alive.

Sitting beside me on the bed, her silver gaze filled with sorrow and something else, something quieter, deeper. Tender. *Terrified.*

My heart lurched. I blinked at her, breath tangled in my throat.

"Isabelle? I—" My voice cracked. "I thought..."

"I know," she said, gently cupping my cheek in her hand. Her touch was warm now, the heat returning to her slowly. "I'm so sorry, Kayden. I never meant for you to find me like that, but there's something you must know."

I reached for her hand, gripping it like it was the only real thing in the room.

"Tell me," I said, heart still racing. "How?"

Fingers curling around mine, she looked down at our hands, then back up. Her voice, when it came again, was barely a breath.

"Every morning, when the sun rises... I *die*."

My stomach dropped. I waited for the punchline, an alternative explanation, but her eyes didn't waver.

"Not a metaphor," she added, like she had heard my thoughts. "It's not emotion. It's literal. My heart stops. My body... *stops*."

The way she had touched me that night came back in full: the way she had trembled, kissed me, held me like it might be her last chance to feel alive. And now, I understand why.

No words came. I couldn't speak.

A shaky breath left her. "It's been this way for nearly a century. Since I was twenty. I've been trapped in this house ever since, reliving the same night again and again, waiting for something to shift."

Her gaze returned to mine, silver and shimmering with pain.

"Until *you*."

What she had given me wasn't just her body. It had been a farewell.

My lips parted. A thousand things rose in my throat, but none made it into sound. Whatever I might have said, it stayed buried beneath the ache.

"I don't understand," I finally managed. But even as I said it, part of me did. Part of me had always known. I had seen her stillness. Her silence. Held her cold body in my arms. Felt what it was to grieve for her and love her all at once.

Love. Even so soon, the word felt right.

"I know," she said. Her thumb stroked gently across the back of my hand. "You're not supposed to. Not yet. But I promise I will tell you everything."

With a hesitant smile, she leaned forward and pressed her forehead to mine.

"I just need you to believe me—*for now.*"

I didn't trust the world I thought I knew anymore.

But I trusted her.

You are the reason I light every candle.
The reason I don't lock the door.
Come back, even if only as a shadow.
Even if only as an ache.

CHAPTER 9

The Flower

The look in his eyes when I told him the truth will stay with me for the rest of my life. It wasn't fear or disbelief. It was sorrow.

I had woken to find him asleep beside me, his face unguarded, softened by exhaustion. Even in sleep, he looked hollowed out. Grief pressed deep into the lines around his mouth, his hands loose but restless, as if he'd been holding vigil through the weight of it alone.

And still, he stayed.

When I told him what I was, what the curse had done to me, he didn't look away. He didn't recoil.

There was no horror in his expression. No sharp intake of breath. Only grief.

Grief for the life I'd been denied. For the truth I had carried alone.

And perhaps, too, for the woman he had held only days before.

The one who had curled into his arms and whispered against his skin. The one who had breathed and wanted and ached beside him.

By morning, I was gone, and in my place remained the quiet aftermath of magic and loss.

But he didn't turn away.

"When I was twenty, in the year 1933, a woman lived in town. Strange and secretive, she moved through whispers. People said she knew things no one else could. She had a son close to my age and claimed she had seen our futures entwined. One afternoon, she came to our home and told my parents we were destined to marry. That she had seen it in the stars. But I was not a bride. I was a promise she had carved from my future and handed to a man I did not love. My father said no. Kindly, but firmly. My parents didn't believe in spells or omens, but they feared her in the way people fear what they don't understand. When she left, I was grateful. I thought it was over."

Kayden's fingers tightened gently around mine. His brow was furrowed, but not with skepticism. Only pain.

"The next morning, I didn't wake up. At least... not in the way I had before. My parents found me cold. Breathless. They thought I had died. My mother collapsed. My father sent for the priest. I remember the sound of him weeping beside my bed when I returned at nightfall."

I paused, looking away from Kayden to the soft shadow of the curtains.

"When she returned a day later, after the priest had prayed over me, she said I would be bound to this house," I began softly. My voice held no tremble, but something inside it had thinned. *Worn.* "That I would die each morning and rise each night until I found true love. Not just love, but a vow. A bond. *Marriage.*"

When he didn't speak, I tightened my grip on his hand and let myself keep going.

"But there was more she didn't tell them that night."

My gaze drifted toward the darkened window again, though I wasn't seeing the glass.

"The curse couldn't be broken while her son still lived... or so she claimed."

That stilled something in him. Although he didn't speak, I saw his face tense.

"That was the real root of it," I said. "The cruel spine beneath her words. She claimed she had seen a premonition. That if her son and I were married, he would live forever. That our union would not only preserve me, but it would elevate him. She believed I was the key to his immortality. So, when we refused her," I said, taking in a deep breath. "She didn't just curse me to die and rise again. She cursed me to be unable to marry. Unable to love. Unable to be free in any way until her son was gone."

I looked down at our joined hands.

"It was never meant to be a lesson. It was a punishment. A lock she sealed with her will—tight, deliberate, impossible to undo from the inside."

I shifted upright slightly, as if needing the steadiness.

"They buried an empty coffin," I said. "My parents couldn't bear to leave me, so they stayed, but my father couldn't let it go. Not the curse. Not the woman who had done this to me. One morning, he left quietly, without a goodbye. I think he meant to find her son. I think he meant to kill him."

My voice thinned.

"But he never came back."

Eyes widening, Kayden swallowed hard.

"My mother waited. Weeks. But there was no letter. No word. And in her silence, I saw what she never said aloud: that the witch had taken him, too."

Outside, the wind pressed softly against the windows, as if listening.

"Months later, my father's body was found, and after that, she faded," I said. "Slowly. Quietly. The house grew still. The staff left."

I blew out a breath, the emotions I'd been suppressing pressing hard against the walls I'd built to keep them in.

"And I stayed. I have stayed ever since. At first, I counted the days. Then the years. Eventually, I stopped. Time became meaningless. The world changed around me. Wars came and went. Radio gave way to televisions, then glowing screens. Music bent and broke into unfamiliar shapes. I watched generations pass outside these windows and through the newspaper dropped through the mail slot until it stopped coming, but I stayed the same. Night after night. Dying with the dawn. Waking with the dusk."

I looked back at him.

"Until you."

Kayden leaned in, resting his forehead gently against mine, his breath warm and anchoring.

"You don't have to be alone anymore," he said. "Not if you don't want to be."

And for the first time in nearly a century, I let myself believe it might be true.

I hadn't planned to tell him tonight. The air still held the last of my confessions like the echo of a storm. I wanted to give him time. Time to breathe. To process. To run, if necessary.

But he hadn't run.

He had stayed.

Even after I gave him my curse, my truth, my body... He had wrapped his arms around all of it and held on.

That changed things.

Then, we lay together in the quiet. His fingers traced light patterns along my arm, each one gentle, patient, and present. He didn't ask more questions. He didn't press. The silence between us had thickened. It wasn't empty anymore. It waited. A space that had become a door, waiting to open.

"Kayden?"

His warm gaze met mine instantly.

"I'm here," he said.

When I sat up, curling my legs beneath me, I was no longer hesitant to talk about my plight. The cool air teased across my bare arms despite the warmth of the blankets. I stared at my hands for a long time, willing them not to tremble.

"There's something else about the curse. Something I haven't told you."

He didn't flinch, but I saw the flicker of concern in his eyes. Still, he didn't turn away. He just nodded once, encouraging me to continue, so I did.

"Marriage can free me from the house, but it doesn't stop the dying."

He blinked, brows knitting as he leaned in.

"What do you mean?"

I exhaled slowly, trying to find the words that wouldn't fracture in my throat.

"No matter what, when the sun rises, my body dies. That part doesn't stop. Not yet. Not until the curse is broken completely."

His expression shifted. Not to fear, but to something more profound. A dawning understanding that cut through him like a tide that couldn't be turned back.

"Then how do we break it?" he asked.

I hesitated. The answer felt too old, too heavy.

"She said the curse was tied to her son's life. That wasn't true... at least I don't think it was. If my suspicions are correct, it was linked to hers. She took something from me. A piece of my soul, I think. That's what keeps me here. *Trapped.* To break it... she has to die. I have to take back what she stole."

Kayden didn't speak right away. I could see it in his eyes, that quiet storm of thought building inside him. Not disbelief. Not retreat. Just a man sorting through the weight of what he now carried.

"I don't know where she is," I added, my voice small. "It's been nearly a century. She's still out there. I know she must be. If she weren't, the curse would've lifted by now. But I don't know where she's hiding, or how to find her."

We sat in the kind of silence that only truth leaves behind. The stillness between us had changed. It was no longer fragile or forced, but steady and present, anchored by everything we had finally said aloud.

"And if we were married," he asked, "you could leave?"

"I would not survive the daylight," I said. "Not until she's gone, but I would not be bound to the house anymore. Not in the same way."

He nodded once, his gaze steady, his voice sure.

"Then we'll marry. And after that, we find her."

Later, after his breathing slowed and the weight of his arms around me eased into sleep, I lay awake, watching the ceiling as shadows curled along the edges of the room.

The echo of my words lingered between us—the ones I'd spoken, and those still caught behind my ribs, waiting for the right breath. There was more. Always more. But I had spoken the heart of it. Enough to make the silence feel like space, not a prison.

The night pressed in.

As the moon kept its watch, I slipped from the bed, pulled a robe around my shoulders, and padded barefoot to the window. Mist hugged the glass. The sea below hissed quietly in the distance. I placed my palm on the pane, letting it cool my skin and grounding me in the present moment. Not the weight of the century that haunted me.

A part of me feared I had said too much. That I had shattered whatever spell had drawn him to me.

But he hadn't left. He hadn't looked at me with fear.

He had stayed, and that meant something.

For a while, I stood in the doorway and watched him sleep. One hand outstretched, as though still reaching for me even in his dreams.

At that moment, for the first time in nearly a hundred years, I did not feel like the girl who died with the dawn.

I felt like someone who might survive until morning.

Knowing I could not sleep, I moved through the familiar still air of the house, trailing my fingers along the banister as I descended to the study. The fire there had long since gone cold. I lit a candle from habit and pulled a thin leather journal from beneath the floorboard. The volume was older than Kayden. I opened it to a blank page, and for the first time in years, I knew what I needed to say.

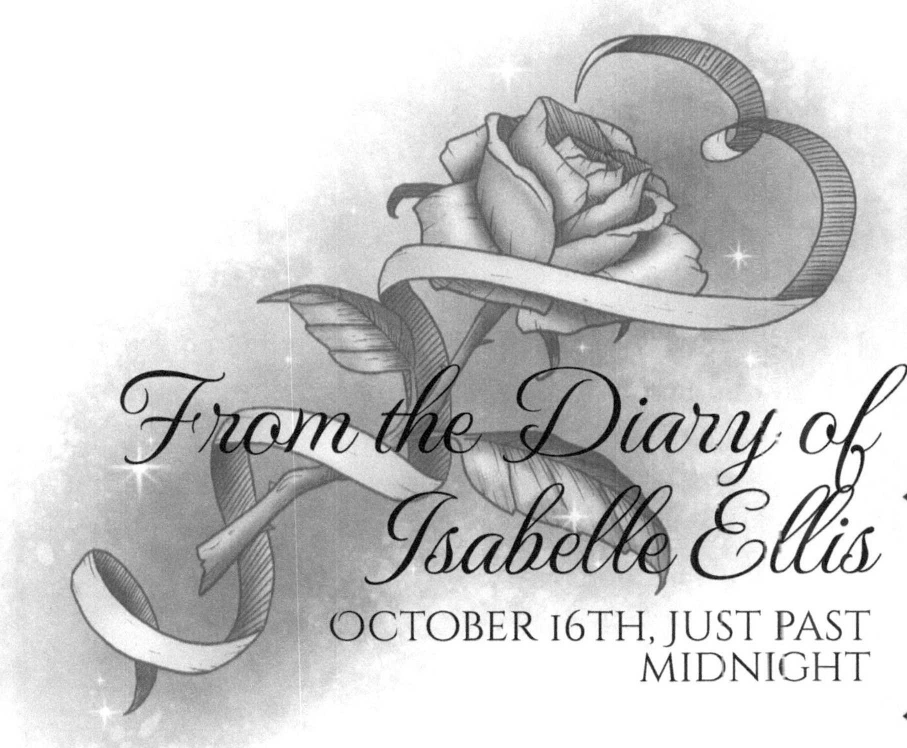

He knows. And still, he stays.

I did not expect that. I bared my soul to him, revealing everything about the death, the curse, the witch, and the vow. I braced for silence. For distance. Perhaps disbelief. Instead, he reached for my hand. He listened. And in his eyes, I saw something I had not been offered in nearly a century: A promise.

He carries my truth now, and I still do not know whether it's a gift or a weight.

The thought of marriage unsettles me, not because the desire is foreign, but because it lives so deeply inside me.

It has waited there quietly, like a prayer I no longer dared to speak.

What would it mean to be chosen? To truly belong to someone who sees me as I am?

I didn't want to be a story or a symbol, bound by old magic, frayed and afraid, longing to be more than the sum of her shadows. I yearned to be a woman he could hold and choose. I craved to trust what he sees when he looks at me. I wanted to believe that the silence, the suffering, and the years all led me here.

To him.

But curses are not broken by hope alone.

And if we should fail... The thought alone sends shivers down my spine.

No. I will not allow myself to imagine the end tonight.

Love, Isabelle

CHAPTER 10

The Keeper

I must have drifted off for a little while, just long enough for dreams to curl around the edges of my thoughts. When I stirred again, the scent of lavender ghosted across my face, and she was still there, warm in my arms.

Isabelle had since drifted off beside me, her breath soft against my shoulder as the wind made ivy tap lightly on the windows. I kept my eyes open, staring into the dark, my thoughts caught somewhere between disbelief and wonder. I watched the pale moonlight slowly shift across the ceiling, trying to let the truth of her presence sink in.

I had believed in many things before I came here. In fate, maybe. Ghosts, on the lonelier nights. But curses? A woman who died with the morning light and rose again at night, like a myth given breath? That had never fit inside my reality.

And yet... I had held her body when it was cold. I had kissed her lips and tasted life in them. I had seen her rise from stillness with breath that belonged to the dark. Disbelief had vanished, leaving only awe, quiet grief, and questions too large to fathom.

She had told me her story with trembling hands and steady eyes. Not as a warning. Not even as a plea. But as a gift. Trust was placed gently in my hands.

That kind of trust didn't ask for words. It asked to be carried, and I didn't know how, but I wanted to.

I looked down at her as I lay there, her cheek resting against my chest, one arm draped over my stomach like I was the one who might slip away. The fire had left her skin warm, and strands of hair fell across her face like moonlight spun into silk. Breathtaking. *Enchanting.*

Mystery still clung to her, but she was no longer untouchable. Not to me. Not tonight.

The curse had made her fragile, but it hadn't broken her.

With a careful breath, I pressed a kiss to her forehead and eased myself out of bed.

The apartment was dim. Only the candle beside the sofa still burned, its flame low and flickering. I poured myself a glass of water and stood at the window, watching the silver slash of the sea under the moonlight.

What did it mean to love someone who only lived by night? What would it mean to marry someone you couldn't share the day with?

I thought of my father. The way he used to say, love isn't supposed to be easy. That's how you know it's real.

And I thought of Isabelle. Of her loneliness. Her quiet strength. The unspoken ache she carried with every breath. She didn't ask to be rescued. She only asked me to believe her, and I did. I couldn't do anything else.

No matter what I had to do, I would find the witch. I would cross whatever distance was needed to be crossed. Even if it took me the rest of my life.

I didn't know how or where to begin, but I would.

For her. For us. For the life she had never been allowed to live.

The room glowed with soft candlelight, golden flames flickering against the walls while shadows danced overhead. Outside, the storm whispered against the windows, the wind sighing low through the old bones of the house. It felt like the kind of night that belonged to no one but us.

Isabelle lay in my arms, her breath steady against my chest, and though the silence between us was peaceful, my mind wouldn't quiet. Everything she had told me still echoed: her curse, the conditions, the impossibility of the life she had endured. Yet none of it gave me pause. Not even close.

That one word, marriage, held so much weight for her, as if she expected it to shatter what we'd built. I saw it in the hesitation in her voice, the way she braced herself when she spoke, but all it did was deepen what I already felt. Her fear told me more than her words ever could. She was bracing—for abandonment, for loss, for what always came next.

But I wasn't going anywhere.

In such a short time, she had become the center of everything, and if she needed proof that she could count on me, then I would give it to her.

Tilting her chin gently with my fingers, I kissed her temple. When she met my eyes, I smiled.

"We'll take each day as it comes, my flower. We can be together tonight, and I'll take care of the rest when the sun rises. I'll start planning. I'll find someone to marry us. I'll get flowers. A cake. Whatever you want, I'll make it happen. I will find a way to give you freedom."

Her smile grew, warming me to my core, and I saw hope bloom in her expression.

"Is that what you want to do?" she asked, her tone unsure.

The kiss she gave me held more than longing. It carried fear, hope, and the fragile trust that comes with surrender. The weight of her voice settled between us as she continued, "It sounds wonderful, Kayden, but I just want to make sure it's what you want. My happiness shouldn't come at the expense of yours."

There was desperation beneath her softness, like she needed to be chosen and couldn't quite believe it. As if love, to her, always came with an expiration date. I still couldn't believe that she thought loving her could ever be a sacrifice.

Maybe I should've questioned it more. Perhaps I should've taken a step back, looked at what little I really knew about her, about this curse, about the risk. But I didn't want to, because despite all of it, despite every reason I shouldn't have felt this sure, I did.

Once her life was her own again, I knew she would need time to heal, to relearn the world, but I would be there for all of it. Her pain. Her joy. Her rediscovery. I pictured her barefoot in sunlight, learning the world again in pieces. Not all of it would be easy. But I wanted it all.

"You don't need to worry about that," I said, brushing a strand of hair from her face. "Being with you is not a sacrifice. If anything, you're making the sacrifice to be with me. Other men might offer you more—wealth, ease, comfort, but none of them would love you the way I do. I only hope that once you're free, you'll still want me beside you."

Her smile turned radiant, eyes glittering as her fingers threaded through my hair.

"Don't be silly, Kayden. When this curse breaks, it'll still be you in my bed at night. Kissing me. Touching me. Making me feel alive."

Her voice dropped to a purr. I felt like a switch inside me flipping. Every thought fell away. All that remained was the urge to touch her, hold her closer, feel her against me.

Lowering her onto the bed, I followed the line of her jaw with my lips, my hand tracing the silky skin along her waist. At that moment, nothing else existed. Only her.

Each shift of her body answered mine, every curve drawn closer as she leaned into my touch.

Need burned low in my chest, it's pulling steadily and consuming. There was no hesitation now. No doubt. Just the weight of wanting her and being wanted in return.

I shifted, drawing her into my lap. Her legs parted as she straddled me, settling with aching slowness. The fire gilded her skin, and I couldn't stop touching her, chasing each shimmer like it was mine to keep. Every movement coaxed a sound from her—quiet at first, then sharper, her breath catching as need bloomed beneath her skin.

She rocked against me, and every movement made it harder to keep myself in check. My hands found her hips, anchoring her, guiding her into a rhythm that made it hard to think, harder still to speak.

"Is that so?" I murmured, lips brushing the hollow of her throat. "You like it when I kiss you... When I touch you, little flower?"

Her breath hitched. That soft gasp—half need, half surrender—answered everything. She moved again, slower this time, grinding down with purpose. My pulse caught. My hands slid over her waist, over the delicate rise of her ribs. Her body rolled into mine, trembling with every new inch of closeness.

She moaned when my mouth returned to her neck, the sound low and broken, filled with a need she didn't bother to hide.

Close to her ear, I whispered, "I love it when you make those sounds."

Hands gripping my shirt, she shivered. "I like it when you kiss and touch me," she said, her breath warm against my neck. Her hips rolled harder, breath catching. "And I love it when you call me your flower."

Those words broke through me.

I was already hers in every way that mattered.

And when she cried my name again, her body trembling beneath mine, the truth hit so hard it left no room for doubt: the curse might still hold, but she was mine, and I wouldn't let her go.

You didn't need to ask for forever.
You only had to look at me
like I was worth staying for.
And in that moment,
I would have vowed anything.

Waking beside the woman I loved, her body breathless and cold, tore through a part of me I hadn't realized was still holding on to. Even knowing she would return, even having watched it happen before with my own eyes, the pain did not dull.

She had vanished again, leaving only stillness behind.

The heaviness of it settled over my chest like stone as I eased out of bed and pulled the blanket gently over her.

I paused at the door, casting one last glance back at the quiet shape beneath the sheets, taken aback by how stunning she was. Even in the dying candlelight, even in the thin line of orange light from the rising sun, she was the most breathtaking woman I'd ever seen.

With the day awakening, I descended the stairs in silence, dread clinging to me like brine-soaked wool. I tried to remind myself that this was her normal. That I would see her again when the sun dipped below the horizon. But knowing and feeling were entirely different beasts.

I stood under the water too long, trying to scrub away what I couldn't fix. My skin burned, but the helplessness stayed. My thoughts spiraled beneath the water, circling her. The way she had looked at me. The way she had clung to me. The way she died, so quietly, it felt like a betrayal.

Back in my own bedroom, I dressed slowly, checking the clock and then glancing up at the ceiling more than once, listening for a sound I knew wouldn't come. It was too early, too bright. She wouldn't return until dusk.

Needing something to do with my hands, I scribbled notes in the back of my notebook. Vows. I didn't need them to have rhyme or rhythm. I needed the truth.

Even if you never walk in the sun again, you won't walk alone.
Even if the world forgets you, I never will.
Even if you vanish each morning, I'll love you through every night.

Once my bleeding heart had been poured into as many words as I could manage, I closed my notebook. There was still so much to do to prepare for our impromptu wedding. I grabbed my keys and laptop, stepped outside, and found myself pausing at the base of the drive, looking up toward the manor. The sun was still climbing, her window still and silent, the curtains drawn. I knew she was safe in her bed. But, even so, that absence sent my stomach tumbling into the rain-soaked ground. No matter how many times it happened, I still wasn't ready for the hollowness she left behind.

The road into town lay wet from the night's rain, the asphalt dark and glistening. Fog drifted low along the fields and sidewalks, moving without urgency, as if it had forgotten where it came from. The air was crisp, but it didn't settle me. My thoughts churned louder than the wind, crowding out the quiet, restless, and thick in my chest.

I wasn't ready for the wedding. It had nothing to do with doubt. I loved her—fully, irreversibly—but what she'd shared with me couldn't be solved with love alone. A curse. A witch. A life measured by nightfall. I needed to understand what we were stepping into. I wasn't hesitating. I just wanted to meet it with both eyes open. For her.

Near the town square, I parked and ducked into the coffee shop. The smell of cinnamon clung to the air, cut through by the bitterness of old espresso grounds.

After ordering a large coffee, I tucked myself into a corner booth, needing the wall at my back and the quiet more than the coffee.. The screen glowed pale and impersonal as I typed her name, *Isabelle Ellis*, into the search bar.

The search returned nothing new. Just the same scattered threads I had seen before. Too few traces for someone who had lived a century.

When it became clear there was nothing left to find, I closed the lid and crossed the street to the Bluff Bar, hoping to see Howard inside.

The place was quieter than usual. The scent of salt and fryer oil clung to the air. Howard sat at the far end of the bar, hunched over his coffee, as if it held more than just heat, as if it were holding him up. I slipped onto the stool beside him.

"You ready to go sailing yet?" he asked without looking over.

"Not today," I said. "Actually... I need a favor."

That got his attention. He turned, studying me with his weather-worn eyes.

"What kind of favor?"

A breath passed before I spoke.

"Do you know anyone who might be willing to talk about the Ellis family? Someone who remembers. Not just the gossip—*really* remembers."

Howard stilled, tapping the side of his cup.

"That house has a long memory," he said at last.

I nodded. "So does she."

Then his eyes found mine, and for a moment, he searched me like he was trying to decide if I meant it. I didn't look away.

After a long pause, he sighed. "Come back just before sunset. There's something I want to show you."

I didn't ask. I didn't have to. The chill in his voice said everything.

The sun hovered low when I returned to the Bluff Bar, staining Crystal Peak in a copper wash. Shadows pooled at the base of the trees, and the sidewalks were streaked in amber and gray, like the remnants of watercolor left out too long to dry. Clouds gathered over the horizon, slow and bruised with weight, as if the sky itself had forgotten how to let go.

I'd spent the afternoon walking along the edge of town, past shuttered shops and rusted signs, letting my thoughts unravel just enough to breathe. I wasn't sure what I was chasing—maybe space, maybe something to quiet the churn. But eventually, my feet led me back here.

The bar was dimmer and quieter than usual when I stepped back inside. Maybe that's why Howard had asked me to come later, or perhaps he'd needed time to decide whether the information was his to share. Either way, I'd done what he asked.

 The amber bulbs overhead flickered faintly, their light soft and warm against the dark wood. A television in the corner muttered a forgotten game, its colors faded to ghosts against the dark.

Howard sat where I'd left him that morning, nursing something more golden than coffee. Seeming to be watching the elderly bartender clean tables across the room, he didn't turn when I walked in. Didn't speak when I eased onto the stool beside him. For a while, we sat in the kind of silence only small towns could manage, the type that didn't need filling.

"You came," he said eventually, his voice a gravelly thing that didn't bother trying to mask its surprise.

"I said I would," I replied, watching the light slide along the rim of his glass.

He nodded, eyes still forward. "You ask a lot of questions about a house that prefers to be left alone."

I didn't interrupt.

He took a sip, seeming to hesitate. "There's an old records office in the back of City Hall. Not many people are aware that it's still there. The town historian used to live upstairs, back when we still had one. She kept paper records of everything: births, deaths, property deeds, the stories no one wanted written down but did anyway. I doubt anyone's touched those files in decades."

My interest piqued. "You think I'll find something about the homeowners there?"

Howard finally turned, his gaze meeting mine sharper than I expected.

"I think if you're going to dig into the history of the home, you need to understand what it's tied to."

Something in my stomach twisted.

"So, you *do* know something."

He exhaled through his nose, the sound rough. "I know that place hasn't shifted in generations. That people whisper behind their hands but never say anything out loud. That once, a long time ago, a young woman vanished from that place overnight, and no one asked why."

His fingers tapped the side of his glass, then stopped. He set it down hard enough that it made a loud echo.

"When I was a boy, my mother wouldn't let me walk past the gates. Said it was cursed. Said the wind didn't sound right when it passed through the trees."

My hands curled around my own cup. The condensation felt like ice.

"You think the young woman who lives there is a part of that?"

Howard turned toward the window. The last light of day was almost gone now, leaving only a thin glow at the edge of the sea.

"I think whatever lives in that house wants to stay hidden," he said. "But she's not what you need to be afraid of."

That stopped me.

"Then what should I be afraid of?"

"If she's part of the original family," he said, his smile grim, "Then it's not her you should fear. It's the one who's kept her there."

The way he said it sent a pulse of unease down my spine. Like he wasn't warning me about superstition, but something he'd felt before.

The air shifted. Reaching into his coat, he pulled out a folded slip of paper, the edges soft from wear. He slid it across the bar without looking.

"Here's the name of the woman who ran the archives. Used to be a librarian. Knew everything there was to know about Crystal Peak. Got a little too into it, if you ask me. If she's still breathing, she might talk to you."

I unfolded the note. On it was a name with an address on the far side of town.

"You didn't hear this from me," Howard muttered, already turning back to his drink.

"Thanks, Howard."

He didn't look at me. Just said, "Be careful. Some truths don't want to be found."

Standing from my stool, I stepped out into the twilight.

The paper in my pocket felt heavier than it should have, and far above the sea, the house on the cliff waited, its windows dark, its walls full of secrets no one dared release, the kind that pressed too long in the dark and changed everything they touched.

The sky had darkened by the time I returned to the house. The last of the sunset clung to the horizon, a smear of dying lavender stitched above the sea. I parked at the top of the long gravel drive, headlights sweeping briefly across the ivy-choked stone of the manor before blinking out and leaving the world in darkness.

The house changed when night fell. Not just in shadow, but in intent. Older somehow. Watchful. Its windows were shuttered tight; its silhouette was jagged against the mist, like something carved from ruin and left behind.

In the passenger seat beside me, a paper bag rested, cradling two warm meals from the café. I hadn't chosen anything elaborate, just something comforting: House pasta. Cherry pie. Something rich and familiar. Something that might feel like the world she hadn't touched in a hundred years. She'd been trapped for so long, fed on memory and solitude. I wanted to give her something that didn't ask anything of her.

Something simple. Human.

Under the faint light of the rising moon, I carried the food carefully down the winding path and into the apartment. The door creaked softly as I opened it, and the space welcomed me with a silence that clicked into place. It had been waiting for me.

Setting the bag on the counter, I lit a few candles, which Isabelle seemed to prefer, and cracked the window just enough to let in the scent of brine and night air.

I never knew the exact moment she returned, only that it came after the sun surrendered completely, when the house seemed to exhale her back into being.

So, I waited. I moved through the space, adjusting the blankets, filling the water glasses, and checking the fire. The kind of motions that keep you from pacing. The kind that said, I'm ready. Come home.

And then I stood at the window, watching the third floor. The curtains were drawn, the windows dark.

But then, there was just barely a flicker. A ripple in the shadows.

Stepping away from the window, I turned toward the door that divided her world from mine, my heart kicking up. When I opened the door, she stood there, wrapped in white and her hair loose around her shoulders, eyes bright and brimming with relief, as if she hadn't truly let herself believe I'd still be here.

"You're here."

I barely had time to answer before she stepped into my arms. Her body pressed close, warm and genuine and unmistakably alive. I held her like I needed the proof, and for a moment, we just stayed like that—no words, no questions, just breath and closeness and the unspoken weight of everything that hadn't broken us.

When we finally parted, her eyes drifted to the paper bag on the table. Her lips parted with a quiet sound of surprise.

"I brought dinner," I said, my voice too loud in the silence. "In case you were hungry."

Her smile was genuine, and it lit something in her face I hadn't seen since the night she first kissed me.

"You didn't have to do that," she said.

"I know," I replied as I ushered her inside. "But I wanted to."

When she stepped into the room, she slipped her arms back around my waist, her face pressed to my chest, and all at once, the space between us felt full again.

I held her tightly, one hand resting in her hair, the other cradling her back. Beneath my ribs, my heartbeat stuttered fast and deep, and I wondered if she could feel it—if it meant anything to hear someone else's life so close to her own.

"Thank you," she murmured, her voice barely audible.

No talk of curses. No mention of the witch. The wedding waited patiently in the hours ahead.

We ate by the fire, her head resting against my shoulder, our legs tangled beneath the blankets. Golden light flickered across the walls, and the tranquility between us felt earned.

Whatever else haunted the house, she didn't feel like part of it now.

She felt real. She felt like mine.

You sleep without breathing.
And still, I speak to you.
As if the sound of my voice
could keep you from slipping back into the veil.

The house had quieted once more, but this time it was different. Gone were the echoes of sorrow and the weight of emptiness. Instead, a gentle sense of calm had taken its place. It was the peace that followed comfort. The quiet that lingers after laughter, after warmth, after the smell of butter cooling in the air. After the feel of his hand brushing against mine across flour-dusted countertops. That quiet remained.

We had finished cleaning the kitchen not long ago. Afterward, he read aloud from a book I had taken off the shelf, filled with fairy tales that had too many teeth, the kind I once held onto when I needed to believe in impossible things. Now, only the hush of time remained between us, the night stretching thin, and the promise of tomorrow looming just beyond the dark.

"Would you cut my hair?"

I blinked, hands stilling against the mug. "Now?"

He nodded, and his mouth tugged into a crooked, almost bashful smile. "It's too long, and if I'm going to marry a cursed woman in a garden of shadows, I should at least look like I tried."

Laughter escaped me before I could stop it—not at his words, but at how much I wanted to say yes.

"All right." My smile only grew wider as I pulled a chair away from the table. "Sit."

The chair scraped faintly across the floorboards as he dragged it to the center of the room. While he settled in, I stepped into the hall. My fingertips trailed the edge of the old sewing drawer until they found the shears. They were heavier than I remembered, familiar in the way a forgotten thing can be when it still knows your touch. They had once cut ribbon, thread, and the occasional stitch from a dress too loved to let go. And once, long ago, my father's hair. His curls had softened at the temples, a touch more unruly at the nape, exactly like Kayden's. The last time I touched them, my fingers hesitated. I hadn't realized it was goodbye. Not until the house fell silent without him. Not until silence transformed into something heavier than grief. Something closer to blame.

When I stepped back into the room, Kayden looked up with quiet expectation, and there was something steadier behind it. A kind of trust I hadn't been given in years.

Moving behind him, I threaded my fingers through his hair. It was soft and a rich shade of brown. A few strands of silver shimmered near his temples, subtle and early for his age, but beautiful all the same.

"How much do you want off?" I asked, hoping my hands would remember what to do.

"Enough to feel like I'm stepping into something."

He shifted slightly, his gaze steady, then softened.

"But not so much that I forget who I was."

I met his eyes for a moment. The breath between us didn't ask for words. It held steady and sure. Then I lifted the shears.

Strands slipped through my fingers and fell in graceful arcs across his shoulders, catching the firelight in quiet flashes. Copper shimmered through the brown in subtle threads, the way my father's hair once had, and for a breath, memory pressed closer than I expected.

"You've done this before," he said after many moments of silence.

Doing my best to keep the grief from my expression, I nodded. "A few times. My father. The last time was the night before he went searching for someone he couldn't save."

He didn't respond right away. He just let the silence remain, undisturbed between us.

I hadn't expected how intimate it would feel, standing behind him with the scissors in my hand. The glow of the flames moved across his face, picking up the angles I'd memorized without trying. I used to spend my days tending quiet spaces—rooms that stayed empty, plants that asked nothing of me. I didn't know how to give care to a person, not like this, but he let me. He sat still and steady, offering nothing but his presence, letting my hands learn the shape of something new. He gave me that without asking, without fear. Just trust. Just him. And all I wanted at that moment was to be good to him.

When I finished, I stepped in front of him, brushing away the stray pieces that clung to his collar. I smoothed his hair with both hands once, then again, letting my fingertips linger along his jaw.

He looked like himself, but something in him had shifted. He seemed lighter. *Braver.* No longer a man bracing for a vow out of duty, but one who had already made the promise in his heart.

"There," I said, my voice quiet, as if I had finally set something right. "Now you look like a man who believes in it."

As he rose, his gaze stayed locked on mine. Taking my hand, he pressed a kiss into the center of my palm, holding it there for a moment, letting the silence carry what neither of us had put into words.

"I do," he murmured. "Every word I've said, and every word I haven't yet, I mean all of them."

Throughout the night, until Kayden fell asleep and I returned to the manor like a ghost, a sense of tranquility enveloped us. It created a space filled with unspoken words and full hearts. The fire crackled softly, its warmth weaving together stories of the past and hopes for the future—an unbroken rhythm as steady as the breaths shared between two souls who had chosen to stay together and would go to the ends of the earth to make that happen.

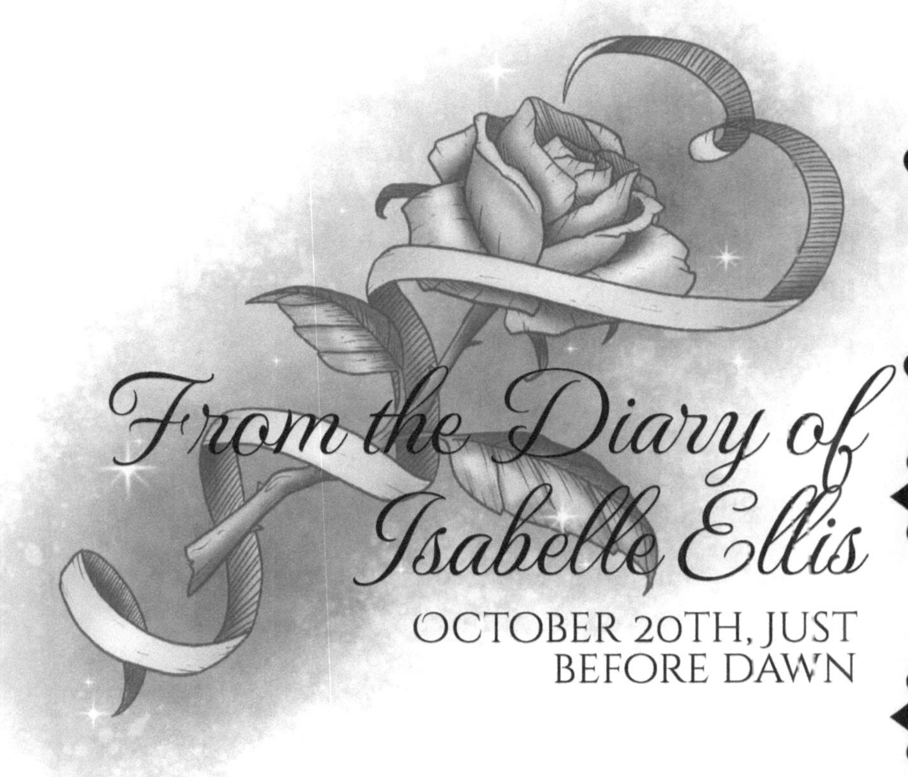

Tonight, I cut his hair.

It was a simple act, yet beneath the surface, it meant more than I expected. He sat still beneath my hands, his breath even, as though the slightest movement might startle something fragile into flight. I trimmed away what no longer belonged: loose strands, the weight of yesterday, and traces of the man he had been.

When I finished, he looked like someone who had made a choice—a quiet one, but certain nonetheless. It was a step toward whatever lies ahead.

He had asked for just enough to feel the change, but not so much that he might forget who he once was. And he chooses, again and again. With every glance. With every touch. With every word he does not speak. His choices, like echoes, reverberate in my bones, a testament to the persistence of change.

The fear, the fear of change, of losing what was familiar, of stepping into the unknown, is still with me, but it no longer binds me.

I do not know what tomorrow may bring. I have never known a tomorrow that stayed.

But tonight, as the herbs steeped in our tea, their aroma filled the air, a comforting reminder of the simple pleasures in life. The bread, warm and fragrant, rose beneath my hands, a symbol of growth and transformation. The lamplight caught the line of his cheek when I kissed him, a fleeting moment of tenderness. A seed was pressed into the garden, a promise of new beginnings. And a man sat quietly while I cut his hair—the same man who will stand beside me beneath the stars when I am free.

And when the sun returns, I shall let it take me. For I believe he will still be there when the night calls me home. And for the first time in a hundred years, I want to return.

Love, Isabelle

Morning returned in a wash of pale light and unsettled thoughts. As expected, Isabelle was gone.

The knowledge that she would return at dusk did nothing to soften the loss. My hand reached instinctively for the space where she had slept. It was still warm, still shaped like her. The pillow bore the shape of her head, a hollow reminder that she had been there and wasn't anymore.

Candle smoke lingered in the air, threaded with the faint scent of flowers. *Her scent.* Her presence clung to the air in a way my body had already learned to expect. Waking up without her had become its own kind of ritual, a mourning I never knew how to live with.

I didn't linger in the stillness she'd left behind. Instead, I showered, dressed, and reached for the slip of paper Howard had given me.

Margaret Whitlow, archivist and former librarian. Her name came with a small address scratched beneath it in Howard's careful script.

The drive took me further inland, past the edges of Crystal Peak, where the houses grew older and more overgrown. The trees arched low over the road, the sky barely visible through the spindly fingers of their bare branches. When I pulled up to the address, I found a cottage abandoned by time, every corner faded, every edge softened by weather and age.

Stepping onto the front porch, it took two knocks before getting a response.

The door opened a crack, just wide enough for a sharp, age-clouded eye to peer through—far from dull. Her face was creased like old linen, soft and deeply lined, framed by wisps of white hair loosely pinned back. A faded cardigan with mismatched buttons hung loosely on her frame. She smelled of mint and old paper, like a woman who'd steeped too long in her own stories.

"You're not from around here," she said, tilting her head just slightly, as though the angle might sharpen the truth of me.

"No, ma'am. I'm staying out at the old Ellis place."

Her eyes narrowed. "Most won't go near that place. Not anymore."

"I was hoping to ask you a few questions," I said, shifting slightly under her gaze.

She hesitated. Then, with a creak and a sigh, the door opened.

Inside, the house was small, lit mainly by candles and scented with dust and dried herbs. Books lined the corners in uneven stacks, while newspapers were bundled into quiet towers resting along the walls. I followed her through the narrow passageway and into a small sitting room cluttered with threadbare cushions and mismatched teacups.

"You want tea?" she asked, gesturing to the nearby kettle.

Although part of me felt like it might be rude to refuse, I shook my head. "No, thank you."

With one more assessing glance at my face, she sank into the armchair, a folded blanket already waiting for her lap.

"Well, then," she said, her tone clipped, though I could see mild curiosity in her expression. "Ask."

I sat forward slightly, resting my elbows on my knees. "What do you know about the Ellis family?"

She tilted her head. "Depends. Which generation are we talking about?"

"The daughter. Isabelle."

Something flickered behind her eyes, the soft twinge of a recollection returning.

"Beautiful girl," she murmured. "Strange story. The kind no one ever tells the same way twice."

The response made something in my chest tighten, but I tried to keep my voice even. "Can you tell me your version?"

Going quiet for a moment, she reached for her tea, stirring it once before setting it back down. She did not meet my eyes as she began. "She was set to be married once, some decades back. Then she vanished. The family stopped attending church. Staff left. Curtains drawn. People said she died, but…" Her voice trailed off, as if the weight of the past was too heavy to bear.

She trailed off for a moment, eyes narrowing as though peering into the past.

"Some claimed she was cursed. That she *lives*."

A chill raced down my spine, forcing me to shift in my seat. Although I already knew Isabelle's truth, part of me didn't want to hear the rumors. I cleared my throat, staying above the spiral. Perhaps there was still a part of me that feared she was a ghost, and that it had all been a delusion.

"There was no body?"

"None that I ever read about," she said, her voice quieter now. "Just a whisper that her parents moved the body themselves. Privately. Quietly. Too quietly."

I didn't respond right away. Even though I knew Isabelle would still return to life when darkness set in, that she must, the room had become heavier.

"And the house?"

"It's old," she said, glancing out the window. "But not empty."

"Some say it's haunted," I offered.

Margaret gave a slow nod, her mouth twisting faintly. "Ghosts are kinder than the things that house has held onto."

The words sent the bitter tang of dread settling into my chest.

Leaning over, she reached beside her chair, pulling a thin ledger from a crooked shelf and sliding it toward me across the cluttered table. I wasn't sure how old it was, but the pages were yellowed and delicate. The first page was dated over eighty years ago in a handwritten script:

Ellis daughter. Rumors of sickness. Sent away? Buried alive? Curse?

"People like to pretend we live in a world with rules," she murmured as I stared down at the small book in my hands. The ink had faded, but the words were still legible. "But we don't."

Even though I knew some of the answers this woman clearly sought, I didn't confirm anything. Not aloud. Not when it could put Isabelle's safety at risk.

"Do you think someone could... still be there from that family?"

My voice came quieter than I expected, like the question had shaped itself before I'd fully realized what I was asking.

Margaret looked at me for a long moment. Her expression didn't change, but something in her eyes did.

"I think someone never left," she said. "Not really."

Then, in a voice so low it might have been meant only for her own ears, she added: "She's not a ghost."

The room felt too small for the weight of those words. With the book still in my hands, I lifted my eyes to hers, waiting for her to continue.

"She's worse," she said, her fingers twisting into the blanket in her lap. "She remembers what it was like to live, but she can never experience life."

Her words landed like a stone dropped into still water. Something in me recoiled, but I did my best not to flinch. Lungs struggling for air, I looked down at the ledger in my lap, curling my fingers tighter around its binding.

Before I could even think to respond, she continued.

"My grandmother used to tell stories about a woman who moved to town," she said, her voice seeming far away, like it, too, came from the past. "Children were warned not to speak her name. She was strange. Cold. No one knew where she came from. They said she practiced strange rites in the woods, cast spells... hexes. My mother said people stopped knocking on her door. Said even the trees kept their distance, branches bowed away from the house without reason."

The image unnerved me more than I cared to admit, and when I looked back at Margaret, I caught her staring into the fireplace. She seemed almost younger, how her eyes caught the firelight, the way old coals sometimes glow again when stirred.

"And then one day, she and her son were gone. Packed up in the night. No forwarding address. Just disappeared."

That was when it clicked into place. She was talking about the witch—the woman who'd cursed Isabelle. I leaned forward. "Do you remember her name?"

"Thorne," Margaret said without hesitation. "Lenora Thorne. That name started to appear in land records just before the Ellis family withdrew from town life. She bought parcels no one wanted. Land that was believed to be cursed. There are stories, old ones, if you know where to look. Perhaps it was simply campfire stories—things meant to scare children into behaving..."

She reached for a small leather-bound notebook tucked beneath her chair. Her fingers moved across the worn pages until she found one marked with a date and a symbol I didn't recognize, a Raven twisted in thorns.

"But she wasn't like the others," Margaret added. "And whatever she started... it didn't end when she left."

The ride back to the house felt longer than it should have. Not in miles, but in weight. Margaret's words circled through me, uninvited but impossible to ignore.

She's worse. She remembers what it was like to live.

Thick fog rolled inland from the sea, slipping over the roadside in slow, restless ribbons. The trees pressed closer with each mile, their bare limbs grazing one another in dry, whispering touches. The manor did not appear all at once. It gathered shape slowly, rising out of the mist the way a half-remembered name rises to the tongue. Its windows revealed nothing. The silhouette held to the fading light, hoarding it the way the lonely hoard warmth.

I parked at the top of the drive and let my hands rest on the wheel, holding still for longer than I meant to.

What was I doing? The question wasn't new, but this time it didn't feel like a rhetorical question. It hit low and deep, landing in the hollow my chest had made for her. I missed her with a kind of ache that didn't wait for a reason. In such a short amount of time, she had become my reason for existing.

And still, the question remained. I was loving a woman who vanished with the dawn. Who woke only after nightfall. Who had waited a hundred years without hope, and somehow, now, was trusting me with the fragile pieces of what came next.

When I finally stepped inside the apartment, I didn't reach for coffee. I didn't light the fire. I dropped my keys on the counter with a metallic clatter that felt too loud, too final, and went straight to my laptop. The screen glowed in the dimness like something expectant.

I opened a blank document and typed the things I knew I had to do, as if putting them down would make them feel real.

Find someone who can marry us. Buy rings, nothing extravagant. Just something true. Call the florist. A cake? Dinner? Clean the apartment. Write vows.

My hands stilled. It wasn't the list that mattered. It was the movement. The sense that something lasting might finally be taking shape.

The screen didn't rush me. It just waited, like it knew the words had to come from someplace deeper. Rubbing my eyes, I tried to focus. Then I started typing into the search bar: *marriage license requirements, Crystal Peak town offices, same-day ceremonies, can you marry someone without ID?*

The questions grew stranger the longer I typed—less practical, more like confessions I didn't know I needed to make.

Eventually, I leaned back in the chair and stared at the screen, empty of answers.

What could I say to a woman who had died a thousand times and still dared to hope?

My fingers drifted back to the keys.

I didn't know what I was writing, only that the words came from somewhere deeper than thought. They unfolded one by one, unfiltered and authentic.

I love you.
I believe in you.
And whatever curse has claimed you, I will fight it with you.
Even if we never see a sunrise together.
Even if this house is the only world we ever know.
I will marry you in the dark,
because you're the only light I've found in years.

The screen's glow pressed faintly against the windowpane, a pale reflection blurred by mist and glass. Outside, the fog thickened, coiling around the manor like a serpent. The house above was silent.

Still, it felt like it was listening.

And the words on the page, however imperfect, felt like I was finally speaking the truth from my soul.

It was a plan. A promise. A beginning.

For the next several hours, Isabelle remained still above, lost to the curse's grip, but the house no longer felt cold. It no longer felt indifferent. The house knew me now—or at least, it knew I wasn't leaving.

Restless, I left the papers and laptop behind and made my way to the atrium. The passageway echoed with each step, the stone underfoot, and the air thick with the weight of age. The old door opened with a familiar groan, and the scent of earth rose up to meet me.

Sunlight filtered through the glass ceiling in a weak haze, illuminating the lavender and creeping vines that clung to the wrought-iron frame. It was warm inside, damp with the breath of growing things. I knelt near one of the empty plots Isabelle had once cleared and reached into my coat for the bundle I'd brought: packets of seeds I had picked up that morning. A few herbs. A wild rose variety. A cluster of deep purple violets labeled moon shade.

The soil gave way easily beneath my fingers. I planted slowly, pressing the seeds into the earth with more care than skill, hoping they would take root despite everything. Hoping they might greet her one day with something alive and beautiful.

She deserved a life that kept growing in the dark—green things that reached toward her, even here. She deserved to wake to more than silence.

Until the sun was nearly gone from the sky, I stayed beneath the lemon tree, my hands in the earth, the quiet settling into me in ways I hadn't expected. This place had held her. Kept her. It was her proof, and now it felt like mine.

The curse returned with a breath I never chose to take. It always came back this way—quiet and abrupt, like surfacing too quickly from deep water. One moment, there was nothing, and the next, there was pain. My chest tightened as the world rushed in all at once: air, ache, awareness. It was a tide I couldn't fight, only survive.

That first breath burned. It always did. My limbs stirred beneath the weight of death's memory, slow and unsteady, but I didn't stay there.

Tonight, I rose.

A faint blue light glowed above the bed. Sunset had long passed, and the sky now wore a twilight veil, with indigo deepening into silence, streaked with the serene backdrop of the approaching night. That light felt more like it belonged to a dream than to the passage of time.

Wrapping a shawl around my shoulders, I stepped into the hall. The manor, as always, stood silent. It wasn't asleep. It never was. It felt as if the walls were suspended between worlds, listening alongside me. I passed the hearth in the west corridor, long gone cold. The broken grandfather clock beside it hadn't ticked in decades, and I chose to touch neither. Some things, I had learned, were meant to remain still. The garden, however, was different.

At the atrium door, the air was warm and humid, rich with lavender and lemon balm. Beneath the glass ceiling, the world remained green. It breathed. It was alive. And it was mine, a sanctuary of tranquility in a world of chaos.

My mother planted it when she was newly married—before the war, before the sorrow, before the curse. It was a refuge for her, a haven for unspoken joys. Time has eroded much of the house, but this garden has endured, a symbol of continuity in a world of change.

Because I gave it what the curse couldn't take.

Near the narrow bed of sage, I lowered myself to the ground and let my hands find the soil. It was soft beneath my fingers, still damp from the atrium's breath. I trimmed the dying edges and brushed the roots back into place. The dirt gathered beneath my nails, and with each motion, I felt a sense of calm wash over me. For a moment, I didn't feel cursed or hollow. I felt real.

"Isabelle?"

Though I had grown accustomed to being alone, his voice didn't startle me. It flowed into the garden as if it had always belonged there.

When I glanced over my shoulder, I saw Kayden standing in the archway, half-lit by the soft glow from the hall. His sleeves were rolled up to his elbows, his collar was undone, and his hair was slightly tousled from sleep. A moment passed before he stepped forward, one hand tucked behind his back while the other brushed against the door frame.

The quiet that surrounded him felt familiar—the kind that fades by morning but leaves a lingering sensation in the air, just barely perceptible.

"I thought I'd find you here."

"You always do," I replied, smiling without hesitation. I had been smiling ever since I met him.

A handsome grin tugged at his lips as he stepped closer, revealing what he carried—a small pot wrapped in brown paper, gently cradled in his hands.

"I brought you something," he said. "It's not much, but it reminded me of you."

Peeling back the paper slowly, I uncovered a glazed flower pot, slightly chipped at the rim. Inside, a young night-blooming plant was nestled, its slender white petals just beginning to open. The scent was warm and thick, rich with promise.

"The woman at the nursery said it only blooms in the dark," he murmured. "I couldn't resist it."

Our eyes met, and something inside me let go. His gaze steadied me with a quiet assurance that didn't demand anything. It simply offered.

As the scent rose between us, my breathing slowed and deepened. "It's perfect."

He knelt beside me without a word, setting the flower gently between us. For a long moment, we simply sat there, breathing in the scent, surrounded by the hush of growing things.

The night held steady around us, not waiting, not ending.

And in the quiet, I felt myself take root again.

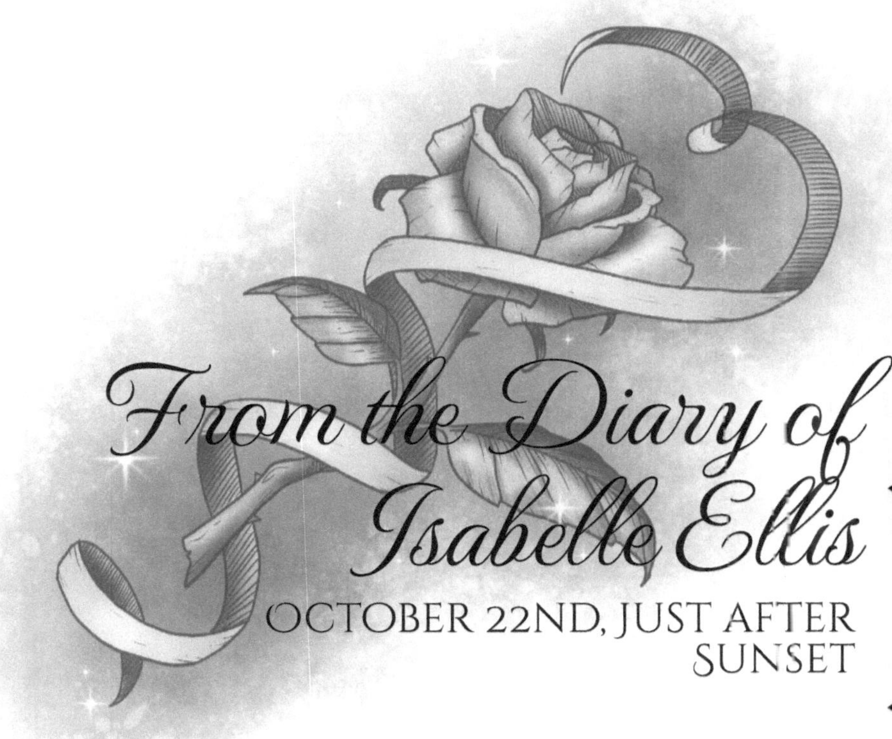

I awoke tonight with the trace of dreams still on my lips, sweet and strange and nearly gone.

Unlike the past, where dread and a suffocating silence greeted my awakening, this time, I was enveloped in a comforting warmth.

He had been there in the dream, standing at the edge of the sea, the hem of his coat caught in the wind. When his gaze found mine, there was no pity. No fear.

Only peace. Only promise.

What we're building isn't a secret, like so much of my life has been. He holds it openly, like something meant to last. He doesn't hide it. And still, I find myself surprised by the gentle care he gives so freely: the candles lit before I wake, the music low and thoughtful, the scent of dinner always warm. Always there.

Always waiting. As though I'd never left. It's a surprise I'm still getting used to.

And somehow, that has begun to feel like home. A word I have not dared to use in years. I never thought I would feel it again.

A word I have not dared to use in years. I never thought I would feel it again.

But there is danger in this kind of love, not because it lies, but because it is real. Because it asks to be believed in, and that comes with the possibility of heartbreak.

Time was once a graveyard, and I measured it in sunrises that I could not survive. Now, I mark it in teacups left warm on the table. How the wax pools at the base of the flame. In the faint echo of laughter, where once there was only silence.

Despite having faced death countless times, the prospect of embracing the life he's crafting for me fills me with a fear I've never known.

Because love, when it arrives unflinching and tender, dares to ask for what I've never known how to offer.

A *future.*

Love, Isabelle

CHAPTER 15

The Flower

When I opened my eyes, I remembered how to belong to the world again.

The sky beyond my window had already turned to velvet, the last traces of sunset fading into shadow. Stars blinked quietly through the mist. The curse had passed. The pain was gone. My lungs drew breath without resistance. My heart remembered how to beat.

I lay there for a long while, letting the peace wrap around me like a second skin.

The house was never truly silent. It breathed and bore witness, its bones creaking like the echo of something never entirely laid to rest.

Yet tonight, the stillness shifted. Beneath it, something faint and familiar stirred.

Music.

It rose from below like candlelight drifting across dark water. Subtle at first, almost fragile, but threaded with warmth. It wasn't the melody I recognized, but the ache in it. The way it wound through the walls was like a question that already knew its answer.

The sky had long since surrendered its color. My limbs ached with the remnants of death's slumber, but the house called to me.

Brushing my hair back from my face, I rose and stepped into the hall.

The portraits watched in silence as I passed, their eyes dulled by time. Near the top of the stairs, I paused. The music had grown clearer, brushed with sorrow, softened by something gentler. Beneath it, I recognized his voice.

He was humming.

A smile tugged at my lips before I could stop it. One step at a time, I descended the stairs, the cool floor beneath my feet grounding me in the moment. At the door, I paused, fingers brushing the frame. It was a simple ritual I hadn't meant to keep, yet one that always seemed to matter.

No words waited beyond the threshold, only welcome. He made space for me in the small things—the warmth of candlelight, the serenity he preserved, the quiet he never tried to fill.

The soft clink of silverware accompanied the scent of oregano and thyme, seasoning the air in gentle waves. A home built not on declarations, but on gestures: small, steady things that carried the shape of devotion. With Kayden there, it was a sanctuary, a place of warmth and comfort.

By the time I crossed the threshold, Kayden was just setting down two plates. It was a simple meal, something he had cooked quietly while I lay in the emptiness above. The roasted vegetables and herbed rice curled through the room, grounded by the comfort of freshly baked bread. He hadn't made dinner for himself. He'd made it for us, turning a mundane act into a gesture of love.

He'd made it for *us*.

When I stepped inside, something in me settled.

"Hey," he said, his hazel eyes lifting to meet mine. It was such a simple word, but it made my heart skip a beat.

For the first time in a century, I didn't feel like a ghost. I felt like a guest. Like a woman. Like someone who had been invited, seen, chosen, and welcomed into something tangible.

When he reached for my hand, I let him take it. His warmth met mine like a quiet promise, not loud or hurried. Just steady. He guided me into the flickering light of the room he had made ready. This room hadn't been lit for solitude. It had been lit for return.

And in that softened moment, surrounded by candlelight and comfort, I felt it whisper, not in words, but in something from within. *You belong here.* It was a feeling of acceptance, of being seen and chosen, that enveloped me in its warmth.

We didn't speak much as we ate, but the silence between us wasn't empty. It was gratitude and devotion. We shared bread and herbed rice by the firelight, fingers brushing now and then as if to say: I'm here. I stayed. When the last of the meal had cooled and the fire settled to embers, we curled together on the couch, his heartbeat pressed to my back. And for just a little while, I let the world fall away.

Kayden looked handsome in the candlelight.

He always did, but tonight something felt different. It wasn't just the way the firelight softened the angles of his face or made the gold in his hazel eyes flicker like embers. It was the steadiness in him. The quiet certainty. The way he looked at me—not like a curse, not like a woman with a century carved into her bones.

He looked at me like he saw a woman. Like he saw a future.

The fire was little more than a glow, flowing like a gentle current against the walls, when I eased myself from Kayden's arms. He didn't wake up. His hand rested near the hollow I'd left, fingers relaxed in the folds of the blanket.

For a moment, I stood against the door frame, just watching him. I committed him to memory, the way others hold on to prayer. His face in sleep was gentler than I ever let myself hope for. All the weight he carried seemed to vanish in those peaceful hours when dreams took him. He looked younger. *Free.* As if the house hadn't touched him yet.

I didn't know how many nights I would have like this. How many mornings he would wake up to an empty bed and the fading ghost of my scent?

But tonight, I could give him something. A fragment of presence. A keepsake for the morning.

Not wanting to wake him, I moved through the apartment in silence. I had learned how the floor gave slightly near the kitchen table. How the cupboard doors whispered when I opened them. In the dim light, I found the small bowl of berries he'd brought from the market and a package of muffin mix left unopened on the counter.

It was simple. *Familiar.* The kind of thing my mother used to make without a recipe. Now mine to give.

Maybe I baked because it let me pretend, just for a little while, that I still belonged to a life with morning in it. Perhaps because it was a ritual I could leave behind for him to find. A way of saying: *I was here. I loved you. I lived, if only for the night.*

The oven creaked softly as it heated. The scent of sugar warmed the air and brought my mother back to me—quiet mornings, flour-dusted counters, her hands gentle at the edge of my memory.

While the muffins baked, I pulled a page from his notebook and sat at the table, a pen in my hand.

What do you leave for someone who already knows your ghosts? Someone who has seen every shadow you carry, and still calls it love.

I wrote:

Don't look for me when the sun rises. You've already found me.

Love, Isabelle

I set the note beside the plate of muffins.

Then, from the pocket of my dress, I drew the small sprig of rosemary I'd picked the night before when we walked through the garden. He hadn't seen me take it, but I had, and I had saved it for this.

A gift. A breath of the garden. A promise.

I placed it gently beside the note, then leaned against the counter for a long while, simply breathing. Letting the scent of baked sugar and rosemary settle into the room.

The sun would come soon, and I would go, but not before I gave him this: a morning that knew he had been loved. Proof that I had been real. Even if only for the night. And if that was all I could give him, I would give it again and again, until morning no longer took me.

CHAPTER 16

The Keeper

I woke to the scent of berries. It drifted quietly through the warm morning air, twining with something softer—rosemary, I realized, as the fragrance enveloped me.

Today was different. The usual silence, heavy with the absence of her, did not weigh down on me like a stone.

For a moment, before my eyes even opened, I let myself believe she was still beside me, that if I rolled over gently enough, I would find Isabelle curled into the blankets, her silver hair fanned softly over the pillow, catching the light like a veil of frost.

She hadn't been a ghost. She had been breathing. She had been present, real, and impossibly close.

But the bed was empty.

The void in the bed next to me still held her warmth. Her body's shape was imprinted in the fabric, and the pillow bore the faint mark of her cheek. I reached out, my hand slipping into the space where she had been, and felt the familiar ache settle in. It wasn't quite grief. It was something softer. A mourning eased by the truth she had left behind.

I sat up slowly, dragging in a breath. Pale morning light pushed gently through the windows, unsure if I was ready for it. The apartment felt unusually still, as though it too was waiting.

The tiles were cool beneath my feet as I stepped into the kitchen.

That's when I saw them.

A plate of muffins sat on the counter, still faintly steaming. The bright scent of berries lingered in the warm air. Beside the plate, a torn scrap of notebook paper rested, held in place by a fresh sprig of rosemary. Her handwriting danced across the page in dark ink:

Don't look for me when the sun rises. You've already found me.
Love, Isabelle

I stared at it for a long moment before I could bring myself to touch it. The slant of her letters, the way she crossed her "t. It was all her, alive on the page.

The paper trembled slightly between my fingers as I picked it up. What we shared wasn't a dream. She had made these muffins and left them for me, not as a good-bye but as a promise to return. That realization eased the pain ever so slightly.

Sitting at the table, I set the note beside me, reaching for one of the muffins and taking a bite. It was still warm and soft at the center. The sweetness curled into me slowly, reminding me of the scent of her skin. I closed my eyes. It wasn't just food. It was a message. A morning created by someone who knew I would still be here to savor it.

She had given me something more powerful than an-swers; she had given me this morning—a morning that didn't begin in grief but in a new memory. A morning that remembered *her*.

As I went through my day, I intended to hold onto that moment, just as I would hold on to her, because even in her absence, Isabelle had found a way to stay, and that mattered more than I'd dared to hope for.

The note remained close to me as I settled down with my laptop. I didn't want to fold it or press it between the pages like something already finished. I wanted it to be visible in the light, so I slipped it onto the cover of my notebook and placed it beside my coffee, treating it like a charm against everything I couldn't control.

The muffins had cooled, but I ate another one, savoring the faint, resinous hint of the rosemary she had chosen. It lingered on my tongue, a thoughtful taste that was unmistakably hers.

And that was precisely what it was: her note, her baking, the tenderness stitched into every detail. It was the closest thing to a vow she could offer while the sun still held her captive, and it was enough to make me believe we could make it to nightfall. *Together.*

I couldn't stay in the quiet forever. If she could give me a morning, I could give her a promise. So, I opened my laptop and began anew.

The screen glowed faintly in the soft morning light as I typed: *Small-town wedding officiant, Crystal Peak.*

Most results pointed to towns more than an hour away. I kept scrolling, feeling restless, until I remembered Howard. If anyone would know of a local officiant, it would be him.

Grabbing my coat and notebook, I stepped out into the dissipating fog.

The town square was still half-asleep when I parked in front of the coffee shop, with rooftops dusted in dew. The air was damp and chilly from the night's low temperatures. Bakery windows glowed warmly from within, while across the street, the florist was arranging fresh buckets of roses, lavender, and lilies, their delicate petals nodding in the gentle dawn breeze.

I paused outside the shop, considering my options before stepping inside, the bell chiming softly above the door. The air was fragrant with blooms and the faint sweetness of dried rose petals and old wood, reminiscent of a photograph tucked away in a linen drawer.

"Something for a wedding," I said, stepping into the fragrant warmth of the shop. "Something... beautiful."

The florist looked up from a bucket of lilies, her expression shifting from surprise to curiosity. "Congratulations," she said, her smile brightening. "Do you have anything in mind?"

"Not really." I glanced around, taking in the riot of petals and stems. "She's... complicated. Soft in ways that matter, sharp in the ways that count. The kind of woman who'd plant herbs next to roses and call it balance."

She let out a short breath, almost a laugh. "I like her already."

I smiled. "Me too."

Setting the lilies aside, she walked toward a table of pale blooms. "White roses," she said, reaching for them. "For devotion. And rosemary—for remembrance. People forget that part, but I always include it when I can."

I nodded. "That's perfect."

As she snipped stems, the room quieted into a kind of rhythm. She worked with quick, precise motions, but there was a tenderness to it, as if the flowers were being chosen for more than just display.

When she was done, I paid in cash, thanked her, and stepped back into the soft light of the morning, the bouquet tucked carefully beneath my arm. It felt less like something I had bought and more like something I had been entrusted with.

Outside, the sky was beginning to brighten. The clouds thinned, and the mist began to retreat.

On a whim, I stepped into the little jewelry shop between the post office and the antique store. Although it was barely open and its windows were still dark, a small bell jingled as I stepped inside.

The interior was dim and faintly smelled of tarnished silver and cedar. Display cases lined the walls, filled with rings and pendants that seemed as old as the building itself. Behind the counter, a man in his seventies polished a silver band with a cloth that had softened over the years. He looked up, met my gaze, and offered a quiet, knowing nod.

"You looking for something specific?" he asked, setting the band aside.

"Something for an engagement," I replied. "She doesn't wear jewelry. She's not flashy—just quietly beautiful. I want something that feels like her."

The man's eyes narrowed slightly, not out of judgment, but in contemplation. "Quietly beautiful, you say..." He tapped a finger on the glass, deep in thought. "Not many come in here looking for something like that. Usually, they want sparkle."

"Not her," I insisted.

With a nod, he turned to a safe. The door opened with a low groan, and from the back, he retrieved a small, timeworn velvet box. He placed it on the counter with the kind of care reserved for items that carried a silent history. Special for just a few

"This one came from a coastal estate outside of Whitcombe," he explained. "No maker's mark, no records, but some say it was part of a long-kept tradition—something old, something meaningful. Silently kept, silently treasured."

He opened the box, revealing a delicate ring crafted from antique gold, shaped like an interwoven branch. The band was slender and textured like bark. Nestled where the two stems met, a small opal shimmered with flecks of violet and blue, reminiscent of moonlight caught beneath water. It didn't demand attention. It whispered.

My breath caught in my throat at how perfect it was. I didn't need to see another.

"That one," I said, the words simple, but anchored. Like I knew it before he even opened the box.

He gave a slight nod, as if he had known all along, too, and carefully boxed it.

With the ring purchased, I slipped the box into my coat and rested my hand there a second longer than I needed to. The weight of it wasn't much, but it pressed against my ribs like she was already part of me, tucked into the space just beneath my heart where I'd been holding her all along.

With the bouquet and the ring in hand, I crossed the street to the Bluff Bar. The door opened slowly, the hinges catching halfway before yielding. Howard was already there, stirring sugar into his coffee.

"You look like a man on a mission," he said without turning.

"I need a name," I told him. "Someone who can marry us."

He glanced over, one brow raised—not in surprise, but as if to confirm what he had suspected. "Victor. My neighbor's son. He's ordained online and has done a few ceremonies. He likes simple things. I can check if he's available tonight... if you're in a hurry."

Without a second thought, he jotted the name on a napkin and slid it across the bar.

"Thank you," I said.

Howard raised his mug but didn't take a sip. "That house has been still for a long time."

Smiling before I could stop it, I looked down at the bouquet. "Not anymore."

He nodded slowly, seeming to have already made peace with the answer. "Congratulations, my friend. I hope I get to meet her."

The sun was already setting as I drove back toward the seaside estate, the car packed with everything I needed for the wedding. Boxes in the backseat rustled softly with each curve of the road, carrying cake, flowers, and rings. Despite the whirlwind of it all, I hadn't hesitated—not once. I should've been nervous, but I wasn't. My hands stayed steady on the wheel. My heart knew where it was going.

As I neared the cliffs, the sky transformed into a soft palette of pastels. Lavender and peach rippled across the surface of the sea, streaked with threads of gold that shimmered like silk. I thought of her skin in the firelight, the way her eyes softened when she spoke of the garden, and the way she pressed her forehead to mine as if it meant more than words ever could.

If we married and found the woman who cursed her, and if everything worked out as she believed it would, she would no longer be forced to miss sunrises. Just imagining her walking barefoot through the flowerbeds at noon, blinking into sunlight that belonged to her again, made my chest ache in the most beautiful way.

I pulled into the gravel drive, the stones crunching beneath the tires. The house loomed ahead, bathed in dusky gold, its windows watching like closed eyes. I glanced up at her third-floor window. Still dark. Still waiting.

After killing the engine, I stepped into the crisp air. The wind from the sea had picked up, sweeping through the trees and stirring the ivy clinging to the stone. I cradled the food containers and flowers in my arms and nudged the door shut with my hip.

The apartment felt different when I stepped inside—warmer, but also expectant, like the stillness had weight to it. Like the place itself was waiting to see if this moment would become real.

Setting the box on the counter, I opened it carefully, like anything too quick might break the spell. The small white cake went into the fridge, its sweet vanilla and buttercream scent swirling through the room. The kind of scent that stirred memories. It smelled like birthdays we hadn't had yet, but would live to see together.

I placed the bouquet beside her note, where it still lived on my notebook. The rosemary was drying at the edges now, but the scent hadn't faded. If anything, it had deepened. I brushed my thumb along the paper, a smile tugging up the side of my lips.

The clock above the stove said just after six. Two hours. Enough time to get ready. Enough time to steady myself.

For a moment, I leaned into the counter with both hands and just let myself be still. Not thinking. Not moving. Just breathing through the ache of anticipation. Then, slowly, I turned toward the bedroom.

The suit hung where I'd left it, waiting. I lifted it from the hanger and ran my hand down the sleeve. The fabric wasn't heavier than yesterday, but it felt heavier. Weighted with what came next. With every word, I was about to speak out loud.

I draped it carefully over the back of the chair and stood there for a moment, staring at it. It looked so ordinary. Just dark fabric and quiet lines, but tonight it would mean something. She would look at me in this. Say *yes* to me in this.

I let out a slow breath, ran a hand through my hair, and headed to the bathroom.

The mirror fogged as I showered, steam curling around me like mist off the sea. I scrubbed the salt from my skin and tried to clear the noise from my thoughts, but it always came back to her—*Isabelle*. Her laugh when she didn't mean to, the soft rasp of it. Her eyes when she was thinking too hard. The way she touched me was like I hung the moon.

She'd looked at me like I mattered. Like I was something she could hold onto in a world that kept losing its shape. And I wasn't ready for that to end—not tonight. *Not ever.*

Yet some truths still lived in silence between us. Howard had agreed to come as a witness, but I hadn't told her that guests would be coming. I didn't know how she would feel about being seen, about opening her life and truth to someone other than me. *Would anyone recognize her from the stories? And if they did... What would they say?*

I wasn't afraid of the stares. I was scared of what they might take from her—the quiet strength she had only just begun to believe in again. We were preparing for her to leave the house, to live again, but the world beyond these cliffs could be cruel to a woman who had outlived her own century.

As I dried off and dressed, my thoughts turned to the shadow that had started it all: the *witch.* The wind tapped against the windows—not violently, but like an exhale the house was struggling to release.

If Isabelle was right, if her soul was still bound to the one who cursed her, then the wedding wasn't just about vows, rings, and hopeful beginnings. It was about drawing the first line in the sand and beginning the fight for her autonomy.

And I wasn't afraid—not of the past. Not of the curse. Only of one thing: that I would carry her all the way to the edge of freedom… and fail to get her through. And if I did—if I lost her at the threshold—I wasn't sure I'd know how to go back.

I will not promise you the sun,
Only a hand that reaches for yours in the dark.
And when the night closes in,
I will be the presence that does not falter.

I will not offer you morning,
Only the softness of night.
And when the silence comes for your name,
I will still be saying it.

I have no spell, no cure,
Only this:
If you fall again,
I will be the one who kneels beside you,
Until you remember how to rise.

CHAPTER 17

The Flower

For all the years I had been cursed, I had always awakened to darkness. It wasn't just the darkness outside the windows. It was the echo inside me that made the silence ache. A loneliness that didn't speak loudly but crept into the spaces between breaths—an unshifting void rooted deep in my ribs.

But tonight, as I stirred from the velvet hush of death, there was light waiting. Soft. Intentional. It felt as if someone had opened the world for me to step into once more.

For a moment, I wondered if I was still dreaming, if this warmth and light belonged to a gentler ending.

I opened my eyes slowly, unsure if what I felt was real. The air was warm with candlelight, and the scent of something familiar wrapped around me: wood smoke, honey, soap, and salt.

Kayden.

Inhaling deeply, I allowed his scent to anchor me. My limbs moved sluggishly, but as I stretched and sat up, the ache of returning felt softer. I turned toward the small table beside the bed and stilled.

At the center stood a crystal vase, its faceted surface catching the candlelight and scattering soft arcs of color across the wall. The white roses within bloomed untouched, their scent subtle yet insistent, the petals curved like secrets not yet spoken.

Beside the vase lay an envelope.

I stared at the envelope for a long time. It had been decades since anyone had written to me with such tenderness and left me flowers. The last time was not a joyous occasion such as this. My fingers trembled as I opened it.

We will say our vows at 8 o'clock, my flower, and I cannot wait to make you my wife.
Love, Kayden

I pressed the page to my heart, closing my eyes and letting the words settle there, allowing them to live inside me—the hope of them, the promise.

A twinge of sadness brushed the edge of my joy as I swung my legs from the bed, the cool floor grounding me. I had imagined this moment once, long ago—my mother standing behind me, fastening buttons with delicate hands, her voice soft as she gave me advice on how to be a good wife. My father waiting in the parlor, smiling in a way that calmed my nerves. Music drifting in from the next room, and the house filled with flowers and laughter from people who knew my name.

But dreams are fragile. They change. They fade. They grow silent. And the people in them sometimes vanish long before the moment arrives.

Tonight, there would be no mother to help me, no father to give me away, no music beneath the chandeliers, and no guests who remembered who I had been before the curse. Just the house. Just the silence. Just Kayden.

But Kayden was everything, and I wouldn't take that for granted.

I gently placed the note back on the table, crossed to the cedar cabinet tucked against the far wall, and opened it. The scent of aged wood and dried lavender spilled out, the familiar aroma evoking a deep ache in my chest.

My mother used to line her drawers with lavender. This scent belonged to her, to safety, to everything I had lost.

Hanging inside, wrapped in plastic, was the dress I would wear to marry the love of my life. It was ivory, simple, and timeless. My mother had chosen it when I came of age, filling her heart with hope for my future, back when the world still felt wide and full of possibilities, back when she believed I would need it.

As I lifted it carefully from the hanger, I turned toward the mirror and held it against my body. The soft fabric shimmered in the candlelight, as if it had been waiting all this time just for me. Perhaps it had.

There was something beautiful about its age, the patience of it, the quiet way it had endured even after everything else had been taken.

Was it too old-fashioned? Did it matter? I didn't think so.

Kayden would see me, not the dress, not the missing years, not the grief braided into the hem.

He would see me, and tonight, that would be enough.

By the time I finished dressing, my hair still warm from the dryer and my pulse fluttering in my throat, the door at the end of the hallway cracked open.

"Isabelle?" Kayden's voice drifted through my bedroom door, sending my heart into a leap. "Is it okay for me to come in?"

One hand pressed to my chest, I tried to steady the butterflies there. For a moment, I couldn't speak. After everything, this moment felt impossibly tender.

"Yes," I said, my tone higher-pitched than I intended. "I'm just about ready."

Sliding into the silk dress, I guided the zipper up my side with trembling fingers. His footsteps approached slowly, giving me time. I smoothed the fabric over my hips, suddenly aware of the enormity of what we were about to do.

At the doorway, he stopped.

Still, my pulse stumbled.

Framed by the low glow of candlelight, Kayden looked handsome in his navy suit. The fabric held a quiet sheen, his hair neater than usual but still soft around the edges. And his eyes... they unraveled something still wound inside me. Something I hadn't known I was still holding tightly. He was *mine*.

Fingers twisting at my sides, I glanced up. "Is it okay?" My voice was barely more than a breath, and I hated how unsure it made me sound. "The dress, I mean."

He didn't say a word. Instead, he walked across the room and wrapped me in his arms, his strength surrounding me like a cocoon. After waking again from death's hold, I let myself truly sink into that embrace, letting go of everything else. When his lips found mine, the kiss was warm, unhurried—a promise more than a question. His hands rested on my waist, steadying me in that quiet moment, making me feel like I had finally found my place again, no longer adrift in the world alone.

"You are absolutely stunning, my flower," he murmured against my cheek. "More beautiful than I ever imagined."

Resting my head against his chest, I blinked once, then again, my vision blurring despite the quiet strength I tried to hold onto. The tears hovered, aching to fall. *Not yet.* Not before the vows.

Pulling back just enough to meet my eyes, he smiled, his expression full of everything we hadn't said. "Are you still sure you want to marry me?"

The laugh came easily, light with joy. "More than ever."

He smiled again, and for a long moment, we simply stood there, foreheads close, hands twined, the world narrowing to nothing but warmth and the promise between us. The moment felt small, but it held everything.

CHAPTER 18

The Flower

Every little girl dreams of her wedding day. They picture satin gowns and lace veils, bouquets of wildflowers, and rooms filled with family, music, and laughter.

I had stopped dreaming long ago. Hope had become too sharp to hold. But standing beside Kayden, I wasn't just dreaming anymore. I was living something real, something I thought only happened in fairy tales.

There were only two guests for our ceremony—a witness and an officiant. No choir or string quartet, and no mother to help me into my dress. But there was Kayden. In his eyes, I saw everything I had ever wanted. It wasn't perfect, but it was ours.

"Isabelle," he said, reaching for my hand as we approached the mantle in the den.

For more than seventy years, I had lived in silence and shadow. But in that moment, beneath the candlelight and with the man I loved by my side, I felt the first stirrings of freedom in my chest.

"Are you ready?" Kayden whispered.

I smiled, feeling hope, joy, and love lighten my heart more than I could ever remember. "Readier than I've ever been."

With the paperwork signed, Victor stepped forward, his glasses glinting in the firelight. Howard stood just behind him, his posture attentive, a hint of a smile softening the lines around his eyes.

Coming from a different time, I didn't know either of the men who were present for our wedding, but I trusted Kayden's judgment that they were safe. We weren't brave enough to share the details of my life, but Kayden sensed that Howard might suspect something was amiss. I couldn't blame him. If he did have his suspicions, however, he kept them to himself. Secrets like mine aren't easily understood, so we both felt it best to keep those details private.

The room went quiet as Kayden and I took our place before Victor. My hands trembled, but Kayden held mine, his grip steady, just like his smile.

Victor opened a small leather-bound book, his soft voice weaving through the flickering light. "Isabelle and Kayden," he began, "tonight you are joined in matrimony—not in grand halls or beneath stained glass, but here, in a place that has known both joy and loss. With fire as your witness, you pledge yourselves not simply to love, but to endure. Let your vows be more than promises. Let them be an anchor. A *beginning*."

My chest tightened when he turned to me first, but I pushed those fears back. No longer would I allow the curse to delay my happiness. I had waited long enough. "Isabelle, please share your vows."

With my pulse pounding like wings in my chest, I drew a breath and looked at Kayden. "For so long, I lived in silence," I said, the backs of my eyes already burning with tears. "In stillness. In shadow. I never thought I would be loved. Not truly. Not as I am. But then you came, and you saw me. You didn't look away. You saw more than my silence. You saw *me*."

Kayden's eyes shimmered just as I knew mine did, but his hands remained steady as I reached for his and slipped the ring gently onto his finger. "You taught me I'm not a burden. That love doesn't weigh me down. It holds me. It lets me grow. With you, I am not fading. I am blooming. And I vow to choose you, not only in light, but in every shadow yet to come."

Victor turned to Kayden. "Kayden?"

Kayden cleared his throat, his voice roughened by emotion. "I came here broken, trying to outrun my past. I didn't expect to find anything but solitude. But you were the silence I didn't know I was listening for. The sentence I couldn't write until I knew you existed."

Taking my hand, he slid the ring onto my finger, a beautiful design made to look like intricately carved tree branches, the opal in the center reflecting the flames. "You are my present. My proof. I vow to carry you when you cannot walk, to wait when you need time, to trust you when the world feels uncertain. And above all, to never let you forget you are loved."

With Kayden's hand in mine and my heart full to the brim, I barely noticed Victor step back. "By the power granted to me by the state," he said, "and by these old walls that bear witness, I now pronounce you husband and wife."

Before he could speak again, Kayden was already kissing me. He kissed me as if there was nothing left to wait for, and I kissed him back as if I knew exactly what I was choosing. It expressed everything words never could.

After we reluctantly pulled apart, Victor offered his warm congratulations and extended a handshake. He lingered a moment before slipping into the night. Howard gave one last look toward the fire and then to us, congratulated us as well, smiled, and then followed Victor out into the darkness.

When the door clicked shut, I turned to Kayden, my chest buzzing with anticipation. We were finally alone, and everything that followed was ours.

He looked at me with wonder in his eyes, a hint of playfulness on the edges. "Well," he said, his voice low, "I can't wait to get that dress off you."

I arched an eyebrow, even though his words sent heat swirling in my belly. "We'll see about that."

He grinned. "But first," he added, lifting the champagne and dinner tray, "wait here."

Before I could reply, he slipped out the back door, moving as if he were orchestrating a secret that the stars might keep.

I didn't follow him, but the knot of tension in my chest tightened behind my smile. The witch had told me that marriage would free me from my prison, but it could have been a lie. I didn't know what would happen if I still couldn't escape. I couldn't bear the thought of remaining trapped, fading away with the morning. Would Kayden still stay with me?

Just as my thoughts began to spiral, he returned with something unreadable in his eyes and crossed the room without saying a word. When he reached me, he wrapped his arms around my waist, and I rose to meet him without hesitation. My arms found his shoulders as if they already belonged there.

"Close your eyes," he whispered. Although I didn't want to miss a single moment, I complied.

The moment he carried me across the threshold, the sharp air struck like the first desperate gasp after surfacing. It poured into me with a force that left my chest aching, as if my lungs had forgotten the weight and fullness of breath. Each inhale tasted like a world I had been denied for decades, a world that had waited just beyond reach until now. *The world of the living.*

Wind coiled along my skin in cool, possessive spirals, threading through my hair, sliding over the curve of my neck until shivers rose in tight succession. Goosebumps bloomed across my arms, chasing the path of each invisible touch. The wind pressed against my lashes, and my eyes stung with a release that had nothing to do with the cold, as if some long-frozen part of me had cracked open. Tears welled before I could stop them, blurring the shape of the horizon, catching light as they slipped free.

When he set me down, the earth accepted me with a softness that made my knees tremble. Grass yielded under my bare feet in uneven textures—plush at first, then edged with the fine prick of individual blades. I flexed my toes into it, savoring the faint resistance of damp soil, the way it gave and then held me, as if testing whether I belonged. Neither of us was quite sure if I did.

Beyond the bluff, the sea breathed its eternal breath, its rhythm spilling into my own. Salt rode the wind to my lips, clinging like something intimate, something claimed. The air was thick with scents that layered and intertwined: the green sweetness of living things, the mineral bite of stone, the restless edge of the tide.

Greedy for the contact, for the raw truth of it, I curled my toes deeper into the ground. I wanted the grit of soil to mark me, the softness to anchor me, the bite of the blades to remind me I had crossed back into the world. After so long living only where the night permitted, I would take this moment and make it mine—without asking, without apology. It may have been the night, and I may have been beneath the moon and not the sun, but

I was outside, and that had to be enough. *For now.*

When I lifted my gaze, Kayden was there, close enough that the heat of him cut through the wind. His eyes were wide, luminous in the fading light, his lips curving into a slow, reverent smile. He looked at me as though he could see the life rushing back into my veins, as though the entire world had shifted to bear witness to this single breath. He understood—not only the step I had taken, but the long, bitter winter I had endured to reach it. And in his eyes, I saw it reflected: the ache, the triumph, and the vow that this would not be taken from me again.

I hadn't stepped outside in nearly a century. The last time I tried, after my mother passed away, it had burned. It wasn't with fire, however, but with something colder. A magic that didn't claw but erased. My vision had blurred, my limbs had locked, and my lungs refused to work. I collapsed before my feet even touched the ground.

I had never spoken of it, not even to Kayden. But tonight, there was no pain. The curse didn't stop me. For the first time in nearly a century, I stood outside—unhindered, unbroken, *free*—and I didn't know what to make of it.

Beside a crackling fire, a thick blanket awaited, ringed with lanterns that flickered like earthbound stars around a scattering of cushions. Above us, the sky opened wide, glowing in the moonlight. For so long, I had watched that same night sky from my third-story window, but it always felt like a distant dream—a life I could see but never live. But being outside, breathing in the air, and standing beneath the heavens with my toes in the grass... that was truly living.

"It's beautiful," I said, my voice no more than a breath.

He reached for me, taking my hand. "Would you like to go closer?"

My feet were already moving as the word left my mouth, eager to explore in every direction at once. "Absolutely."

The stars above us opened like a map to something we had longed for but could finally reach. And for once, I didn't look back.

CHAPTER 19

The Keeper

The fire burned low beside us, its golden breath spilling over the folds of the blanket and catching in Isabelle's hair like starlight braided into silver. The silk of her dress clung to her in delicate waves, moon-pale and unhurried, pooling around her knees as she sat beneath the open sky. Wind threaded through the cliffs behind us, bending the grasses in a slow, restless sway.

The firelight rendered her almost otherworldly, yet the weight of her presence held her here. She was not a ghost, nor a dream, but Isabelle. *Mine.*

Her eyes lingered on the fire as though she wasn't ready to believe it yet, as if touching the moment too directly might wake her from it. And I didn't rush her. I didn't speak. I just watched her, afraid that touching this moment might cause it to vanish as well.

"I still can't believe I'm out here," she murmured finally, her voice nearly lost to the wind. "That the world didn't end when I stepped across the door."

"It's only just beginning," I said, meaning every word. "We have an entire life to build moments like these."

She turned to me then, slowly, and the fire in her gaze turned her irises to molten silver—fragile with hope, luminous with uncertainty. The world seemed to pause around us until a soft sound rose from her belly, and she laughed, pressing a hand to her middle. "Apparently, I'm starving."

The unrehearsed sound of her laughter, the raw sound of her joy at simply being alive, nearly undid me. I would have given her anything at that moment. A thousand meals. A hundred lifetimes. Just to hear her laugh like that again.

"Then let's feed the bride," I said, reaching for the containers of food at our feet. "I wanted to try the Italian restaurant in town. Howard spoke highly of it."

Steam unfurled as I lifted the lid, revealing the eggplant cream sauce over angel hair pasta with a side of roasted vegetables beneath.

Isabelle leaned closer, a smile gracing her lips as she took in the scent. "It smells... divine."

After having been alone for so long and living off her garden, food storage, and the baskets left by a mysterious gifter for decades, Isabelle's food options had become simple and scarce. I realized quickly that introducing new foods to her was one of my new goals in life, just to see that look of curiosity and excitement on her face. To create moments with her that could finally overshadow all the bad and lonely ones.

Setting the lid aside, I reached for a fork. "It's not fancy, but it is something new for you to try. I think you'll enjoy it."

Her smile was slow—a kind of blooming. She leaned closer, letting the first forkful pass between her lips. Her eyes closed, and she moaned softly as she chewed, a sound so tender and unguarded it reached straight through my chest and settled there.

"I'd forgotten how joy could taste."

Sitting cross-legged beneath the stars, we ate out of the same plate, passing the fork between us like a shared secret. Each brush of her fingers sent a low current through me. She laughed more easily now. Her posture had unknotted. Her gaze held mine longer, and I watched the shadows on her collarbones, the curve of her lips, the way the firelight softened the worry that had once lived behind her eyes.

When the plate was nearly empty, she stole the last bite with a triumphant grin.

"Thief," I said, my voice low, my tone teasing.

Eyes never leaving mine, she licked a smear of sauce from her finger. "You married me anyway."

"I did."

And I would again. A thousand times.

Her mouth curved faintly as she reached for her wine, only to pause halfway. Her gaze dropped to my lips, and the glass found its way back to the tray without a sip taken, as though setting it down meant surrendering to something else entirely.

I stayed still, holding the moment, feeling the quiet thrum between us coil tighter. It was not rushed, just inevitable. The way the flyer had found me in the streets, how my father's death had sent me across the country looking for a fresh start, it all served to bring us together.

Crawling across the blankets, heat flared in her eyes as she closed the distance between us. Her hand slid up to cup my jaw, the kind of touch that claimed without asking. She didn't need to ask. I was already hers.

She didn't speak. Didn't give me a chance to. Instead, her lips found mine, opening with a need that stole thought entirely, leaving only breath, heat, and the steady pulse of her—alive beneath my hands. The world narrowed to only us. Nothing else mattered in that moment.

With more confidence than I'd ever seen in her eyes, she moved over me, her thighs settling around my hips. Her lips were soft, that familiar taste of honeysuckle intoxicating my senses just like the first night she kissed me. My hands found her waist, her ribs, the silk of her dress slipping beneath my palms. Every inch of her felt like proof—proof that she was real, that I hadn't imagined every moment with the woman who had changed my life.

"I thought the dress might be your favorite part," she whispered, breathless, her lips ghosting across my jaw.

I chuckled, tracing the fabric where it curved around her thighs. "Oh, it is... but what's underneath... that might ruin me."

She laughed, low and wicked in my ear. "Then be ruined."

The firelight gilded her skin as I eased her down onto the blanket, the skirt of her dress still a barrier I was determined to breach. Moonlight brushed her collarbone, glinting in the silver of her eyes. She was every kind of beautiful I'd never known how to ask for. No woman could ever hold a candle to her.

Her eyes found mine as I crawled over her. The hunger reflected in them was something I knew all too well. The way her hands slid into my hair and pulled me back into the kiss told me everything I needed to know. Although it was her first time beneath the open sky in decades, her sole focus was on me... *us*. This moment.

Kissing down the line of her neck, I took my time on every inch of her skin. She arched into me, breath hitching as my hands slid beneath the fabric of her dress, pushing it higher until I could see the lace of her panties, already wet for me. She was warm beneath my palms, trembling, needing my touch as much as I needed to touch her.

A soft sound escaped her, half sigh and half whimper, as I kissed her pulse and then peeled the top of her dress down her body until I uncovered her breasts. I pressed my lips to the skin above her heart, savoring how fast it beat for me.

"I want you, Kayden. *Please.*" Her fingers tightened in my hair, not to stop me, but to hold on.

"Patience, my flower," I said against the soft skin of her belly. It quivered, her breath coming faster.

Giving in to her plea, I slid the dress down the rest of the way, drinking in the sight of her laid bare for me. Her porcelain skin, flushed in places where my hands had lingered, the firelight dancing across every curve. I bent, closing my mouth around one tight peak, then the other, drawing from her the sounds I'd waited all night to hear.

"You're so beautiful," was all I could say, not knowing how to put into words how I felt.

My fingers hooked in the lace at her hips, drawing it down slowly. She parted for me without hesitation, the cool air raising gooseflesh along her body as I lowered myself between her thighs.

The moment my tongue slid through her folds, she gasped, hips rising to meet me. Her taste hit me like a drug, obliterating the last of my restraint. I sucked her clit gently, teasing her with the flat of my tongue before sliding a finger inside, then another, curling until I found the spot that made her breath catch and her legs tighten around my neck.

Her hips rocked in a slow, desperate rhythm against my mouth, seeking more friction. I gave her what she wanted, increasing the pressure until her moans deepened into something even the stars could hear.

She screamed my name when the tension inside her snapped, her voice breaking on each syllable. Her body shook, thighs trembling against my shoulders as her climax took her. I stayed with her through every pulse, every shiver, my mouth softening its strokes until she sagged against the blanket, spent and utterly breathtaking.

When I finally kissed my way back up her body, her eyes were still half-closed, her breathing ragged. She pulled me down and kissed me, tasting herself on my lips, panting against my mouth as if she couldn't bear to be apart for even a breath.

With her body still quaking, her fingers traced the line of my hip before slipping beneath the waistband, each inch of skin they covered setting off a low burn in my chest. I let her slide my trousers down my hips, needing to be inside her more than I needed oxygen in my lungs.

Pressing my palm to the blanket beside her head, I entered her slowly, inch by deliberate inch, until I was fully seated. Her sharp inhale cut through the night, her head tilting back as her body accepted me. The sensation gripped every nerve I had—tight, warm, and perfect.

I stilled, needing to feel this, to feel her, before anything else. Her hands skimmed down my back, nails grazing my skin, her eyes locked on mine as though I was the only thing she saw. I kissed her slowly until she moved beneath me, urging me into rhythm.

Each stroke was deep, meant to show her how much I needed her, meant to make her feel every inch of what I couldn't put into words. Her body lifted to meet each thrust, every whimper driving me to give her more of me. Even as I clenched my jaw and tensed my muscles, my climax begged to break free, but I fought it with every stroke, needing her to come again. Although it wasn't our first night together, it was our wedding night. I wanted her to remember it for the rest of my life—to think back to this moment of passion in her darkest moments and know how much she was wanted.

"Please," she gasped, her back rolling off the blankets as she pulled me into another kiss.

Knowing what she needed, I gripped her thigh and lifted it to hook over my shoulder so I could drive in deeper.

Her release took her in a rush, her walls clenching around me in pulses that nearly broke through the fragile hold I had on my restraint. I kept moving, chasing the edge that burned low in my spine. She pulled my lips back down to hers, her mouth fierce against mine, her lips rocking to meet every thrust.

The pleasure built too fast, too strong, until I was seconds from breaking. Then she whispered, voice ragged, "Come inside me."

No longer able to hold on, I let the coil break, groaning into her neck as I buried myself as deep as I could go. Hot release tore through me, the pleasure unrelenting, until every last tremor left me breathless against her skin.

For several long heartbeats, I remained inside her, unwilling to let go of her warmth, wishing on every star that I could keep her when the sun returned. With her heart beating against mine, she looked up at me, eyes glassy in the firelight, and for a long moment, there was nothing else—no curse, no dawn—*just us*.

For a long while, we didn't move. The fire whispered beside us, its glow dimming with the breeze. She shifted only to press her lips to my temple, a quiet touch that stayed long after she pulled back.

When the air became too frigid to remain outside, I carried her back across the threshold, holding her tightly enough that I might keep her through the dawn.

I knew the sunrise would still take her, but tonight—this night—she was mine, and I would carry her to bed for as many nights as it took until she never had to leave me again.

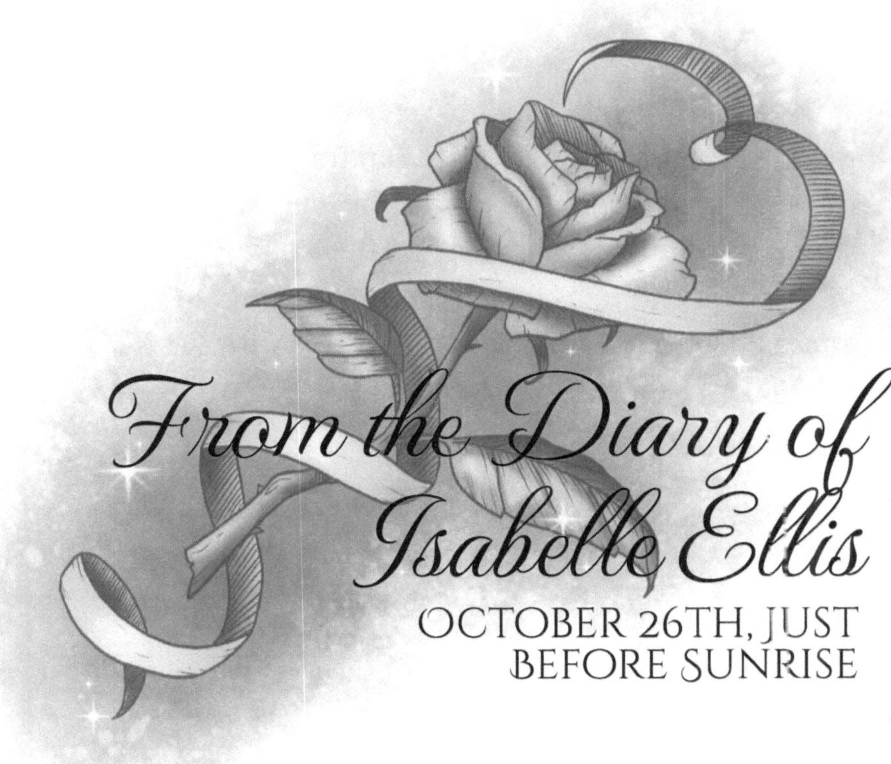

Sleep rarely comes for me in the hours before dawn. Instead, I spend the night by the fire, wrapped in Kayden's flannel, with my mother's journals spread across my lap like relics unearthed from another life. The pages are soft with age, and the ink has faded, but her voice reaches me there in careful loops, whispering love and grief—everything she had hoped for in my life. I read until my eyes burn, until the candle on the sill has nearly burned down to its wick, and the ache begins in my chest.

That's when I know the sun is near. It's ironic how it brings life to so many things, yet it brings death to me. It feels like nothing more than a cruel joke.

Trying to enjoy our night, we didn't talk much about the curse, but we decided to remain at the manor for the time being while we looked for her. When the truth comes to light, and when we find the woman who cursed me, we will end it, as long as she doesn't end us first. It's a fate I cannot fathom, so I dip my pen into the ink and push that possibility away.

Now, I sit at the edge of the bed, my new husband's scent clinging to my skin as I watch him sleep. Kayden lies tangled in the blankets, one hand stretched across the sheets, as if reaching for me even in his dreams. His chest rises and falls in a steady rhythm. He's peaceful, alive.

I will not wake him. Instead, I study the curve of his mouth, the soft fan of his lashes, and the warmth of his presence filling the space we've begun to share. I wonder what it might feel like to stay, to remain alive as he does, even as the birds begin their song on a golden new day.

But I cannot. The curse may be loosening, but the sunrise still claims me. It reaches me even here, safe in my bed.

There will be no garden walk today, no quiet step beyond the stones, no sunlit grass beneath my feet. Only this: the hush of the air, the memory of his touch, and the warmth of a life I never thought I'd hold. Instead, I lie back beside him, resting one hand over the blanket that covers his chest, letting his heartbeat calm me.

Once, I believed the garden was the only place I belonged. But last night, I learned that belonging can take the shape of arms, of breath, of being seen and chosen all the same.

This doesn't feel like a farewell. Not this time.

As the first light stirs the horizon, I close my eyes and let the day take me. But this time, I go knowing I'm not vanishing into nothing, because someone will be waiting for me when I return.

Love, Isabelle

CHAPTER 20

The Keeper

I woke to the sound of birdsong. It wasn't loud or insistent, just the gentle stretch of wings welcoming the morning, a melody woven with the soft rustle of wind through the trees and the distant murmuring of the tide. The fire in the hearth had burned down to a cradle of ash, and the apartment carried a faint scent of lavender and wood smoke—her essence still lingering in the air.

Beside me, Isabelle lay still. Her skin felt cool but not cold, and her breath was absent, but the memory of it remained. I curled my fingers around hers, my thumb brushing over the shape of her knuckles. There was no pulse or response—just silence. But it wasn't the silence of death anymore; it was a waiting silence. The kind of pause a seed takes beneath the snow—quiet, patient, and full of the promise of what might bloom if the sun were to return.

This ritual was becoming familiar: waking beside the stillness and learning not to flinch. The ache was still present, but it had dulled to something my heart could handle. I no longer panicked. I simply missed her.

"I miss you already," I whispered, pressing a kiss to the back of her hand. She couldn't hear me, not in the way I wanted, but I still hoped she dreamed of something soft and sweet, something that didn't carry the weight of remembrance.

Sliding off the bed, I pulled on a hoodie. I reached for two mugs before I caught myself, and poured coffee into both, knowing Isabelle's would grow cold by the time she could drink it. It was no longer depression that slowed my movements during the day, but a somber resignation that weighed me down while the woman I loved lay without breath.

Up the stairs, the atrium windows were cracked open just enough to let in the wind. The breeze carried a sharper edge than yesterday, threaded with the scent of wet stone and pine. I stepped barefoot onto the cool tile of the atrium and walked the length of the garden path, the warm mug comforting in my hands.

The beds we had recently cleared were holding their ground. A few brave sprouts had begun to break through, pressing toward the light as if they trusted it would last. I crouched beside one of them, my thumb brushing against the edge of a young basil leaf. It smelled green—alive. Resilient. Like her.

When I stepped back into the main house, an eerie silence filled the air, as if it had been listening all along.

The table near the window was scattered with papers: Margaret's scrawled notes, Isabelle's half-formed memories, and the things we had tried to piece together from town records and brittle deeds. There were maps with margins filled with circled names and addresses crossed out and rewritten. So many roads led to dead ends, but one line began to stand out—*a cottage near the woods, moss-covered stone, Thorne.*

The name settled heavily in my mind. It was not a conclusion, just a thread; a single note in a song we hadn't yet finished playing. If we could find that land, or a record, or even a whisper buried in the right margin, we might find a way to end the curse.

I glanced at the clock. There were still hours until sunset, still hours until Isabelle breathed again.

When she did, I didn't want to greet her with empty hands. I wanted something more than just memories. I was determined to find answers or, if nothing else, a better question that could lead us to the truth.

Needing to keep my head and hands busy, I spent the afternoon at the kitchen table, sifting through the countless pieces of research we'd stitched together, hoping something would pop out at me that I had missed. I went through the pages until I knew I would see the faded ink in my dreams.

As the light shifted across the room, I moved through the house, allowing myself to fall into motion. I fixed a few small things I had been meaning to deal with—the crooked frame in the hall, the bulb in the laundry room, and the hinge on the bathroom door that always squealed when I opened it too quickly. It wasn't really about the house. It was about the rhythm, the doing, the waiting, helping Isabelle in any way I could.

I swept the corners of the entryway where the dust had crept back in and wiped down the counters. Finding a pile of books she had meant to shelve, I returned them to their place. It was the kind of cleaning that didn't look like much when it was done, but felt good to have it out of the way.

By the time I made it back to the kitchen, the sky had slipped into that early evening blue. I stared at the pantry shelves for a long time, not really hungry but knowing I should eat. My hands reached out without thinking for flour, eggs, and milk. It was something simple. Something warm.

I made pancakes.

The batter was a little lumpy, and I should have let the pan heat longer, but they came out all right. I scrambled a few eggs while they cooked and poured a second cup of coffee, reheated from the pot I had made that morning. It was nothing special, but it smelled good and filled the quiet. It would take time for me to fine-tune my domestic skills, and I hoped it was something Isabelle and I could do together.

I prepared plates for two, as I always did since Isabelle became part of my life, and set hers aside, hoping the aroma would draw her from the veil.

There were no candles, no bread warmed on the side. Just a plate of pancakes and eggs and a mug of coffee waiting for her when she returned. I sat at the table and let the steam rise, listening to the house breathe.

Outside, the wind shifted. The sun hovered just above the horizon, casting long shadows across the floor, and I knew it wouldn't be long before my wife opened her eyes again. Until she did, I intended to wait for her.

CHAPTER 21

The Flower

The scent of butter and warm maple syrup filled the air as I took my first breath, transporting me back to my childhood. Memories of Mama in the kitchen, cooking enough to feed the entire town, flooded my mind. At the same time, I could picture Papa on the back deck, sipping his morning coffee. These thoughts brought a veil of sadness, yet my lips curled into a smile at the thought of Kayden, my husband, my savior. My emotional journey was filled with memories of the past and the warmth of the present.

The aroma of a home-cooked breakfast, coupled with the realization of who had prepared it for me, gently pulled me from the silence, like a comforting thread woven through the ache of waking. I took slow, deep breaths. The pain lingered—an echo in my ribs, a pull in my spine—but it felt softer than usual, dulled by the warmth of the fire and the faint sweetness in the air. It was a bittersweet moment, a reminder of the love that surrounded me and the struggles I faced.

When I finally opened my eyes, the first thing I saw was the flicker of the low, crackling fire in the hearth. Candlelight illuminated every surface. On the nightstand beside the bed sat a small plate with a stack of slightly uneven pancakes, accompanied by scrambled eggs and a drizzle of syrup pooling around the edges. A chipped mug featuring a smiling cat rested beside it.

He had cooked for me and had fallen asleep waiting for my return.

Sitting up slowly, I wrapped the blanket around my shoulders and reached for the plate. The first bite made my eyes sting. The pancakes were soft and imperfect, slightly overcooked at the edges, but I didn't mind at all, because he had made them for me.

Across the room, Kayden stirred. Like so many other nights, he was slumped in the chair by the door, his body curled slightly, one arm across his chest and the other limp at his side. It was clear he had tried to stay awake for me but had eventually nodded off. His head was tilted against the cushion, and his mouth was parted. His hoodie was slung over the back of the chair where he had fallen asleep, and an empty mug sat on the windowsill, probably from that morning. This room, once dim, cold, and sealed from the world, now pulsed with life. It no longer felt like a tomb; it felt like a home.

He woke with a quiet inhale as I stepped closer, pushing himself up in the chair. "You're back," he whispered, his voice rough with sleep.

I brought my hand to his lips and kissed his knuckles. "I never really left."

His fingers curled around mine, and the way his eyes lit up with his smile made my heart flutter. "I've missed you."

"You made my breakfast," I said, excited to take another bite. I was hungry, but I couldn't help but go to him as soon as I saw him.

He blinked. "Pancakes. Not my best work."

"Better than instant noodles," I teased. "You're evolving."

For the next few hours, I ate while Kayden and I went over some documents on the table, sifting through those he had pulled aside as important. Later, we wandered to the atrium, tending to the plants together in the moonlit tranquility, our fingers working the soil and pruning where necessary. By the time we returned to the den, the fire was low, and the air between us had grown charged. We made love in front of the flames, his hands and lips expressing everything that words could not.

Afterward, he stretched out on the rug beside me, our limbs tangled together, the heat from the hearth sinking into our skin. I lay against his chest, listening to the steady thrum of his heart, the sound growing slower and softer. His arms tightened around me once before relaxing, his breath evening into the deep rhythm of sleep.

I stayed there, watching the shadows ebb and sway along the walls, feeling the comforting weight of him beside me. The night outside was vast and alive, but here, within these four walls, everything I needed was already in my arms.

Once Kayden drifted off to sleep, I slipped off the couch, wrapping myself in his flannel shirt and moving barefoot through the darkened manor. I didn't light a candle. I didn't need to. My body knew these halls by memory. The floorboards and corners were still shaped by the girl who once ran through them barefoot, too. The familiarity of these surroundings brought a sense of security, like a warm embrace in the cold night.

After decades of wandering the dark halls of the manor alone,if only to keep myself from going crazy, I rarely had a destination in mind. That night was no different. I didn't begin this walk intending to find anything, but the longer I moved, the more a thought began to press against the quiet—something that had followed me since the night before when I looked over Margaret's notes again. My introspection was a constant companion, guiding my thoughts and actions.

Cillian.

His name hadn't been written clearly—not at first—but it was there, tucked in the margins, next to places only hinted at: initials, vague landmarks, half-forgotten roles. A stable boy. A groundskeeper. Someone who had once worked at the manor. Someone who had vanished, only to return years later—not through the front door, but through offerings left quietly on the steps: candles, salt, soap. Always what I needed. Never more. Never less.

For a long time, I had told myself those baskets were from her—from the witch. It made more sense that way. It felt safer to believe they were laced with manipulation than to admit the possibility of kindness. Hope was dangerous in captivity; it softened the edges and made you forget the bars.

But now, after reading what Margaret had left behind, I couldn't ignore the possibility that Cillian was the witch's son. If he had truly been the one watching over me all that time, maybe the letters were not what I initially thought. Perhaps I was mistaken; possibly he had genuinely cared about me. Maybe he wasn't behind his mother's decision to curse me for rejecting his proposal.

I found myself standing in front of the pantry door. The hinges groaned as I opened it, the sound quickly swallowed by the stillness inside. The air was cool and dry, heavy with the scent of vinegar, beeswax, and dust. Shelves lined the walls, some fully stocked while others stood bare. Jars of jam, pickled beets, and dried herbs filled the space. I had filled this room over the years, preserving everything I could—food, memories, the illusion of control.

Stepping inside, I crossed to the far shelf, where an old tin box waited behind a row of empty jars. I had hidden it long ago, too afraid of what opening it might mean. Hope or manipulation—either one would be dangerous.

The latch gave with a soft click, and inside, I found the letters. Neatly folded and still bound with the same ribbon I had wrapped them in decades ago, they were tucked among sprigs of dried lavender and wax-sealed cloth. I had kept them all, even when I couldn't bear to read them. At the time, they felt like poison I needed to store out of reach.

But now, with Margaret's clues humming softly in my mind, they felt like something more. They were not salvation or absolution, but perhaps they could be a trail.

I pulled one from the stack at random, uncertain of how long ago he had left it. My name was written on the front in the same careful handwriting I remembered from all those years ago.

> *Isabelle,*
> *I don't know if you read these. Still, I hope you know I think of you. The baskets, the offerings—I leave what I can, though I don't know if it helps. May the salt still protect. May the candles still burn. More than anything, I hope you're well. And I hope you know I meant no harm.*
> *—Cillian*

The letter trembled in my hand. He hadn't saved me, but perhaps he'd tried. And now, after all this time, it wasn't just kindness I needed from him. It was answers.

I didn't rest that day—not after the hours I'd spent with-out breath, and not after the letter I'd just read.

Even curled into Kayden's arms, my mind refused to quiet. Thoughts pressed in from every side: the pantry, the brittle jars, the fading supplies, and Cillian's words folded between my palms. The quiet weight of what might still be waiting in the shadows we hadn't searched loomed over me.

Instead of sleeping, I lay still beside him, watching the soft lines of his face in sleep. I let my fingers move gently across the curve of his cheekbone, the line of his jaw, and felt the steady warmth of his breath. The peace on his face looked hard-earned, something I didn't want to disturb.

But I couldn't stop thinking. If Cillian was the witch's son—and I believed now that he was—then the answers weren't in town. They weren't buried in ledgers or old records. They were in the woods, in places we hadn't dared to go, and maybe, just maybe, in the words he'd left behind. I didn't have much time, but I had enough to start.

Slipping from the bed, I pulled on Kayden's flannel again and made my way to the kitchen. The apartment was quiet, with the fire still throwing low light across the floor. I picked up his notebook from the table and opened it to a blank page.

The pen felt heavier than it should have. It had been so long since I tried to organize my thoughts on paper, aside from my diary, and so long since I believed there was a future worth preparing for. But now I had Kayden, and that changed everything.

With my mind cluttered with a chaos of thoughts, I began writing what I remembered—not just the obvious things like names, places, and bits of stories I'd heard before my curse and from my parents after that day—but the details that had stuck with me without explanation. Landmarks from dreams, faces I'd only glimpsed once, sounds, phrases, and half-formed memories I used to dismiss but now felt the need to chase. With so much at stake, no detail was too small.

When the words began to blur and the ache in my fingers caught up with me, I stood up again and crept to the bathroom. The air was still warm from Kayden's earlier shower, the scent of his soap lingering, clean and soft with a hint of sandalwood.

Turning on the faucet, I watched the water run, letting the steam curl into the space around me. For years, I had bathed only to survive—quick rinses, cold water, with no heat left to waste and no time to indulge. It was something that broke the time between living and dying.

Tonight, however, I lingered, allowing the warmth to soak into my skin, loosening everything the day had tightened. I sank deeper, the water curling around me like a second heartbeat. Steam blurred the edges of the room, softening the sharp thoughts that waited beyond these walls.

For the first time in longer than I could remember, I allowed myself to simply be—to feel the weight of the water, the slow pull of breath, and the heat easing into my bones. Tomorrow and the days after would demand more of me than I had ever given. But tonight, I could surrender to the quiet, to the steady rhythm of warmth, and pretend, just for a little while, that nothing waited beyond the door.

CHAPTER 22

The Keeper

I woke to the soft sound of water running, too close to be the rain or the sea. For a moment, I wasn't sure if it was real or if some half-memory had followed me into waking, but then her scent reached me.

Honey and lavender. The warmth of her skin, clean steam rising off the tile. The air held the echo of her, as if the room remembered her better than I did.

I turned my head just as she stepped from the bathroom, wrapped in one of my towels, hair damp and curling against her shoulders. Candlelight flickered at her back, gilding the steam behind her like a veil of smoke. A smile touched her lips when she saw me, her bottom lip caught briefly between her teeth. She was exquisite.

Her eyes met mine, and in that gaze I found no sorrow, no fear. Only peace—aching, fragile, almost unbearable in its beauty. Neither of us had ever found it alone, but together, we had.

Without hesitation, she crossed the room, footsteps whispering against the rug, eyes locked on mine. Rising from the chair, I let the blanket slip from my waist and reached for her. The moment her arms wound around my neck, I pulled her into my lap, desperate to close the distance.

Her lips found mine, and just like the first time—and every time since—the kiss was nothing short of magic. Before Isabelle, I had never believed such a connection existed. Now I knew better. She was the fire that kept me alive, the one I would give everything for. She was everything.

Her mouth moved slowly, every kiss heavy with need. The moment pressed down on us, but instead of breaking beneath it, we gave ourselves to it.

The towel loosened at her hips as her fingers sank into my hair. I caught the slipping edge in one hand—not to cover her, but to savor the gift she was. Isabelle carried a grace that demanded devotion, and I would worship her on my knees if she asked it of me.

"I thought I dreamed of you," I murmured, my breath grazing her jaw.

Her lips brushed mine again in answer, a whisper of warmth. "I'm real. At least for tonight."

Lifting her into my arms, I carried her to the bed. Her legs tightened around my waist, and I was already aching for her. I didn't just want her, I needed her, needed to feel that she lived, that we lived.

When I laid her down and let the towel fall away, I took a moment just to look at her. Candlelight gilded her damp hair, her breath coming too fast with anticipation, her eyes darkened by lust. My heart ached, desire tempered by the raw ache of awe.

Everything about her was soft: her skin, her hair, the sound of her breath when I kissed the inside of her thigh. The way her eyes never left mine made it hard to undress myself, because all I wanted was to lose myself in her warmth, to give her everything before the sun came to steal her away.

We kissed more than spoke, trying to make the best of the little time we had before sunrise.

When she pulled me down into her, the world narrowed to heat and breath, to the rhythm of us colliding. Her hands tangled in my hair, tugging me closer. Fingers traced down my spine, then curled hard, keeping me where she wanted me. Her thighs clamped around my hips, dragging me deeper until every stroke felt like surrender.

The room filled with the sounds of skin against skin, her breath breaking in my ear, my own groan spilling against her throat. She moved with me, not passively but insistently, her body demanding more. I kissed her jaw, her mouth, the place beneath her ear where her pulse fluttered wild and frantic.

Her climax caught her suddenly, trembling waves that rippled through her body, clenching around me until I lost rhythm. She pressed her mouth to my shoulder, muffling the cry that still shivered through both of us. I pushed harder, faster, my control unraveling in seconds.

Hot release tore through me as she trembled, leaving me buried inside her, gasping against her neck. My forehead fell to hers, our mouths brushing, our chests heaving in unison. For a breathless span of moments, we shared everything—pulse, heat, and the fragile proof of life between us.

But slowly, her warmth began to slip away. She did not vanish, but the shift was undeniable. Her breath stilled, her hand slackened, her body settling into silence that hollowed me.

I stayed with her for a long time, holding her against me even as her body cooled in my arms. She had told me not to be afraid, that this was only a pause and not an ending, but the stillness settling over her was more challenging to endure than I had imagined.

When the warmth finally left her skin, I bent close and whispered into her hair—words that belonged to her alone. Then, with every step heavier than the last, I forced myself to rise and leave the room.

The morning light was thin through the windows, the sky still caught in that in-between place where dawn lingers and shadows haven't yet fled. I slipped into a sweater and stepped barefoot into the atrium.

The tile was cold under my feet, but the air was warming already. Bees moved lazily between blossoms. The lemon tree's leaves were still damp with condensation. I knelt in the soil and dragged my fingers through the rosemary, breathing in the sharp, green bite of it. That earthy scent helped more than I wanted to admit.

I understood why the atrium meant so much to her. Amid all the death, it was life.

Back inside, I cleared the dirty dishes from the table. Isabelle's mug still sat on the windowsill, the remaining tea long cold. I rinsed it and placed it in the dishwasher, and then washed the pans in silence. The hum of the kettle on the stove was the only sound in the apartment. It was easier to pretend she was simply sleeping.

With the kitchen clean, I spread Margaret's notes across the table once more. My own scribbled pages joined them—some folded, others scrawled in the dark. Isabelle's handwriting was there too, a presence woven between the lines.

Flipping to a fresh sheet of paper, I wrote one name across the top: *Cillian.*

Then I began to search.

By late morning, my eyes burned from scanning faded records online—deeds without names, census entries with only initials, news clippings that read more like superstition than fact. A boarding house in 1952. A handwritten ledger noting a caretaker who never signed his full name. No addresses that matched. No family trees I could trace.

They were just breadcrumbs.

Eventually, I stepped away from the desk. The kettle was still warm, so I poured more water and brought the mug with me to the atrium. The scent of herbs hung in the air, mixing with lemon and damp stone.

I sat on the low stone wall beside the lavender beds and let the sun settle on my shoulders from the large windows overhead.

The garden did not ask anything of me. That was what I loved about it. It grew when it could and rested when it needed to. Some of the seedlings we'd planted were already beginning to show signs of stubborn life—thin shoots curling toward the light, green despite the cold.

I didn't talk to her aloud. I didn't need to, but I carried her with me in every glance at the basil, in the way I smoothed the stones at the edge of the beds, the way I touched the honeysuckle and brought my hand to my face just to breathe her in. She was in every part of this place.

When the sun shifted lower in the sky, I returned to the main house. The papers waited. The questions waited, but I wasn't looking for a breakthrough, at least not yet. Still, I needed to move forward, even if it was slow.

As dusk settled over the house, I lit the candles the way Isabelle always had, their glow softening the room and holding the dark at bay. At the table, I spread out my notes again and began to redraw the map from Margaret's journal, layering in every strange detail she had once recorded: the cottage in Vaughn Hollow, a raven carved above a door, a son who loved Isabelle, even the place where her father's body had been found.

Whenever something refused to fit, I circled it. When it echoed one of Isabelle's half-memories, I marked it again.

If Cillian or the witch had left even the faintest trace, I intended to be the one to follow it, no matter how far into the dark it led.

I held you until the warmth left,
pretending silence was only sleep.
Your breath was gone,
but you lingered in the rosemary.

The first thing I saw when I woke up was light. For a heartbeat, I lay still, allowing the shape of it to settle around me. It was not sunlight, which had no place in my world, but the warm flicker of candlelight. The light danced along the walls in gentle patterns, as if it were breath made visible, brushing against the bookshelves and the curve of Kayden's shoulder. The scent of the sea lingered in the air, mingling with parchment, tea, and the faint sweetness of smoke.

"You were reading again," I said, nodding toward the cluttered table beside us.

"And waiting," he replied, lifting my hand to his lips. "But I may have found something."

He reached for a small leather-bound journal, one I hadn't noticed before. The binding was cracked, and the pages were soft with age. Margaret's handwriting curved across the paper like a ghost still trying to speak.

"There's a passage here," he said, scanning the text with his eyes. "A cottage near the forest. And… a raven carved into the door."

A chill moved through me—not exactly fear, but recognition.

"I remember that raven," I murmured. "I saw it once in a dream when I was young. Just a glimpse. It seemed out of place, like it was watching, even after I woke."

Kayden looked up, his expression sharpening. "Margaret says it was a symbol used by a hedge witch cult in the 1800s. They supposedly disbanded, but there's a note in the margin: *one region still whispers the old names.*"

He turned the journal toward me, his finger pressed against a single underlined phrase.

Vaughn Hollow.

The name echoed in my chest before it left my lips.

"Vaughn Hollow," I whispered.

Kayden let the name hang in the air, as if saying it aloud might change something. Then he asked, "You've heard of it?"

I hesitated, slowly flipping through a few pages Kayden had stacked beside the journal. "Not in words, but there was a case I remember from years ago. My father's body was found in a forest, not far from where he vanished. I never knew the details, and the police didn't tell my mother much. Back then, they kept everything quiet, especially from women. I wasn't allowed to ask questions, and even if I had, I couldn't have followed any leads. I was already bound to this house. No one knew I was still alive, except for a few who kept the secret. My parents buried an empty casket to protect me, terrified the town would believe something wicked had taken root in our family. A daughter who couldn't die, not in an era that feared anything it didn't understand. They were afraid I'd be labeled a witch, that I'd be hunted for something I never chose. So, they hid me."

I looked down at the page, my fingers brushing the edge. "I've dreamed of forests like that, but I've never been to Vaughn Hollow. Still... something about it makes sense."

"It sounds like the kind of place she would go," he said. "Somewhere forgotten. Hidden by choice."

I nodded slowly. "It feels right. Or at least... less wrong than everything else we've found."

Setting his pen down, he closed the journal. "Margaret marked a few references to that region in some of her later notes. Not enough to chart a course, but enough to know it exists. It's not on modern maps, but if the old ones are even halfway accurate, it's a few days' drive north. Mostly forest. Untouched land now, or at least it used to be."

"So if there's a cottage still standing out there, it's deep enough to stay hidden," I said. "And far enough away that we'd have to take a real risk to reach it."

"Exactly. It's not a casual day trip."

"And I still die every morning," I added quietly. "That will complicate things."

"Yeah," he agreed. "But you can leave now. That's a beginning."

For a moment, neither of us spoke. My thoughts ran in slow, looping circles: the journey ahead, the strange pull of Vaughn Hollow, the risk of chasing a place that might not even exist. *What if we were wrong? What if we reached the edge of the forest and found only rot and ruin? Or worse, nothing at all?*

I glanced at Kayden, wondering if he was thinking the same thing, if he felt the fragile weight of hope pressing hard enough to hurt.

The tea he'd poured earlier had cooled slightly, but he handed it to me anyway. I took a sip, letting it settle in my chest. "What if we go all that way and find nothing?"

"Then we come home and try something else."

I searched his handsome face. There was no fear in his eyes, only conviction.

"You really believe it might be there," I stated rather than asked.

"I believe it's the best lead we've had, and we have to follow something."

Glancing back down at the notes, I shrugged. "Even if most of it came to me in dreams?"

"Especially because it did."

I let out a slow breath, my nod forced. "It will take planning: supplies, somewhere safe to stop during the day."

Kayden nodded. "Then we plan."

After we finished our dinner, which consisted of left-overs from the night before, the fire settled into a bed of glowing coals, its warmth reaching only as far as the hearth. I rose to stretch, my limbs feeling sluggish from stillness, yet a restless energy surged through my veins. The sky beyond the windows had deepened into full night, stars scattered like salt above the cliffs.

Kayden watched me from his spot on the couch for a moment before standing. "Come outside with me," he said gently as he rose. "Just for a bit."

Outside, a chill had settled in, a subtle reminder that winter was approaching. The heavy snows we received in Crystal Peak would only make traveling north more difficult. I knew we could not wait, no matter how much trepidation I felt.

The stones held the warmth of the sun, and the air smelled of the salty sea. Barefoot on the path, I let the dew kiss my skin. It struck me how strange and beautiful it was to walk freely in the night after so many years confined behind windows.

We walked slowly, our hands brushing, then intertwining. I let my head fall against his shoulder as we passed the fire pit where we had dined and made love on our wedding night. Heat flushed my cheeks as I remembered how he had made me scream to the stars that night.

Slowing near the cliffs, Kayden turned to me. "When we go, I want to make time—not just to reach our destination, but for you to see and feel things again. The beach, ice cream, movies—things you've only watched from your window or read about in books. It's time for you to feel like part of the world again, not like a ghost watching from the shadows."

My throat tightened. "You don't have to do all that. You already gave me my freedom."

"That wasn't enough," he said softly, tucking a lock of hair behind my ear. "You remember what life used to feel like. I want to give some of that back, even if it's just a little."

His touch sent a shiver through me that had little to do with the cold, and the sincerity in his voice unraveled something within me. I turned to him, intertwining my fingers with his.

"I'm scared," I admitted. "Not of the journey, but of what I might lose. What you might lose."

He pulled me into his arms as my words trailed off. Tears burned at the edges of my eyes, but I forced them back. The days of mourning the life I had lost were over. A future was attainable with Kayden in my life, if only I could be brave enough to fight for it. "Then let's create the kind of memories that make the risk worth it."

The Flower

The first inhale clawed its way through my lungs. It wasn't fire or pain—just the deep, seizing ache of being reminded that I was alive, of awareness rushing in before my heartbeat had fully returned. My limbs felt heavy, touched by the kind of chill that lingers after frost.

For a moment, I couldn't move. I listened to the faint crackle of candlelight, the murmur of waves beyond the cliff, and the quiet pulse of existence that didn't yet feel like mine.

Bathed in the soft light of the candles, Kayden sat near-by—his body half-turned toward me, his eyes lost some-where between thought and waiting. His notebook lay open, the last line of whatever he'd been writing trailing off mid-sentence.

"You're back," he murmured. It was the line he always said, even though we both knew I hadn't really left, not really.

A slow breath steadied in my chest as I reached for the blanket, pulling it tighter around my shoulders in silent acknowledgment as I pushed myself upright. The ache of stillness clung to me, but tonight, it felt less like a cage and more like the shedding of old skin.

My body remembered. It always did, in time.

Rising from his chair, Kayden crossed the room and sank to his knees beside the bed. His steady fingers sought mine and held them gently.

"I found something," he said.

From the cluttered edge of the table, he retrieved a folded slip of paper. The edges were yellowed, and the handwriting was familiar—too familiar.

The moment I saw the script, my breath caught—not just because I recognized it, but because I could almost feel the brush of her arm against mine, the faint scent of lavender and ink clinging to her sleeves. My mother hadn't written anything in decades, and yet here she was, whispering through the paper.

He read it aloud: "If something happens to us, look where rosemary never dies."

The words didn't all emerge at once. They unfolded slowly, like something pressed beneath stone—fragile yet alive in their return. The sound of his voice reading her handwriting hollowed me. They would never meet. My mother would never know that I had finally found love.

As I tried to process my mother's note, I turned toward the window. The candlelight cast faint halos against the glass, and beyond it, the moon blurred in its watchful glow. Something inside me tightened—a thread knotted by time and loss, cinching close to the place where her voice used to live.

"My mother," I said softly.

Kayden nodded once, saying nothing, allowing the silence to convey more than words could express.

I reached for a sweater draped across the chair and pulled it over my dress, needing the familiar weight of the fabric as I rose. Kayden fetched the lantern and a spade. The rosemary was waiting for us.

Moonlight stretched long and silver across the stones, guided by a quiet we dared not disturb. Each step pressed deeper into the weight of the place.

We passed the overgrown rosemary hedge, its sharp green scent rising like a memory itself. My fingertips brushed the leaves, and for a moment, I could almost see my mother's hands in the same spot, tucking sprigs into her pockets.

Kayden moved beside me, his shoulder brushing mine now and then, grounding me as my chest tightened with every step we took.

At the far corner, I lowered myself to the ground, pressing my palms into the soil. The sharp scent rose instantly, taking me back to the countless days my mother spent in this garden, teaching me how to grow my own food.

Kayden crouched beside me, lowering the lantern before setting the spade to the ground. The sound of metal striking something solid sent a shock through me. My pulse quickened. I dropped to my knees, pushing his hand aside to claw through the dirt myself. Soil packed beneath my nails, cold and damp, but I barely noticed. I needed to touch it, whatever it was.

The spade caught on an edge, and together we cleared the soil until a shape revealed itself: a small, rusted tin box. My throat tightened as I pulled it free with both hands; the rust flaked against my palms, and its weight was heavier than I expected.

I set the box in my lap and forced the lid open. Inside, cushioned in a lining of faded cloth, lay a key no larger than my thumb. My breath hitched. For so long, my parents had lived only in memory, but here was something real—something I could hold. My chest ached with emotion.

Beside the key rested a folded scrap of paper, its edges curled with age. My fingers shook as I lifted it, terrified it might fall apart before I could even read what it said.

Isabelle,
This opens the place where your father kept his treasures.
I hope one day it brings you something worth finding and
helps you create the life you've always deserved.
—Mama

The words blurred before my eyes. It wasn't just ink on paper. It was her voice, her hand, her love reaching across decades to touch me again.

My breath caught as I stared at the words, their meaning striking harder than they should have.

"He used to say that," I murmured, the loss of my father opening a barely healed wound in my chest. "After he passed away, my mother became a shell of herself. There was no more planning for the future."

Kayden's expression revealed tenderness as he looked at me. "What?"

"When I was little, his desk drawer was always locked. When I asked why, he told me it was where he kept his treasure."

A faint smile tugged at my lips, memories blooming through the ache. "I thought he meant coins or maps. Secrets, maybe. I didn't realize it might hold real treasure."

Kayden's gaze dropped to the key in my hand.

"So, it's not just a drawer," I whispered. "It's a clue."

I closed my fingers around the key, the metal cool against my skin. The sharp scent of rosemary rose again, grounding me as I stood.

We lingered in the stillness for a few heartbeats longer. The garden whispered with night sounds—the hush of lavender brushing against itself, the rhythmic sigh of waves far below, and the rustle of leaves in the breeze.

My gaze fell on the key once more, its ridges catching the moonlight like a memory etched in metal, before lifting to meet Kayden's eyes.

Our gaze locked, and in that suspended moment, the curse, the forest, the witch—none of it mattered.

Only this: the touch of our hands and the ghost of the woman who left me the first breadcrumb home.

His thumb traced across my cheek with a tenderness that quieted my thoughts.

I leaned into his touch, needing it more than he realized.

Another glance at the key, heavy with more than age, drew my thoughts back to the curse.

A certainty stirred within me: I didn't know what awaited us beyond this, but I would face it with open eyes.

"This is where it starts," I said, my voice barely above the night.

"No," he whispered. "We changed fate."

We didn't return to bed.

Instead, we carried the key back inside, but I didn't stop at the table. We passed through the kitchen and into the corridor that hadn't been warmed in years, not stopping until I reached my father's study tucked behind the east wing.

After so much time locking the ghosts away, the door-knob stuck. Kayden reached past me and gave it a firm twist. It opened with a soft groan, and the air inside was colder than I remembered. Everything was still, undisturbed, as if no one had crossed its threshold in decades.

I stepped in first, lifting the candle to see better.

A shiver skittered down my spine, reminding me why the room was so devoid of life. My father had fought to save me and died trying. It was a guilt I could never wash from my hands, even though I had not been the one to utter the curse.

The room smelled of dust, cedar, and faint cigar smoke. A window, long cracked open just a little, had rusted into place. The desk sat against the wall beside it, covered in a thick layer of dust.

I crossed the room and knelt beside the small drawer on the left, the one my father had always called his treasure. The key resisted the lock, but after a bit of coaxing, it yielded to me.

Inside lay a single journal. The cover was leather-bound, its edges worn with age. Resting atop it was a dagger. Although dulled by time, its blade shimmered faintly in the candlelight, and its hilt was wrapped in cracked leather.

For a moment, all I could do was stare. I had never known my father to hide weapons like this.

Near the base of the blade, a raven symbol was etched, its beak turned downward. The sight of it unsettled me, dragging me back to the raven in my dreams—the wrongness of it all. Hand trembling, I set the candle on the desk and lifted the dagger as I slowly stood.

"I saw something like this in Margaret's sketches," Kayden said. "This was meant to protect someone."

I nodded, my fingers still curled around the hilt. "We'll need weapons if we're going after her. This can't just be research anymore. We need to be ready to defend ourselves."

Even as I said it, the words rang hollow. I couldn't imagine striking anyone with such a weapon, no matter what they had done to me. I wasn't sure Kayden could either. Kill. Would that be what it took to earn my freedom?

When I looked up at him, his expression had shifted. If he was unsure, he hid it well—not with fear, but with understanding. "We'll bring it with us. And a gun. I have my father's pistol. Anything that gives us a chance. If she's still out there, we're not going in unarmed."

We fell quiet, the weight of it settling between us.

It took me a moment to remember the journal still in the drawer, left by my mother after my father never returned. Setting the dagger on the desk beside the candle, I lifted the journal and opened it to the first page.

The ink was smudged, and the handwriting was shaky, but I recognized it immediately as my father's. His notes filled the pages: sketches, theories, and fragments of research on how to break my curse. Plans to visit Vaughn Hollow. As time went on, the words grew more frantic and less coherent. One line repeated over and over: she can't have Isabelle.

A tear slid down my cheek before I could stop it, and I wiped it away with my sleeve, hating the guilt that undid me.

"He tried," I whispered, closing my eyes as Kayden's hand brushed my back. "He tried to save me...but he had no idea what he was walking into." I couldn't finish that thought. Neither of us knew what we were walking into, either.

Kayden's arm slid around my waist, steadying me. "He left this for you, my flower, so you could take your life back."

Although the idea filled me with more fear than I'd ever known, I nodded and set the journal down.

"He left this for me to take my life back," I said softly, "and that's exactly what I'm going to do."

With the dagger and the journal in hand, we returned to the apartment. The silence felt heavier now, weighed down by what we had unearthed. Kayden poured two glasses of wine, and we sat at the table with the journal, the dagger, and the scattered research spread between us.

For a moment, we didn't speak. We simply glanced at everything laid out before us, the candlelight reflecting off the blade and casting its lethal intent back at me.

Then Kayden opened his notebook, and in that small moment, something shifted. The first outlines of a plan began to take shape on the page: routes to Vaughn Hollow and landmarks connected to the forest whispered about in my father's notes.

Once the plan was laid out, we rose from the table and started gathering what we thought we might need, even though it was all guesswork. We had no idea what we were stepping into. I wasn't sure if human-made weapons could stand against her. Lenora Thorne hadn't used anything from this world to take my life, and I doubted this world could provide me with the means to take it back.

While Kayden packed his clothes for our journey into the unknown, I returned to the butler's pantry upstairs. Tucked on the same shelf where I had left it was the box of Cilian's letters. There were still some I hadn't read, and perhaps within them lay something more we needed.

With the box beneath my arm, I pushed aside jars of stewed tomatoes and reached for another one I hadn't opened in years. Inside, resting above a small stack of photographs, was a rosemary charm tied with a faded ivory ribbon. I had kept it since I was a child—stored in coats, drawers, and beside my bed through the long years of the curse. Eventually, when the ribbon unraveled and the rosemary dried to brittle dust, I tucked it away for safekeeping.

There were only a few things that could survive the decades I had haunted these halls. This was one of the few reminders of my mother that I could still carry with me.

She hadn't studied the occult. She hadn't known how to wield a curse. But she believed in Old Wives' Tales passed down through generations. Rosemary, she always said, would hold on. It protected. Sometimes the earth remembered when people did not.

It wasn't magic in the way curses were magic, but it was memory. And it was mine.

I couldn't imagine leaving without it.

The manor was full of sunlight. Warmth pooled across the floorboards, catching motes of dust in slow spirals. The windows stood open, curtains breathing in and out

like lungs. A soft breeze drifted through the house, laced with the scent of lemon balm and old books. The light touched everything as if it had missed the opportunity for years and meant to make up for it. I stood barefoot in the atrium.

For a moment, I just took it in. It had been so long since I'd felt the sun on my skin.

The tiles beneath my feet were warm from the sun. Rosemary had grown thick and wild beside me, its scent sharp and green—rich with memory. Vines stretched taller than I remembered, brushing gently against the glass ceiling as though they were reaching for something. The garden had grown in my absence, or perhaps I had simply forgotten how full it could feel.

It was morning, and I was alive.

Laughter caught my ears from down the corridor, sending a prickle down my spine. My mother's gentle voice rose like a song nearly lost to time. My father answered, his tone lower, humming alongside her. I turned toward the sound, drawn forward by an unseen thread coiled around my ribs, tugging with the weight of something I thought I'd forgotten. There was a part of me that knew it must be a trick, that it couldn't possibly be real, but an even bigger part of me needed it to be.

The hallway stretched as I walked, longer than it should have been. Doors opened on either side, rooms I hadn't seen in decades. A cradle, long forgotten, lingered in one, but no baby cried from within. Faded wallpaper clung to the walls like memory. The music room with the cracked piano. A corridor of portraits, their eyes following in silence. Memories pressed in from all directions, scent and sound and shadow layering over each other until time began to slip. The house was too large for one person, or even two, leaving room for the spirits of the past to linger.

I passed them all, barefoot and breathless. The farther I went, the colder the air became. It crept along my skin like mist, stealing warmth in increments, reminding me that not everything familiar was safe.

At the end of the hall, one door waited half-open. Symbols palpitated beneath the wood like veins. It was no longer carved, but grown, as if the door had bled itself into being. The sigils pulsed with a rhythm not mine, a chant I could not hear. I didn't recognize the language, but something within my body did. Perhaps that part of me Lenora had left behind when she took a piece of me.

A dark pit swirled inside my chest, thinning the stale air until I could barely breathe, but still I stepped forward, my body drawn by an invisible force.

Beyond it lay a garden. It wasn't the one Kayden and I had tended with our hands and hope, nor the ones outside that had been neglected by time. This garden was darker.

Wilder. Its edges blurred, but it wasn't by fog, but by a lapse in memory.

The plants choked together, towering in dense tangles. Vines wrapped tightly around the stone. Overhead, the sky held no color, only a pale silver veil. Still, the garden pulsed with life, but it was all wrong.

Without a sun to feed it, the rosemary bloomed black. Lavender drooped low, its tips brushing the earth. The yarrow curled inward, hiding something it had never meant to reveal. This garden did not give life, but took it away.

Swallowing back the fear that paralyzed me, I stepped around the dying lemon tree, its fruit black with rot. Up ahead, in the center of the path, stood a woman. Standing motionless, she faced away from me. Her hair was dark as ink, the streaks of silver standing out in her tight braid. Bare feet disappeared into the soil, and her dress shifted faintly, though the garden held no wind.

Although she remained still, not turning to look into my eyes, the uneasy feeling in my chest told me who she was. Lenora. The witch who cursed me.

As I watched her from several feet away, my feet paralyzed by fear, she raised one arm and pointed. Beside her appeared a door, freestanding in the middle of the garden. It was tall, weathered, and impossibly still, but just like *the door I'd entered through, it was covered in sigils that glowed faintly in the low light.*

A key waited in the lock, and above the key, a raven had been carved into the wood, its wings outstretched and its beak turned downward.

A moment later, the woman disappeared, and life pulled me from the darkness once more.

CHAPTER 25

The Flower

When I stepped outside the following morning, I forgot to breathe, paralyzed by fear as silence pressed harder than sound ever could. Although I had been able to leave the manor for several days, I hadn't yet found the courage to step beyond its borders until now. But I summoned the strength, knowing that if I wished to find Lenora and end my curse, I had no choice but to face the world beyond the gates.

The night felt different here. It wasn't confined by walls or imprisoned in corners. Instead, it moved freely, uncontained, brushing against my cheek and trailing down my throat. The wind slipped through my hair, whispering across the back of my neck as if reacquainting itself with skin it hadn't touched in decades.

There was meaning in that breeze. It was an invitation to a world I no longer belonged to. For the first time in more than eighty years, the world opened itself to me, and it smelled of brine, damp earth, and a future I still didn't know how to embrace.

I stood beside the car as Kayden placed the last of our supplies in the trunk, my hands curling into the folds of my coat. The last rays of sunlight spilled across the sea, scattering like petals torn from a fading bloom. Above the cliffs, the sky was in transition—lavender fading into indigo, folding into black. The stars blinked slowly into place, uncertain at first. Like me, they needed convincing that they were allowed to shine.

Inside me, the curse loosened. The invisible tether that had bound me to the manor pulled taut, then snapped like a thread drawn too tight, just as it had on our wedding night. The weight slipped from my shoulders in quiet increments—faded but still lingering, like a ghost slowly regaining its shape.

Knowing what this journey represented and what its outcome could mean, I lingered there for a long while. I listened to the wind in the hedgerow, the crunch of gravel beneath Kayden's boots, and the silence that no longer felt like a cage but rather like a doorway, open wide and waiting for me to step through.

Breathing deeply, I inhaled the salt carried in on the sea breeze. Lavender still clung faintly to my collar, a reminder that some things rooted in the past could follow us into the future. The road stretched ahead, dark and ribbon-thin, unspooling toward the edge of what we knew.

Behind us, the manor waited in its usual stillness—shrouded now, watching, perhaps remembering me. I knew every echo held in its walls, every shuttered window, and every breath it had ever contained, but I no longer belonged to it. At least for this moment, I was free.

When Kayden finished loading the car, he opened the door for me and waited, never rushing me forward until I was ready. I looked at him, then at the open road, and finally back at the house that had held me for so long. My pulse beat like a second heart, as though it could run ahead and clear the path for me.

This moment was real, and it was happening, even though I was afraid. My heart raced, my hands trembled, and a knot of fear and anticipation tightened in my chest.

I slid into the seat, and he closed the door. The leather was cold against my legs, unfamiliar in its smoothness. The car came to life with a hum that startled me more than it soothed. I flinched, just slightly, but enough for him to notice. Automobiles had been simpler when I left the world. They hadn't been so bright, so loud, so alive with voices and music conjured from within their frames.

His hand reached across the console and found mine, brushing gently over my knuckles—a different kind of tether.

"Okay?" he asked, his voice low.

I nodded, though my hands still trembled. The world beyond the windshield felt too wide, too loud, too fast. I still wasn't sure I belonged in it.

The manor lingered in the rear view mirror longer than it should have, its doors closed and its windows vacant—a tomb we had both walked out of.

It was goodbye... for now. Ahead, the road unspooled into darkness, and though fear still pressed at my ribs, I held Kayden's hand tighter and let the night carry us toward whatever awaited.

The cemetery sat at the edge of town, half-swallowed by trees that leaned inward, as though trying to listen to the spirits they guarded. The iron gate sagged on rusted hinges, heavy with moss and the weight of time. Kayden pulled the car onto the gravel shoulder beneath a crooked oak, whose skeletal branches reached across the windshield, scratching lightly in protest of our arrival.

He opened the door for me, his gaze filled with depthless empathy. Having just lost his father, he understood how such a loss could feel. "Do you want me to come with you?"

I hesitated. The wind caught the hem of my coat and tugged it forward, a gentle urging. My fingers closed around the edge of the dried violet I had tucked into my pocket, now flattened and fragile, and I shook my head. "No," I said, my voice thin enough to vanish. "Not this time."

He didn't question my decision. Instead, he nodded once, and his words were filled with reassurance. "I'll be right here."

The cold beyond the gate was unlike the ocean wind I had come to know. It was less wild, more rooted. It clung low to the earth and sank into my old bones. This was the chill of stone and sorrow, not of the sea. A hush lingered over the ground, heavy with the weight of things buried but never gone.

The gravel path had softened with moss and rainwater, the stones muted beneath curling weeds. I moved through the moonlit dark, each step a reckoning. I had never come here before. Not once. I had watched their deaths from behind locked doors, trapped in a house that had stolen the hours from me. By the time their bodies were lowered into the ground, the world already thought me dead.

As I rounded the curve in the path and saw the markers—two simple headstones beneath the sweep of a leaning pine—I knew this was where I had always been meant to arrive. The weather had softened the lettering, but the truth remained, etched deep and refusing to be forgotten. I had loved my parents dearly, but grief, like everything else, fades over time. Still, a wound deep within me stirred, aching as though it had never healed.

I sank to my knees before them, pressing my hand to the cold surface of my mother's stone. The chill of it climbed up my arm like a ghost. I didn't cry. There was no wailing or collapse, just an ache so deep it felt like it had always lived in my body, waiting for permission to rise.

"I'm sorry I never came," I whispered, hoping they could hear me from wherever they were.

The wind stirred through the branches above, sifting moonlight into broken patterns across the earth. It wasn't a reply, but it wasn't silence, either.

"I thought, for a long time, that if I waited quietly, the world might heal on its own. That I would wake one night and everything would be whole again. But the truth is... time doesn't mend what we aren't brave enough to face."

The words fell to no one, but I spoke them anyway.

My hand moved to my father's stone, reminiscing about the sound of his voice when he read aloud, the scratch of his pen, and the warmth of his eyes when he shared a story. He had believed in answers and action. He had tried to save me, and in the end, the curse took him too. "I found the journal," I said softly. "The dagger. The letter you never finished. I know what you were trying to do, and I will finish it. I promise you."

From my coat pocket, I drew the pressed violet. It had spent so many nights between the pages and in silence, and now I laid it gently on the cold stone, fragile against its strength.

Turning back to my mother's name, I traced each letter with my fingertips. Her hands had always smelled of lavender and woodsmoke. She had braided my hair with a gentleness that stayed with me even now, and when she sang, she needed no words, only melody and breath. "I've missed you," I whispered, and this time the ache bloomed wider than I could hold.

A leaf drifted down through the branches and came to rest beside my knee.

I closed my eyes and bowed my head. Not in prayer, but in surrender, to the weight of memory, to the softness of presence, to the unspoken truth that they had never truly left me.

When I rose, the stars had hidden behind clouds, darkening the sky. The air felt unchanged, but something in me was lighter. Before I walked away, I looked once more at the stones. It wasn't to say goodbye, but to acknowledge them, to honor what had been lost and what still remained.

Kayden stood beneath the crooked oak, still as stone, haloed in the ghostly wash of the headlights. His silhouette hadn't shifted since I left him. He hadn't come to intervene or pull me from my grief. Instead, he had come to bear witness, to hold space in the silence I could no longer carry alone. That support meant more than he knew.

I walked to him slowly, my steps muffled by the moss-soft path, the weight of their absence still pressing against my ribs, though it no longer pulled me under. Even in my sadness, I kept walking forward. Not because the ache had vanished. Grief, I had learned, does not dissolve. It lingers. It softens. It changes shape. But tonight, for the first time, I felt it settle beside me instead of behind me.

Their absence would never stop echoing, but it no longer consumed me. It walked with me now—a presence carved from love and sorrow, from unfinished words and remembered touch. Not a burden strapped to my back, but a quiet company at my side. Enough to keep them alive within me.

Returning to the road, we entered the edge of a town that was completely foreign to me. It was more than just unfamiliar; it was unlike anything I had ever known. Light shimmered from every corner, too bright to be natural. It spilled from the windows of buildings I couldn't recognize and poured from blinking signs that pulsed in colors I struggled to follow. Everything looked polished, bright, and designed to be noticed rather than understood.

I shifted in my seat and gripped the armrest tightly. My stomach turned from the overwhelming experience. The world outside moved too quickly, and even its quiet seemed hurried.

The buildings looked sterile compared to the manor. There were no vines clinging to their surfaces, no soot-softened bricks, and no ivy tucked around the windows—just flat walls and lights that never dimmed or flickered.

Suddenly, a woman stepped onto the sidewalk. Her jacket was the color of crushed roses, and her metallic boots shone. A wireless phone was pressed to her ear as though it were a part of her. A group of boys crossed the street, glowing rectangles in their hands illuminating their faces like ghostly lanterns. Laughter erupted from behind tinted windows, only to vanish as the car moved on.

No one looked at me, but I found it impossible to take my eyes off them.

Kayden pulled into a parking lot beneath a canopy of humming lights, which buzzed above in a constant mechanical rhythm. The building in front of us glowed from within, illuminated too brightly and unnaturally, as if a sun had been trapped inside.

He stepped out of the car first and came around to open my door. "Are you okay?" he asked, offering his hand.

Though I wasn't sure, I took it. His fingers were warm—real and human. "I don't know," I admitted. "It feels... like the world moved on without me."

"It did," he said, his voice incredibly gentle. "But you're still allowed to belong to it."

I wasn't certain I fit in or belonged at all, but I trusted him, so I took his hand.

Gravel shifted beneath my boots as I stepped out. The cold air tightened in my throat, infused with the scent of oil and asphalt, or at least that's what Kayden told me. I had never smelled either before. Beneath it all was something artificial, plastic warmed by fluorescent light, the scent of the modern world reaching out before it spoke.

The doors parted as we approached, sighing open with a mechanical breath. Cold air spilled out, edged with sugar and frost. It smelled like childhood re-designed by machines—stripped of warmth and un-touched by life.

Inside, the world transformed.

Fluorescent lights buzzed overhead, humming across a ceiling that felt both oppressively low and endlessly far away. The air was dry and sterile, scrubbed clean of anything that seemed alive. The floor gleamed, and shelves loomed, stocked with items I didn't recognize, their surfaces too smooth and too bright. Everything shimmered. Everything shouted for attention. There was no texture, no weight, and no invitation to touch.

Boxes lined the aisles, displaying names in bold, jagged letters. Colors clashed like arguments. I saw no fingerprints, no warmth, and no traces of the hands that had shaped anything. Everything felt untethered from the earth, from time.

I paused near a rack of magazines. Dozens of faces stared out at me with perfect teeth and vacant eyes, their symmetry unnerving. Headlines twisted across the covers like riddles meant for people who had never lived through silence. I didn't recognize a single name.

The tightness in my chest forced me to turn away. A bell chimed at the entrance, the sound sudden and sharp, pulling my shoulders taut.

Realizing I was overwhelmed, Kayden's hand found mine. His thumb pressed softly against my fingers—a tether he always offered when I needed it. "It's just the door," he said. "Nothing more."

Blowing out a breath to ease my racing heart, I let him guide me past coolers that hissed in rhythm, past shelves lit from within, casting their contents in an unnatural glow. Bottles and cans lined up in rows, their colors impossible. Fog curled from the seams of the glass like breath that had waited too long to be released.

I reached out, my fingertips skimming the glass. On the bottom shelf, a row of pale cartons waited in neat, silent formation. Absent were the bright colors and boastful fonts. Only a modest label remained, and a shape my body seemed to recognize before my mind could catch up.

"Ice cream," I whispered.

Kayden leaned closer, his gaze following mine. "You remember?"

"Almost." My voice was thin, wrapped in distance. "It feels like something I once glimpsed in someone else's life—a flicker from another room. A joy that never had my name on it."

He opened the case. The door gave way with a quiet pull, and cold air spilled into the space between us, curling against my arms until I shivered.

"Pick one," he said.

I hesitated, staring at the rows of cartons lined up like strangers waiting to be chosen. The colors were loud, the names unfamiliar. For a moment, I feared I wouldn't know how to decide, that even in something so simple, the world would remind me I no longer belonged to it.

Then my hand moved on its own, guided by something deeper than thought—an instinct reaching through the blur. My fingers rested on a carton stamped with small, quiet lettering: vanilla bean.

It wasn't the loudest or the brightest. It didn't demand attention. It simply felt like something I had once loved and perhaps could love again.

For a long while, we sat on the hood of the car beneath a flickering streetlamp. Shadows stretched across the empty lot, shifting in and out of view as if uncertain whether to stay or slip away. The world felt paused in that moment—forgotten by time, yet somehow safe in its stillness, unlike the inside of the market.

The wind moved gently around us, stirring strands of my hair and tugging at the hem of my coat with a quiet insistence. Above us, the sky still flickered with starlight.

Between us, the spoon clicked softly against the rim of the cup as we passed it back and forth. The ice cream was sweet and soft, colder than I remembered, but familiar in the way a scent can be—how it tugs at something buried, something you didn't know you'd forgotten. Each bite melted slowly, bringing with it a flicker of warmth. A moment. A shadow. A trace of joy.

"I remember eating this on a porch once," I said, the memory forming as I spoke. "My father let it melt too long. It ran down my chin in ribbons, and he laughed. He said that was always the best part."

Kayden remained quiet, his gaze steady, anchoring me to the present without words. He was simply there.

"These moments," I added more softly, "they're what make it feel real. Not the curse. Not the silence. Just... this. A flicker of something ordinary."

Reaching out, he tucked a piece of hair behind my ear, his fingers lingering for a breath at my temple before falling away. I turned my head toward the glowing windows of the store, and then to the distant silhouettes of people I didn't know, living in a world that had moved forward while I remained still. In only hours, dawn would return and take me from this world again, while they continued to live. It was a reminder that no matter how much I wanted to belong, I couldn't—not while Lenora still lived.

We arrived at the inn during the hollow hours of night when time thins, and everything feels just a little farther away. The inn was modest, salt-worn, and weathered by years of ocean wind. Wind-bent pines crowded close, their silhouettes swaying against the gentle lapping of the sea. The siding had silvered with age, and a hanging sign creaked softly above the porch.

The Crescent Shore Inn

Kayden pulled into a narrow space near the back, where gravel surrendered to sand. The presence of the sea behind us calmed me in a way. It was a backdrop I had lived with for so long, even if I would soon lie in a bed that was not my own...die in a bed that was not my own.

Inside, the innkeeper was a middle-aged woman with long black hair pulled up into a bun. Her demeanor was calm, almost sleepy, but she was kind.

Once Kayden finished checking in, she handed him a silver key. "I put you two in room four. It's upstairs, facing the ocean."

Floorboards groaned beneath our feet as we climbed the narrow staircase. Vines twined across faded wallpaper, softened by time into a quiet motif of green and gold. A single sconce flickered near the landing, setting the wainscoting in shadows. The inn did not smell of dust or dampness. Instead, the scent of lavender and saltwater lingered, woven through with linen and wood polish.

The room was small but lovingly kept. A white cover-let lay neatly folded at the foot of the bed. A ceramic lamp glowed softly on the nightstand beside a shallow dish of dried herbs. From the half-open window, a breeze curled into the room, carrying with it the scent of the sea and something faintly floral from a garden below.

I crossed the room and stood for a long moment, letting it all settle around me: the absence of haunted walls, the peace of borrowed space.

"This is the first time I've ever spent the night some-where else," I said at last, still watching the dark be-yond the glass.

Behind me, Kayden stepped closer. "How does it feel?"

It took me a moment to respond because I wasn't sure of the answer. "Freeing, but part of me is afraid to return with the curse still intact."

I turned to him and allowed him to pull me in close.

"You won't," he said. There was no hesitation in his voice, but I couldn't miss the unsure look in his eyes. "We'll find her. We'll end this."

Neither of us knew what we would find on this jour-ney. Hope was all we had. Hope, and the will to carry it into the dark.

I leaned against him, listening to the cadence of his breath, the steady drum of his heart beneath my ear. Beyond the window, the ocean sighed against the shore, a rhythm older than both of us, reminding me that the world had kept turning even through my silence.

Tomorrow, we would follow the road deeper into the unknown. Tomorrow, I would step closer to the woman who had stolen nearly a century of my life. But tonight, here, in this small room by the sea, I allowed myself to rest in his arms, even knowing the dawn would claim me again.

CHAPTER 26
The Flower

Tonight, I stood at the edge of the sea, and it did not try to swallow me.

This was not the sea I remembered. It wasn't the snarling, restless force that clawed at the cliffs beneath the manor, always out of reach, always whispering my name without mercy. This sea was gentle, breathing against the sand with the slow, patient rhythm of something ancient. Within that rhythm, it made room for me. There was no resistance, no warning.

After I returned to the world of the living, Kayden and I ate in a charming diner, and then he took a detour without explaining why. When I asked, he simply smiled, his fingers relaxed on the wheel, his gaze fixed ahead. I watched as the road narrowed, widened again, and finally vanished beneath pale dunes. When it ended, he parked beside a weathered wooden fence and came around to open my door.

"I thought you might want to see it up close," he said. "Just once."

He didn't need to explain further.

For a time, we walked along the shoreline, something we could never do at the manor until he married me. We spoke of everything and nothing. It was unexpected, but that only made it more romantic. In all my years, I don't think I had ever felt so much like a young woman in love, rather than one condemned.

I carried my shoes in my hand, sand working its way between my toes, a stark contrast to the worn wooden floors I had known for so long. We walked for a while, but then I ran.

Not far, not fast, but enough. Enough for breath to rush into my lungs, making them burn. Enough to crack open the stillness that had long hardened around my bones. The waves reached for me, and I reached back. They caught my calves, soaked the hem of my dress, and I didn't care.

I hadn't run since the day my world narrowed to walls, when motion lost meaning and stillness became survival. Now, with salt on my skin and wind tearing through my hair, I felt decades slough away like a second skin I no longer needed.

A ragged laugh tore loose, carried by something fiercer than joy. It felt closer to surrender. I laughed until my ribs ached and my throat burned, until joy surged through me with the force of a tide. For an instant, I feared it—the brightness, the unfamiliarity of happiness—but I didn't stop.

I danced in the shallows under the moonlight, spinning and splashing, uncaring of how drenched I became. It was one of the most exhilarating moments of my life.

From the shore, I saw the look I had come to cherish bloom across Kayden's face. When I laughed, he laughed too.

"You're going to freeze," he called, kicking off his shoes.

Breathless and grinning, I turned toward him. "I've been frozen for years!"

Another wave curled around my feet, and for the first time in a century, I welcomed the cold. It felt like defiance, like baptism—proof that I was still here.

When I turned back, soaked and burning with life, he was already coming toward me. He slipped off his coat and draped it over my shoulders. His hands lingered as he pulled the collar close at my throat, his fingers warm against the curve of my neck.

"You're soaked," he murmured, leaning forward to kiss me.

"I'm alive," I whispered, as though saying it aloud might make it true. At least for the moment, it was.

After the beach, we drove until we found neon lights. They were harsher than moonlight and louder than fire. Red and blue lights pulsed above a squat building at the edge of town, nestled beneath a fringe of black pines. Warm light steamed against the windows, and a crooked sign hung like a weary smile above the door:

Rosie's Diner – Open All Night.

We passed it without stopping, but just beyond—tucked beside a shuttered pharmacy covered in dust—stood the theater. It had only two screens and one box office. A faded marquee spelled out its offerings in brittle plastic letters:

7:30 – Stars Among Us
10:00 – Shadows of the Hollow

By the time we purchased a large slushie and a bucket of popcorn that took both of my hands to carry, the lights in the theater had already dimmed. Darkness draped the aisles like velvet, pierced only by the soft glow of the screen. Although other people were there, the room went quiet as the previews began.

Kayden guided me down the carpeted aisle to a pair of seats near the back. My coat whispered against my knees with each step, and the floor beneath us clung faintly with something sticky—evidence of joy spilled and left behind. As I eased into the chair beside him, the cushion gave a soft sigh, and for a moment, I forgot to breathe.

When the screen came to life, I flinched just enough to feel it spark in my chest. Color bloomed, sound followed, and motion poured forward like unbound magic. It was too large, too alive, and too immediate. This wasn't the murmur of a book or the hush of a phonograph. It was radiant and relentless light conjured from darkness, a cathedral of dreams.

Without thinking, I reached for Kayden's arm. He leaned toward me, his breath warm at my ear. "It's alright," he murmured. "You'll get used to it." But part of me hoped I wouldn't.

There was something profound in this gathering of strangers in a darkened room—a shared ritual of stillness and wonder. A hundred quiet heartbeats, all watching the light and hoping for something.

And I watched everything. Not only the story unfolding on the screen but also the spaces between it—the flicker of heartbreak in a stranger's eyes, the way silence stretched and shimmered between sentences, hands that almost touched, and breaths that hovered just short of speech. The camera lingered on stillness and longing, and I followed it like a thread drawn through a dream I almost remembered.

Then a girl appeared. She stood alone at the edge of a cliff, her dress whipping in the wind, her mouth shaped around something unsaid. Her arms hung frozen at her sides, as though she no longer trusted them to reach. Her eyes were fixed on the horizon, wide and waiting for someone who would never come back.

I didn't know her, but I knew how she felt. Something inside me gave way—quiet at first, then sudden. The sorrow in her body echoed deep within mine, and before I understood it, my throat tightened. Tears flowed without permission, and I didn't try to stop them.

I turned slightly, brushing the back of my hand across my cheek, not wanting Kayden to see. But of course, he noticed. Kayden said nothing. He didn't ask or press. He only passed me a napkin and leaned close, his lips grazing my temple.

For the first time in what felt like forever, I let myself cry openly. Not for the girl on the screen, but for the girl I had been—the one who lived behind windows, who watched from the far side of glass, wondering if she would ever be allowed to return to the world she remembered.

Kayden held my hand across the center console as we drove to the next stop on our trip, headlights stitching through the dark. The smell of butter and salt still clung to my sleeves. I leaned into it like proof that the night had happened, something I could carry with me. Even when the lights went out. Even when morning came. Even when the stillness returned.

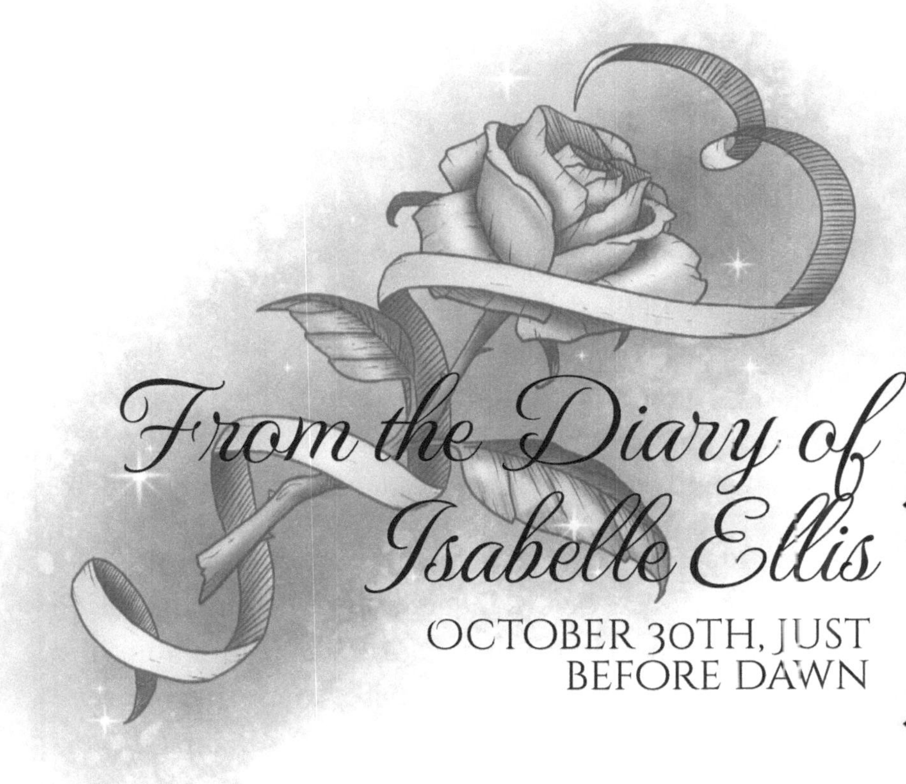

From the Diary of Isabelle Ellis

OCTOBER 30TH, JUST BEFORE DAWN

Tonight, I truly lived. Not in the quiet, spectral way I endured for so many years, hidden in silence and buried in shadow, but openly—without caution, without retreat.

I was among strangers and light, with salt in my hair and starlight in my eyes. Laughter danced upon my lips, and the ocean clung to my skin as though it remembered me.

Kayden called me wild, but I think he meant free. He watched me run barefoot into the surf and made no move to stop me. He only smiled, waiting with a coat and open arms.

Before going to the beach, we found a diner that smelled of butter and nostalgia. I enjoyed pancakes beneath flickering lamps, their hum low and steady, like an old radio drifting through someone else's home. Syrup gleamed like amber in the light. A thin, blue straw rested in my glass, and I held it as though it might break, laughing until my chest ached, until the world beyond our small booth seemed to fade away. For the first time in a long while, I stopped being careful. I stopped measuring every breath.

He took me to the cinema. I had never seen anything like it. The screen rose before me like a second moon, casting silver light and sound into the darkness. For an hour and forty-two minutes, I forgot I had ever died. Strangers fell in love beneath starlight, and I believed in them. One girl stood at the edge of the sea, her hair wild in the wind, her gaze fixed on a horizon that offered no answers. I don't know why she undid me, only that she did. Perhaps she reminded me of the girl I once was, or the one I still hope to be.

When the story ended, I couldn't move. I feared breaking the spell the night had cast. Kayden didn't rush me. He simply reached for my hand, as though it had always belonged there.

And when we returned to the inn, something shifted within me. I realized I was no longer mourning what I had lost. I was falling in love with what I had found.

This journey was supposed to be an ending, a final walk into the dark, a search for the woman who cursed me. Yet, tonight felt like a beginning, borrowed from a life not yet lived. I was not a ghost, but a girl being written back into the story.

And if it ends tomorrow, if I wake beneath the trees and confront her, I will carry this with me: the sand, the syrup, the silver glow of the screen, the man who kissed me beneath neon lights and made me believe I was still worth holding onto, the quiet between us that felt like trust, and the warmth of his hand in mine.

I lived tonight. I chose it. And I will carry it with me.

Love, Isabelle

CHAPTER 27

The Flower

The road stretched out before us, narrow and unfamiliar. Moonlight traced pale lines across the windshield as we ventured deeper into the hills. The trees here were taller and older, their branches arching overhead in solemn shadows, as if the forest itself were listening. A bird of prey swooped overhead, disappearing into the canopy.

Outside the glass, the landscape shifted in slow, breathing shapes. Clouds gathered thick above us, and it felt less like we were driving beneath the sky and more like we were passing through veils, each layer drawing us further into a place long forgotten. The scent of pine thickened in the air, mingling with the cool, metallic smell of damp earth beneath it, like freshly broken stone. With every mile, something inside me seemed to peel away.

Needing to concentrate on the vague directions, Kayden drove without speaking much, the headlights cutting narrow tunnels through the fog as shadows shifted between the trees—too swift to catch and too strange to forget. His hand rested on my knee, its warmth steady against me, a tether that held without demand. I let my fingers drift to his wrist, tracing the measured beat of his pulse. The hush between us was heavy—not empty, but promising, suspended in the stillness that bound us together. There was a notable tension in the air, but it was not between us; it pressed in around us.

I leaned my forehead against the window. The glass was cold enough to bite. "Do you think she knows we're coming?"

His voice barely disturbed the silence when he replied, "If she's still alive... perhaps. If not, then whatever remains of her will know."

His answer did not settle easily in my bones. It slipped through them, dripping acid into my blood. If she wasn't there and I couldn't end my curse, I didn't know how I could go on.

After several hours of driving through dense forests, we passed through a nameless town where a solitary traffic light blinked red into the fog. A shuttered gas station hunched at the corner like a mausoleum. In the distance, a diner glowed faintly, its light illuminating a fogged glass door.

The sight stirred something deep within me. I thought of my parents, of things they had never spoken aloud, of warnings hidden in lullabies and whispered behind closed doors. Some places are forgotten for a reason.

For a moment, my eyes drifted shut, and memories resurfaced without permission—memories of my mother's voice, speaking so low I could barely hear her: "You do not walk into the forest after dark. If you hear your name, you do not answer. If the wind goes still, you run."

Now we were driving straight into that stillness, and I didn't know if we would find our way out.

"It feels closer tonight," I murmured. "As though the woods are breathing."

Kayden squeezed my hand—not tightly, just enough to let me know he heard me. I smiled because there was nothing else to do. No map could guide us to where we were going, and no journal could tell us what we would find there.

The road stretched on for hours. The signal had gone silent on Kayden's phone miles ago, and the map lay abandoned in his lap. Nothing remained but trees and darkness. Vaughn Hollow was still hours ahead, according to the chart, but time itself had begun to blur.

The heater hummed softly, but the air in the car grew colder. Branches pressed inward until the pavement narrowed, and the woods closed around us, making the night even darker. There may have been stars and a moon in the sky, but from our place in the trees, their light could not reach us. We were utterly alone.

We did not venture further into the woods. When the road forked and the trees closed in, Kayden eased the car into a gravel pull-off. The headlights illuminated a weathered sign, its paint nearly obscured by mist:

Cliffside Inn – Vacancy

The lodge crouched among the trees, its cedar frame worn silver with age, ivy climbing the stones as if trying to hold them upright. A single porch light glowed faintly, haloed by the fog. Most of the windows were dark, except for one where lamplight flickered steadily.

After parking in front of the building, Kayden cut the engine. For a moment, neither of us moved.

"It's far enough," I said, my voice softer than I intended.

He nodded, his jaw tight. "We'll rest and leave early tomorrow. I can drive while you are... well, away."

The thought of being in a moving car while I was no longer in my body made my throat burn with dread, but I trusted Kayden wholeheartedly, so I said nothing.

The boards creaked beneath our steps as we climbed the porch. Inside, the air smelled of cedar and cinnamon, with a faint trace of chamomile that had been steeped long ago. Behind the counter sat a woman with pale hands and an open book resting in her lap.

She looked up slowly, her gaze lingering longer than necessary before she closed the book. "Room seven," she said, sliding the guestbook forward.

Her name tag read simply: *Maris*.

We signed our names, received a brass key on a velvet tag, and followed the narrow hall into the shadows.

The room was small but welcoming. A quilt lay folded at the foot of the bed, its floral pattern faded by time. Two chairs faced a stone hearth where a single log waited to be lit. Beyond the window, mist wound its way between the trees, pale ribbons against the darkness.

While Kayden put our bags down and lit the fire, I took off my coat and poured us each a glass of water. The heat seeped into my skin, loosening the tension that the road had left behind.

"Are you still with me?" Kayden asked as he set down his map and notebook.

I nodded, because I always would be. "Just listening."

Curiosity flashed in his hazel eyes as he looked up at me. "Listening to what?"

"The trees," I replied. "They sound different here—as though they have been waiting."

As he came up behind me, his arms wrapped around my waist, his chin resting on my shoulder. We swayed in the quiet, letting the fire chase away the bitter chill.

His lips brushed the curve of my neck, sending goose-flesh down my body. "You're tired."

"I am always tired," I murmured, unable to stop the sleepy smile that rose on my lips. "But I am glad we stopped."

It was true, but I knew I wouldn't sleep, and if I did, it wouldn't be restful. Still, I knew Kayden needed sleep, and if I were being honest, I wasn't ready to face Lenora. Not yet.

His embrace tightened as an anchor, not a possession. For a while, he said nothing, yet his touch was its own assurance: *I am here.*

His mouth found my throat again, slower this time, and I turned into him, slipping my hands beneath his shirt. My fingers skimmed muscle I already knew by memory. There was no urgency between us, no pretense. This was not a discovery. It was a return to each other.

I melted into the kiss he offered, deepening it until breath no longer mattered. His hand found the zipper of my dress, easing it down. The fabric sighed from my shoulders and pooled at my feet.

Without breaking eye contact, his hands traced my skin, gliding from the slope of my shoulders to the curve of my waist, then lower still, until he gathered me close. His lips followed, brushing the hollow of my collarbone, then lower, leaving a path of fire across my skin.

Needing the press of him against me, I drew his shirt over his head. My palms moved across his chest, the hard plane of muscle alive beneath my touch, a reminder that he was no phantom but flesh—the anchor to my long-buried hunger. I kissed him deeply, and in that kiss was every unspoken yearning of the years I had been denied.

When we reached the bed, he eased me down, his mouth never leaving mine. The quilt beneath me was rough with age, but his body was heat, weight, and strength, and it was all I wanted. A gasp broke from me when his hands slid down my thighs and his lips followed, pressing gentle kisses along the way.

The first stroke of his tongue against me stole my voice. My back arched, my fingers clutched at the quilt, and I cried his name, broken and desperate. He lingered there, unhurried, tasting me with a patience that unraveled me thread by thread. His mouth closed over me, his tongue moving in slow circles that tightened until I was writhing, trembling, begging without words.

When he slid a finger inside me, I nearly sobbed at the fullness, at the exquisite pressure of being opened after so many years of silence. It was not our first time together, but every time still felt like it was new. The passion still burned bright, and the pleasure he brought me was more than I ever thought I could feel.

His eyes lifted, watching me as he added another, his fingers curling just enough to draw shivers from the depths of me. The rhythm of his mouth and hand pulled me higher, taut with need, until I could no longer hold it.

A cry tore from my throat as my climax broke over me, sending pleasure through me in waves. I convulsed against him, my body clamping around his hand, his tongue never ceasing until I was shaking with the force of release. He kissed the inside of my thigh softly, reverently, as though to soothe me even in the aftermath.

Still trembling, I pulled him upward, needing him fully. My hands guided him, wrapping around his length, slick with desire. He entered me slowly, deeply, filling me until nothing remained between us but the sharp ache of completion.

I clung to him as he moved, my legs twining around his hips as his body pressed into mine. Each thrust was deep, forcing sounds from me that I could not silence. His hands framed my face, his mouth claiming mine as though to seal us together. I met him eagerly, hips rising to welcome each movement, the ache inside me unfurling into something consuming.

When his pace quickened, his breath came ragged, his muscles trembling as he drove harder, deeper, striking the place that made me cry out. My nails raked his back as ecstasy mounted again, until the pressure broke and I shattered once more, my body bowing beneath him, my cry muffled against his shoulder.

But he did not let go, not yet, only giving me more pleasure, until I thought I might burst. His rhythm faltered into desperation before he drove deep, his groan rough in my ear as his release tore through him. His body convulsed above me, every tremor spilling into me until I felt entirely claimed, entirely his.

Tangled and trembling, we collapsed together, our bodies slick with sweat. His chest pressed hard against mine, his weight grounding me in a way that felt like belonging. I closed my eyes, not to hide, but to linger.

Because I wanted to hold this moment until the light claimed me. Even if dawn would take me, tonight I had chosen life. Tonight, I had chosen him. And when I returned with the night tomorrow, I would choose him again.

CHAPTER 28
The Keeper

We left the inn just after sunrise.

That morning, she had died again. I held her through it, dressed her, and packed what we needed. Then, I placed her body beneath a blanket in the back seat, cringing at how wrong it felt.

The car carried a chill that hadn't been there the night before. Instinct moved before thought: my hand reached into the backseat, searching for warmth, and found only stillness. She lay without breath, her skin pale, her shoulder cool even through the fabric.

Gently, I adjusted the blanket and tucked it higher, then brushed a kiss to her temple. The contact was cold as stone, where life should have been. One finger had snagged the edge of the cover, curled loosely against her chest. I freed it and pressed a kiss to her wedding ring.

"I'm still here," I whispered. "You're not alone."

The dashboard clock glowed faintly as I drove, its pale numbers casting just enough light to catch on the rim of my notebook. Isabelle's shawl had slipped across it in the night, soft fringe trailing like a veil. The car smelled faintly of her—lavender clinging to the wool, smoke from the night before woven into the fibers of my coat. Not strong. Just lingering. Like a memory refusing to fade.

Even the silence seemed alive. Just like the manor, it was neither peaceful nor hostile. It was simply aware. I drove carefully, afraid that if I disturbed it too abruptly, something around us might shatter.

At a stop, I let the engine idle and reached for the map folded on the passenger seat. Sixty miles, maybe more, though the roads ahead had already begun to blur into absence. Segments were missing and trails rerouted or marked impassable. It felt as though the forest was already erasing the path before we reached it.

With no signal, not even my cellphone worked anymore, leaving us entirely vulnerable to whatever might happen. I realized quickly that we would have to finish the rest by feel, which made my stomach tighten uncomfortably. All I wanted was to free her from her curse and keep her safe, but the further we drove into the unknown, the more I realized I was not in control at all.

Thankfully, having spent some of my childhood in the scouts, I had packed our supplies methodically. If we got lost in the forest, I wanted to ensure we had everything we needed to survive for a few days. Inside two backpacks in the trunk were rope, a fire starter, a tent, food, and spare blankets. The dagger from Isabelle's father's drawer lay wrapped in cloth at my side, heavy in a way no blade should be. I had never been a fighter, but I wasn't foolish enough to enter the woods unarmed. Isabelle's journal was tucked into the top flap of her backpack, a sachet of rosemary beside it. She said her mother had given it to her, and that it was part memory, and part protection. In my pocket, a folded note she had written rested close to my leg. I hadn't opened it. I wasn't sure I could.

At a red light, I glanced into the rear-view mirror. One of her hands had slipped free of the blanket, fingers relaxed in a shape that almost resembled sleep. I reached back, took it gently in mine, and tucked it back against her body.

"I'll get us there," I said quietly. "Even if the forest takes everything but my bones."

She didn't answer, but I held her hand a moment longer, choosing to believe she heard me.

After about an hour, the road narrowed quickly. Gravel gave way to broken asphalt, then to packed earth still damp from an old rainstorm. Within minutes, the trees leaned inward on either side, their limbs lacing overhead like ribs closing around a heart. Light fractured through the canopy in sharp, uneven shards. At the same time, mist drifted low across the forest floor, curling in pale threads along the ditches like an exhale rising from something long buried.

I drove slowly, as though each mile were tightening its hold on me.

In the back seat, Isabelle lay beneath her blanket, her head resting against the rolled coat I had tucked beneath it. My eyes returned to the mirror again and again, half-expecting, half-praying for the faintest movement. She remained still—my flower at rest.

Sometimes I spoke to her. Soft words, fragments of memory, details of what passed outside the window. I told her where we were, what I saw, and what I remembered. As though speech itself might slip beneath the veil she wore and give her something to cling to until she could wake, but I knew she wouldn't. Not until the sun sank below the horizon.

The air inside the car grew denser with each passing mile. Not warm or cold, but saturated, as though the forest had seeped in through the vents and filled the space with its own essence. The farther we drove, the more it seemed the trees were closing ranks, the road narrowing not only beneath the tires but above us, until the car itself felt swallowed, carried forward in a procession we had not chosen.

The GPS had surrendered a day ago. The paper map sprawled across the passenger seat, edges warped where damp had seeped in. Its lines no longer resembled roads but instead the half-formed guesses of someone trying to draw memory from a dream.

Twice the road forked without warning, the forest demanding I choose. The first time, I trusted my instinct and turned left. The second, I circled back after arriving at a clearing that seemed too familiar. I marked a tree with charcoal, a hard black slash across its pale bark. Yet fifteen minutes later, I passed the same mark again.

The forest no longer felt like a place. It had become a memory itself, uneven, shifting, and watchful.

By late afternoon, the light thinned to silver instead of gold, wrong for the hour. Shadows stretched too long, and the trees no longer swayed. They leaned instead, blocking out what little light remained.

I pulled into a hollow beside a dry stream bed and killed the engine. The cold reached me at once, seeping through my coat and curling tight around my ribs. An eerie silence pressed in around it. Only an occasional rustle disturbed it—too soft to place, too near to ignore.

Opening the hatch, I checked our supplies. Everything remained as I had packed it. From the bag, I took out a water bottle and drank slowly, the brittle crackle of plastic loud against the quiet. I wiped my mouth and stood for a while beside the car, scanning the tree line.

There were no birds. No insects. No wind. Only mist shifting at the edges, only time bending strangely out of shape. Although I couldn't see anyone, eyes seemed to be watching me from all around. The prickle of awareness sent my arm hair standing on end, but I brushed it off, trying to be braver than I felt. For Isabelle, I had to be fearless, but I had no idea what we were stepping into.

Setting the water bottle down, I retrieved Isabelle's journal and sank against the front bumper. I turned the pages carefully, searching for anything—symbols, names, directions. Some fragment of a dream that might now serve as a map, but all I found was her voice: grief and wonder, the shape of hope etched into words I already knew by heart.

Still, I read. Until the light dimmed. Until the cold deepened. Until the sky turned that strange lavender shade that always came before true nightfall.

Closing the book, I stretched my back and returned to the car.

The passenger door gave a soft creak as I opened it and reached inside, brushing a hand along her cheek. It was still cool, but the night was coming, so I slid in beside her. With the heater in the car already running, I settled against the quiet of her body, laid my hand over hers, and waited for her to return to me.

Isabelle woke with a gasp, the sound jagged enough to cut through the stillness. Her body convulsed as though some unseen hand had hurled her back into herself. It was always like this—never gradual, never merciful. A brutal reclaiming. The lungs dragged open. The heart struck hard against the ribs. The shudder of a soul wrenched out of shadow.

Her chest heaved in uneven bursts, and her lips parted, drawing air with a wet rattle. Then her eyes snapped open. They were glazed, enormous, and filled with light that did not belong to the world of the living. A guttural sound broke from her throat, and she arched upward once, spine rigid, before collapsing back against the seat.

Her gaze found mine instantly.

"You're safe," I said, my voice scarcely more than breath as I smoothed the hair out of her eyes. "I've got you."

Her fingers stirred, reaching blindly. Cold, faltering, they fumbled through the space between us until I caught them. I held her hand in both of mine and bent over it, pressing my lips to her knuckles. Already the stone was softening, though the chill still clung to her like a second skin. Her eyes, dull moments ago, now carried the fragile shimmer of life.

We sat in the aftermath, the quiet inside the car wrapping us like gauze. Outside, the forest had no song, no voice of bird or insect. Instead, the ground itself seemed to whisper beneath the roots in a low hum. The sound was layered, ceaseless, unsettling in its patience.

Pulling the blanket closer, Isabelle turned toward the window. Her palm pressed faintly to the glass, leaving a fragile print against the misted pane. "We're close," she whispered, her voice thin, already sounding claimed by the trees. "I can feel it."

I nodded. "The roads are gone. What remains is hardly a road at all. But we're almost there."

Her movements were slow, stiff, the motions of a body relearning how to live. She touched the window again, as though trying to read the dark through her skin. "Everything feels different here," she murmured. "Like we've stepped into a place time no longer claims."

"Or one that casts time aside," I said.

Our eyes met—hers dark, mine darker, each unflinching, but I knew she was as afraid as I was.

"This is where she is," she said, the words landing heavy in my chest, but I tried to keep my expression blank.

Knowing she needed to eat, I passed her the thermos and a protein bar. She accepted them in silence, sipping cautiously. Yet her eyes betrayed her unease—darting back to the treeline again and again, as though the woods might rearrange themselves if she dared to look away.

"Do you think she's already watching us?" I asked, although I already knew the answer. Even though Lenora was not a part of my past, I still felt her.

"I think she always has been."

The pause that followed was heavier than silence, heavier than fear. It was the weight of memory, the shape of dread given body. Readiness, though not yet courage.

"I'm not ready," she admitted softly. "But I don't think I will ever be."

I touched her cheek, cupping it as warmth returned little by little. "I'll be with you," I said. "Every step of the way."

She leaned into my hand, closing her eyes for the space of a heartbeat. Then she kissed me, and although the future was not guaranteed, it wasn't rushed.

When we finally pulled apart and she finished eating, we stepped from the car together. The air met us like a blade, cold and damp, laced with rot and leaf-mold. Soaked leaves sighed beneath our boots, and overhead, a branch gave a long, hollow creak, like the exhalation of something too large to see.

I tightened the straps of her pack, pulled each buckle secure, then lifted my own backpack over my shoulders. She drew her hood into place, her movements steadier now, and brushed a leaf from my shoulder with fingers still pale from the grave.

"Promise me we'll come back," she said, uncertainty trembling at the edges of her gaze.

"I promise," I answered, forcing confidence into a voice that betrayed my fear. "Even if we have to carve the path ourselves."

Hand in hand, we stepped into the forest that had already begun to forget the names of those who entered, leaving the car and the last trace of safety behind us.

The forest did not welcome me. It recognized me.

No branches lifted to make room, no roots shifted to ease our steps. The trees stood in solemn silence, unyielding as stone, their presence heavy with judgment. Their watchfulness carried no warmth and no malice, only the still weight of awareness.

Beneath our boots, the moss yielded faintly, damp beneath the tread. The air pressed against my skin, thick and close, while the silence clung like a shroud I could not shake.

Kayden said nothing. His hand remained in mine, and the lantern he carried swung a slow, flickering arc through the dark. Its flame skimmed across frost-slick leaves, caught on tangled roots, and traced the bark of trees still wet from yesterday's mist. Now and then, his thumb brushed my knuckle, reminding me that we were in this together.

Yet the forest had felt me long before Kayden ever took my hand. It knew the mark carved into my life, the silence pressed into me by another's will. The curse had left its echo, and that echo lingered here. This place had not forgotten the woman who bound me, or the shadow of her work that still clung to my skin.

I slipped one hand into my coat pocket and found the coil of rosemary bound with a faded ribbon. My mother had given it to me when I was a child for protection. I had not believed in charms then, yet I carried it still. The ribbon was worn thin, the herb brittle, its weight a memory I refused to release. Even now, part of me hoped she walked beside me. Perhaps she always had.

Above us, the sky had vanished. Branches locked together in dense lattices overhead, blotting out the stars until even the heavens seemed forgotten. No wind stirred. No rustle broke the stillness. The air tasted of moss, rust, and wet stone, cold in a way that did not belong to any season.

I paused beside a birch, its bark peeling in pale curls like parchment. My palm pressed against the trunk, and at once my chest tightened. Symbols carved deep into the wood stared back at me—familiar before my eyes could even register them.

Kayden stepped close. "What is it?"

"These," I whispered, my fingertips tracing the etched lines. "I've seen these in my dreams. I never knew they were real."

He crouched at the roots, brushing away the moss from the sigils. "Do you think we're close?"

Although I did not know where the certainty came from, a tightness coiled beneath my ribs. "I think we're already inside."

Shifting the weight of his pack, he rose to stand beside me. He said nothing further.

We walked for what felt like hours, until the path narrowed and frayed into nothing. Roots writhed beneath our feet, slick with moss and unstable. Each step sank as though the earth wished to swallow us. The deeper we went, the dimmer the lantern burned. There was still plenty of oil inside, but the darkness itself seemed to absorb the glow.

Neither of us spoke. Intuition guided me, nothing more. There was no space for words, no need for them. The world pressed too close, too heavy for sound. All that remained was the rhythm of boots against the earth, each step a surrender to whatever fate waited in the depths ahead.

Sometime around midnight, we crested a shallow rise where the trees parted just enough for a single shaft of moonlight to break through. It fell across the forest floor in a narrow band of silver, cutting the dark as cleanly as a blade laid flat between what we had been and what we were about to become.

The clearing ahead gaped like a wound.

At its center stood a ring of stones, uneven in height, their faces worn smooth by centuries yet still carved with symbols that had resisted time itself. Moss curled in heavy coils around their bases, softening their edges without diminishing their severity. I could not read the inscriptions, but I did not need to. My body knew them before my mind did, the way a dream can settle in the bones long after the details have dissolved. Bile rose in my throat as I circled the perimeter, recognizing them as the same sigils carved into the door from my dream—the door Lenora had pointed toward before vanishing.

Kayden stepped closer, his hand brushing my shoulder before sliding down to entwine with mine, and with his nearness came a faint, acrid scent rising from the ground, ash and damp earth clinging in the air. It clung in my lungs until I coughed, stinging with the unmistakable residue of fire. Something had burned here long ago, and the forest had never allowed the ember to fade. A ritual interrupted. A wound reopened.

"You think this is where it began?" His whisper barely disturbed the silence. If she were nearby, we couldn't risk drawing her attention.

"Something began here," I breathed. "Or ended."

I did not touch the stones. Their weight had already entered me, pressing against my ribs, anchoring itself in a place I had never been able to cleanse.

This was not her forest. Yet it remembered her. And it had not forgotten what she had done.

The silence was shattered as a branch snapped somewhere in the dark, sharp as bone giving way. My heart lurched, plunging into my stomach, while my throat tightened until the air itself seemed stolen from me. I strained to catch another sound, every muscle locked, the rush of blood in my ears so loud I feared it would betray us.

A tremor rippled through me, impossible to hide. Kayden's hand closed more firmly around mine, steadying me, and I knew he had felt it. I swallowed against the rising panic, unwilling to glance behind us, terrified of what might be waiting if I dared.

My body screamed to run, but my legs refused, locked tight as if the earth itself had claimed them. I forced reason into my thoughts—it was only a branch, only wood breaking beneath some passing weight. Yet beneath that fragile lie, dread coiled sharp and certain. The sound had not been random. It had been meant for me.

Later, after we unwrapped sandwiches from their paper and ate them in the half-light, we pitched the tent where the ground dipped between two broad roots. It was no fortress, only canvas and seams. Yet, Kayden insisted it was enough to keep us sheltered, a small gesture of safety even while the forest pressed close on every side. He smoothed the earth beneath the bedrolls, coaxed the fire until it burned low but steady, and only then allowed himself to rest.

"Sleep," I whispered, brushing my hand against his as he lingered near me. "I'll keep watch."

His fingers clung to mine before he let go. Reluctance showed in the weight of his touch, yet he lay down at last, his breathing lengthening until the rhythm of sleep carried him away.

I stayed near the tent flap, feeding the fire with small sticks. The flame snapped weakly, refusing to rise higher, but it held. Mist wound itself through the clearing, drifting low across the embers as if testing their resolve. The silence was heavier here than it had been at the stones. It pressed on my skin, patient but watchful, until every part of me felt strung tight.

Time slipped strangely. I could not have said whether minutes passed or hours, only that the stillness deepened with each moment I sat there, refusing to close my eyes. I listened for change—for the shift that would tell me the forest had grown tired of waiting.

At last, it came.

Branches shifted in the dark, their tips tilting inward until what little sky remained was sealed away. Roots stirred faintly, withdrawing into the soil with the slow creak of something ancient. No true path appeared, only a sliver of opening ahead, not made by chance but by decision. The forest had chosen to let me through.

Mist drifted lower, curling at the threshold of the tent. Kayden slept within, his face softened in repose, his hand curled near where mine had been. He did not stir, did not sense the world reordering itself just beyond his dreams. I should have woken him. I should have told him what was happening, but I had no choice.

The summons wound through me in a way I could not deny. It coiled in my marrow and would not release me. My body rose before thought could protest, dread tangling with inevitability in my chest. Every instinct screamed to stay, to cling to the fragile safety Kayden had built, yet my feet moved toward the opening.

The fire guttered to ash. The mist clung closer to the ground.

And behind me, as I stepped into the waiting trees, the forest closed its mouth around meI walked for what felt like an hour, though time had already begun to unravel in this place. The forest pressed in so closely that I lost all sense of direction; every tree mirrored the last, and every shadow seemed designed to mislead. My legs ached, but still, I moved, drawn forward by something I could neither resist nor name.

At last, the trees began to thin. Moonlight broke through in fractured shafts, silver light spilling across a clearing that looked as if it had been carved open by an ancient wound.

In the middle of that clearing stood not a cottage, but a crypt.

The forest drew me onward, each step a trespass I could not take back. Behind me, the firelight from our camp dwindled to a faint glow, then vanished altogether, swallowed by trees that leaned inward as if conspiring to hide me from the world I had left behind.

The lantern in my hand fought against the dark, its flame guttering in defiance, though the oil was full. Mist dragged at my skirts, winding cold fingers around my ankles until I stumbled. The air itself had changed—thick with the metallic sting of rust and stone, so sharp on my tongue that I had to remind myself to breathe.

Symbols emerged in my path. They clung to bark and cut into roots that should have been only wood and earth, their edges catching the lantern light with a faint, inner pulse. I knew them before I truly saw them. The same lines I had drawn in my journals without meaning to. The same sigils that haunted my dreams.

Something cracked behind me, and I froze, but it was only a branch echoing too long in the stillness. Nothing moved when I turned. Only the silence watching.

Though my body trembled for retreat, I pressed forward.

I walked for what felt like an hour, though time had already begun to unravel in this place. The forest pressed in so closely that I lost all sense of direction, every tree a mirror of the last, every shadow shaped to mislead. My legs ached, but still I moved, drawn forward by something I could neither resist nor name.

At last, the trees began to thin. Moonlight broke through in fractured shafts, silver falling across a clearing that looked carved open by an ancient wound.

And in the middle of that clearing stood, not a cottage, but a crypt.

Half-sunken into the earth, its stones swallowed by moss and ivy, it waited like a clenched jaw. The door was bound in iron, carved with symbols too deep for time to wear away. Above the lintel perched a raven, black feathers glossy as wet ink, eyes glinting like coins struck in firelight.

It cawed once. The sound split the night and hung in the air, cruelly long, until the forest itself seemed to absorb it.

For several slow heartbeats, I stood rooted. Fear swept through me in a trembling wave, but resistance was useless. The curse pulled me forward. My feet crossed the moss without command, carrying me toward that black threshold.

As I neared, the raven shifted, wings spreading in a dry shudder before folding once more. It was still watching. Still waiting.

The door loomed close, its carvings alive with a faint pulse that echoed inside my chest. Though I tried to stop it, my hand lifted on its own. Cold iron met my palm. The hinges groaned, and the crypt opened.

CHAPTER 30

The Keeper

The fire had collapsed into itself during the night, leaving only a dull red pulse beneath its veil of ash. It gave no warmth now, only the faint memory of it. A coldness crept along my spine as I stirred. The dampness of the forest floor had seeped through my coat, clinging to my ribs with the chill of stone.

I reached across the bedroll, but the space beside me was smooth and untouched. There was no warmth, no weight, only a hollow impression in the fabric where she should have been. Her pack was gone, and sunrise wasn't far off.

For a moment, I couldn't move. My lungs locked, refusing to take in air. When I finally managed to breathe, the gasp was too thin, too sharp. I lurched upright, my heart hammering, already searching the shadows as if I would find her gone forever.

"Isabelle?"

Fog coiled low between the roots, thick and reluctant to rise. It swallowed sound before it could echo, so even her name dissolved before it could carry. The forest seemed to be waiting for my question, and it had already decided not to answer.

The blanket slipped from my lap as I staggered to my feet. Leaves crackled too loudly beneath my boots, their certainty offensive in a place where nothing else would speak. Turning slowly in a circle, I searched the shadows, straining for the slightest sign of movement, but nothing stirred.

"Isabelle!"

Silence enveloped me, shifting to fill the space she had left behind, the branches above adjusting to her absence.

I circled the small clearing, my heart pounding like a drum against the stillness. The lantern was gone. Her side of the bedroll was untouched, but the ground around it was too neat. There were no footprints, no signs of a struggle, nothing disturbed except for her absence. It wasn't the careless trace of someone wandering off in sleep. It was a deliberate departure, careful enough that it seemed intentional.

At the far edge of the clearing, where roots thrust upward like ribs, something glimmered faintly. Dropping to my knees, I brushed aside a patch of damp moss. My fingers closed around a coil of faded ivory ribbon, still tied around a sprig of dried rosemary.

Her mother's charm.

The copper thread had dulled, and the rosemary had withered to brittleness. Still, the scent lingered faintly, carrying the memory of her touch. She would not have left it behind, and yet here it was, neither hidden nor lost, but set apart.

It was as if the forest itself had unraveled it in her wake. It wasn't a trail, but a marker; a way of saying, "She passed through here."

And I was meant to follow.

I kept the charm in my hand, hoping it would lead me to her. The weight of my pack pressed heavily on my shoulders, a burden I could not cast aside. Whatever lay beyond the trees had already made its move. She was ahead of me now, and I was determined to find her.

The forest didn't open for me. It swallowed me whole. Each step felt stolen, the ground muffling sound, conspiring to trip me and keep me lost. Moss absorbed the weight of my boots. Branches leaned too close, and even the air felt different here. It was dense and resistant, moving with the disinterest of something that no longer wished to let me breathe.

I moved as cautiously as I could, my eyes scanning the ground for the faintest signs of passage: a bend in the ferns, a depression in the moss, or a careful absence where something might have brushed by, but there was no trail, no mark I could trust. Only suggestion, instinct, and the tightening thread of dread that wound through me with every step.

Light filtered down in thin, pale patches, more imitation than illumination. It carried no warmth, no weight, only the flickering quality of light you cannot trust, the kind that seems to waver even when the trees remain still.

Twice I halted, certain I had circled back to the same crooked pine. At last, I scored an X into its bark with the edge of my knife, the wound stark against the pale wood. Yet when I returned, the trunk stood unblemished, whole, the mark erased as if the forest itself had closed the cut and denied my proof.

It was not guiding me through. It was studying me.

Still, I pressed forward. The charm remained warm and steady against my palm. I didn't know if it was guiding me or simply reminding me that I was not entirely alone.

Somewhere in the distance, a sound stirred. It was neither voice nor footstep, but the weight of a presence shifting against the silence. Each time I turned toward it, the fog thickened, rising like a wall to bar my way.

I called her name softly, testing the silence with my low voice. The sound barely escaped my lips before the forest swallowed it, the trees responding with nothing but their heavy stillness. Suddenly, my boot caught on a root, pitching me forward, and I grasped a branch that hadn't been there a heartbeat earlier. The bark felt slick beneath my palm, a reminder from the forest that I was not moving through its depths unnoticed.

"You don't get to take her," I whispered into the silence.

For the first time, the fog responded. It did not retreat. Instead, it deepened, curling inward and drawing me further into its embrace.

As I watched the unending chaos of green ahead of me, something formed—a low, square shape wrapped in ivy. It was neither a ruin nor a dwelling, but an unsettling blend of the two, half-real and half-conjured from the dark.

I stepped closer, and the fog surged, but when it cleared, the shape had vanished.

The ground beneath me shifted, and roots twisted in circles where none had been before. Symbols scratched themselves into the soil—marks that could not have been made by human hands. One of them I recognized instantly: a spiral, broken at the edge. Isabelle had drawn it repeatedly in her journals. A fragment of her dreams brought to life on the earth before me.

With shaking hands, I lifted the lantern at my side and raised the charm to my lips.

"Show me where she went."

As though in answer, the trees began to thin, their ranks loosening with reluctance, as if the forest weighed upon me and, for this moment only, allowed me to pass through. The fog loosened just enough to reveal a small clearing sunk deep within the woods. The air there was unnaturally still, its silence drawn so tight it felt ready to snap.

At the center of the clearing waited a stone bench. It leaned slightly to one side, its surface cracked through the middle, with moss curling thick around its base as if it meant to devour the stone itself. The sight struck me like a blow. Recognition came first, followed by a wave of disbelief that hollowed me out from within.

My boots sank into the damp earth as I drew closer. Each step felt weighted, heavy with the uncanny familiarity that pressed into my chest until I could hardly breathe. I had seen this bench before. I had sat upon it countless times in the atrium, surrounded by ivy climbing the glass walls, the sunlight dulled by the haze above. The tilt was the same. The fracture was identical. Even the moss, clinging stubbornly to the cracks, mirrored what my memory insisted had always been there.

My hand lifted before I realized it had moved, my fingertips brushing against the cold stone.

As I tried to make sense of what I was seeing, a voice slipped through the clearing.

"Kayden."

It was soft, barely more than a whisper, yet it struck me like thunder. It was spoken with such aching patience that I could almost believe she had stood there for years, repeating my name into the silence until I finally answered.

I turned too quickly, stumbling two steps forward, and there she was.

Isabelle.

She stood at the edge of the clearing, half-consumed by shadow, her dress pale against the dark, her hair falling loose around her shoulders—the way I had first seen her at the manor. My chest seized, and her name tore from my throat, jagged and broken.

"Isabelle—"

Desperate to close the distance, I lurched toward her. My heart crashed wildly against my ribs, every instinct screaming to seize her hand before the forest could steal her away again.

But the fog thickened. It rose in curling coils around her legs, climbing higher until it blurred her outline. Her eyes held no light, and her smile spread too late and too wide, as though something had rehearsed the expression without understanding the shape of love. A blade of dread sliced through my chest.

I stumbled forward another step, my arm outstretched, panic burning in my lungs, and then she dissolved.

She was gone.

The clearing warped in her absence. The bench vanished, the trees shifting quietly, realigning and correcting themselves the instant I stopped believing. My knees buckled. Air tore ragged from my throat, too thin to steady me. The forest had granted me what I longed for, dangled it in front of me, and then ripped it away before I could touch it.

Turning in a desperate circle, I searched for anything that remained, but the ground where the bench had stood was nothing but uneven soil and moss. The fog pressed closer, suffocating me.

My heel caught on a root, and I staggered, pitching sideways before I caught myself against a tree trunk, the bark slick beneath my palm. The forest wanted me to feel its presence.

For a long moment, there was nothing but the brutal hammer of my pulse, pounding in my ears loud enough to drown everything else. My chest heaved, my throat raw with a name I no longer had the strength to call.

This was no dream, and it was no memory.

The forest had given me what I longed for and then stripped it away.

My fingers closed around the charm, crushing it so hard that the rosemary bit into my skin. The pain steadied me more than the ground beneath my feet. I forced myself to move—one step, then another. Because if I stayed here, I would break.

Longing would not bring her back. Only movement might.

I had been walking for what felt like hours, though time inside the forest no longer seemed to follow its own rules. Each step bled into the next, and the distance I had covered dissolved behind me, leaving only the weight of forward motion.

The ground tilted without warning, my boot skidding across moss slick with rain. The stone beneath me shifted treacherously under the fog. I caught myself against a tree, its bark clammy and damp, the cold of it seeping through my hand. My chest strained for air that would not come. Each breath was shallow and sharp, begrudged by the forest itself.

Ahead, the trees rose taller and darker, their trunks bent inward as if remembering a collapse. Fog thickened at their roots, rolling low and heavy, causing every step to feel uncertain—each one questioning whether the ground would hold me or open beneath my feet.

I stumbled again, dropping to one knee as the slope pitched downward. The mossy root beneath my grip offered the only solidity in a world that no longer wished to keep me steady. My ribs burned with the effort to pull in air, my pulse hammering loudly enough to drown out the silence pressing in from all sides.

Still, the trees closed tighter around me, their branches knitting overhead and shutting me out from even the faintest promise of sky. There was no path now, only shadow upon shadow, absence upon absence, the forest intent on enclosing her away where I could never follow.

I tore the compass from my pocket, but the needle spun in wild, aimless circles before settling with no conviction at all. Time itself had loosened its grip. I could not say whether I had been walking for minutes or hours. Both forward and backward had dissolved, leaving only the labyrinth.

"She's here," I said aloud, the words raw against my throat. "She has to be."

That single conviction was all I had left. Isabelle was here, somewhere in the dark, and she was waiting for me.

The forest pressed close, but I forced my body to move forward, my lungs burning and my legs trembling with exhaustion. Still, I pressed on, half-stumbling, half-running, driven by devotion as much as fear, by the refusal to let her be claimed by the silence that hunted us both. The forest could tighten, the fog could close in, but I would not stop, because stopping meant surrender, and surrender would mean losing her forever.

CHAPTER 31
The Flower

I surfaced slowly, as if my body were remembering itself one fragment at a time. Coldness pressed into me first, merciless in its depth, seeping into my bones until I could no longer separate it from my own flesh. The stone beneath me held fast against my spine, its weight pinning me to the earth. When air finally tore its way into my lungs, it came jagged and scraping, carrying the bitter taste of lichen and wax. The dampness was more than a mere scent. It filled the chamber and soaked into the walls until silence itself seemed to settle over my skin.

Lying still, I allowed the moment to stretch, my mind gathering itself unevenly, fumbling to piece together what had been shattered but never wholly lost. The floor beneath me was slick and irregular, the cold pressing into my spine. Pain burned along my shoulder where I had struck the ground, a dull reminder of how I had fallen. Slowly, I raised one hand and found rough stone beneath my palm, grooves carved deep into its surface. Symbols lay there, their edges blurred by time yet still noticeable, still waiting. I knew them without knowing how: patterns from dreams, sketches that had emerged in my journals when I could not recall ever drawing them.

Above, a narrow seam in the ceiling released a thin blade of silver moonlight, the changing color outside telling me sunrise was coming. Faint pastels bled across the crypt, just enough to reveal what lay at my side.

A body, arranged with care, arms folded across the chest. His hair was dark, streaked with silver at the temples. Around his throat hung a chain, and the pendant at its end caught the moonlight with a glint of blood-colored stone.

Cillian.

The name rose without shock. I did not gasp or cry. There was only quiet recognition, a truth my silence had always carried. Beneath the rhythm of the curse and the hollow years it had forced upon me, I had always known who he was, what he had offered, and how he had been remade into something I could neither wholly love nor fully mourn, thrust upon me by his deranged mother.

My hand pressed against the stone between us, not his skin. I could not cross that boundary. To touch him would have felt too much like seeking forgiveness I had no right to claim. He had been gentle, and I had looked away, seeing it as a manipulation of his mother's. But looking at him now, I no longer saw it that way.

I wasn't sure how he had ended up in the crypt, but it did not grieve him. It only kept him, and I wonder if his mother had meant to lure me here all along. The air was thick with unspoken truths, pressing down on me without release, and the walls seemed to close in with every breath I drew.

In that suffocating stillness, terror gripped me as I realized I was sealed inside. The door had closed behind me when I fell, and I had been too disoriented to notice until it was too late. And Kayden—Kayden was still out there. He must have woken up to find me missing, probably stumbling through a forest that twisted time against him, carrying what little he could: our weapons, his sorrow, and perhaps, if mercy prevailed, the rosemary charm my mother once pressed into my hand. By the time I realized I had dropped it, it was already too late. But if he found it, perhaps it would protect him or lead him to me. The thought of him searching while I wasted away here made my chest ache.

The pendant on Cillian's chest glimmered softly in the light, catching my attention. I had never seen anything like it before. It was clearly an antique.

My throat burned with the urge to scream, to tear at the sealed walls, to claw my way free, but no sound escaped me. Instead, my body betrayed me, trembling, unsteady, already weakening with the coming of daylight. The warmth within me had begun to slip, my edges dissolving into something less than myself.

There was no serenity in this death, no readiness. There was only the sick inevitability of the curse advancing, stripping me away piece by piece.

Above me, the fading moonlight crawled slowly across the chamber, inch by inch, until it reached my skin. Turning toward Cillian, I lay back down on the stone, but my body began to fold under its own failing weight. Silence had cornered me here, and there was no path left to resist it.

My limbs felt heavy, and my thoughts began to fade. Panic welled up inside me as darkness closed in around me. Without uttering a word, I silently begged Kayden to hurry and to find me before it was too late. But when the light finally reached me, I could no longer resist. The dawn claimed me once more.

The darkness unraveled, not into light but into shape—shadow arranging itself into the likeness of a world I once knew.

I stood in the garden behind the manor. At first, it seemed unchanged, but the wrongness crept in slowly, frost spreading through the cracks of glass. The hedges loomed higher than walls, swallowing the horizon. The stones beneath my feet no longer felt firm. They yielded under my weight, earth pretending at permanence.

The rosemary beds had transformed most of all. Where my mother's hands had once kept them ordered, they now grew monstrous, vines as thick as ropes climbing the walls, their green threads pulsing faintly beneath the surface. The sharp scent filled my lungs until it suffocated, turning comfort into poison.

Above me stretched a sky the color of ash. It was dusk, but the shadows reached too far, lengthening unnaturally, bending into warped shapes that leaned close as if to listen.

At the garden's edge stood a woman wrapped in gray. Her shawl clung to her like a burial cloth, her form shifting *from sharp to blurred with every breath. She had no face I could hold onto. It was never still, never human long enough to name.*

Beside her waited a young man with downcast eyes, dark hair falling loose around his temples. He carried a bouquet of white violets in his trembling hands, but he did not meet my gaze.

Cillian.

A knot tightened in my throat, making it hard to breathe. He appeared younger than I remembered, though perhaps it was guilt that had always aged him in my mind. His hands trembled faintly around the flowers, yet his posture held with the resignation of someone who had already accepted an answer I had never spoken aloud.

Stepping forward, he lifted the violets toward me, their pale faces trembling in his grip. The sight forced me backward, retreating before I knew I had moved. My lips parted, trying to form his name, but no sound came. Instead, my throat locked, as if the dream itself had sealed it shut, forbidding me even the mercy of speaking what my heart had carried for so long.

As I stared at Cillian, the woman's voice slipped into the air, though her mouth never moved.

"She could have loved you," she whispered. "You were good. You were kind. And still she turned away."

The words struck me like blows. My knees weakened beneath their weight.

"Cillian—" I tried again, but the sound cracked uselessly in my throat.

Even as I struggled, he would not meet my eyes. His gaze stayed fixed on the violets, as if their pale faces might explain my betrayal better than I ever could.

"No," I rasped, but the denial wavered. "I never meant—"

The woman drifted nearer, her shawl sweeping the stones. "You let him die with your silence."

My stomach hollowed. Shame rose hot and suffocating, heavier than the air itself. "I was afraid," I whispered, the confession scraping out like blood drawn from a wound. "I thought if I looked away, it would pass me by. I thought I could pretend—"

But my words fell apart in the stillness.

In Cillian's hands, the violets blackened. Their petals shriveled and curled inward, collapsing into rot. His fingers still trembled, but he would not look at me. He never looked.

Filled with guilt, I felt a heavy ache in my chest as I reached out to him, desperate to explain that my feelings were not a reflection of any flaw in him. I wanted to convey that fear should not be mistaken for cruelty, but he remained out of my reach. The flowers between us crumbled into dust.

The garden collapsed. Shadows warped into ribs. The path split open into roots, roots twisted into bone, until the whole place buckled and dissolved.

I screamed as I fell through the open wound below me, and when I stopped falling, I was back in the crypt.

But even within the stone walls, silence did not reign. Just like in my dreams, the chamber pulsed with a merciless rhythm that was not mine, the curse pressing close, reclaiming what it had always claimed.

Beside me, the pendant on Cillian's chest flared once, crimson light straining desperately to hold the dark at bay.

It faltered and then failed as I watched, and then the darkness closed in, swallowing everything I could not say.

CHAPTER 32

The Keeper

The forest did not yield. It pressed tighter around me, branches weaving into a ceiling that smothered the last of the sky. Each stroke of the machete cracked the silence but left no echo. The sound was devoured the moment it was made. Fog clung to my legs like sodden cloth, and the lantern in my other hand sputtered against the damp, its glow trembling, unwilling to spread far.

Roots writhed across the ground, slick with moss, forcing my steps to falter. More than once, I caught myself against a trunk, the cold bark leaching into my skin until I could not tell where the forest ended and I began. Time became unreliable. Minutes stretched, warped, unmoored from themselves. Still, I pressed forward. Isabelle's charm locked in my fist, the blade in my other hand the only weapon I could trust to cut a way through.

At last, the trees thinned. Fog widened across the ground, revealing stone where none should have been. What opened before me was no clearing but a wound, an old gash in the earth that had never healed.

The crypt rose from its center, half buried, its walls strangled in roots that swelled like veins. Ivy clung wet against pale stone, slick with rain. The arch above the door had cracked down the middle, as though something within had once pressed hard against it, testing the weight of its own confinement.

I halted at the threshold. The air was stale, steeped in iron and old wax, coating my tongue with a residue that made it hard to swallow. It was an unnatural stillness, a silence that did not wait but endured. And beneath it all, I knew. I felt her before I allowed myself to acknowledge it. Isabelle was inside.

Taking a step forward, I laid my palm on the door. The iron burned with cold, centuries of sorrow clinging to it like frost. Pain lanced through my ribs as I braced my shoulder and forced it open. The weight ground deep into the stone, reluctant, before shifting at last with a groan that seemed to shake the chamber from within.

Darkness spilled outward, flooding the ground like water loosed from a wound.

I raised the lantern high, its glow straining against the weight of the shadows, and stepped across the threshold.

I lifted the lantern higher, its trembling glow barely illuminating the corners of the chamber. The light slid across the floor and stopped on her hand—Isabelle's hand, pale against the stone. My knees weakened, and I nearly fell beside her.

"Isabelle—"

Her name broke as it escaped my throat, and I staggered forward, dropping to her side. She looked impossibly still, her hair fanned out in silver strands across the stone, her face tilted faintly toward the ceiling, too serene for the horror of this place. I took her hand in mine. It was cold from the day, but nightfall was only a few hours away, and I had to believe she would return to me. My forehead pressed against her temple. "You're not alone," I whispered, though the words fractured in my throat.

The lantern's glow shifted further across the stone, revealing another body beside her. A man, arranged with deliberate care, arms folded across his chest. His hair was dark, streaked heavily with silver at the temples. He looked to be in his forties when he died, but with Isabelle lying beside him, untouched by age, I couldn't be certain. Around his throat hung a pendant on a tarnished chain, its surface catching the faint light before sinking back into shadow.

The air shifted before I could gather her closer. It thickened, pressing like unseen hands against my chest. I felt it before I saw her.

Lenora Thorne.

At first, she was nothing more than weight—the unbearable sense that the chamber itself had bent inward. Then the shadows knitted themselves into shape, and she emerged at the far edge of the lantern's glow: tall, unmoving, her body cloaked in fabric that whispered faintly when it stirred, yet never touched the ground. Her face hung half in shadow, smooth in places, eroded in others, like time itself had tried to strip her away, but the world refused to forget.

I forced myself upright, standing over Isabelle, though my ribs screamed. My hand hovered near the dagger inside my coat, but I did not draw it yet. Something told me that steel alone would never be enough, not against her.

Without speaking, her head tilted, a subtle, unsettling study, like she was inspecting a fracture in stone rather than the man before her. Her eyes narrowed, free of surprise or fury, holding only recognition, and the slow burn of a memory she had carried for centuries.

Her voice echoed through the crypt like dry paper dragged across stone. "You've come far."

The words pressed into the walls and lingered there, swallowed by stone that refused to release them.

I tightened my grip on the lantern. "She came farther than you ever expected her to."

A fleeting expression crossed her face, some remnant of love twisted into a curse, morphed into something unclean.

"You step into a grave that was never yours," she said, her tone softer than the ruin of her words. "Do you even know what waits here?"

I swallowed the ache tearing through my ribs and forced the words past it. "I know *who* waits. My wife. And I'll tear this crypt apart stone by stone before I leave her in it."

Her lips curved faintly, not in amusement but in some private cruelty. "Such certainty, from one who bleeds. Do you think a mortal vow can reach where eternity has laid its claim?"

"She's my wife," I rasped, my voice breaking under the weight of it. "And I would follow her into hell itself before I let you keep her."

She moved forward, and the crypt leaned with her. Cold bled into the stones. Shadows climbed the walls, narrowing the space until only she remained. She did not walk. She claimed, every corner bending in acknowledgment.

"She was his," Lenora said, her tone more incantation than speech. "Long before you knew her name. His heart beats still through her silence. You cannot take that from him."

For a moment, I faltered. *His heart beats still.* My gaze flicked toward the body lying beside Isabelle, where Cillian was folded carefully into death, a pendant resting motionless against his chest. Whatever heart had once been his was long stilled. The words made no sense, yet Lenora spoke them with a certainty that chilled me, as if she believed the man's presence still pulsed through Isabelle's curse.

My eyes fell then to the other pendant—the one glinting faintly against Isabelle's still body. My fingers brushed its edge, not lifting it, only touching. Yet the change in Lenora was immediate: the twitch in her jaw, the faint tightening of her shoulders.

"She chose no one," I said, forcing my voice steady despite the knot of dread in my chest. "That was what you couldn't bear."

Her gaze sharpened until her eyes looked carved from iron. "She was ungrateful."

I swallowed hard, but I did not look away. "She was young and afraid. The choice should have been hers to make."

The silence between us coiled tighter, the tension thinning the air.

"She should have loved him," she whispered, her voice low and curling like smoke. "He would have given her everything."

"He would not have forced her," I said, my hand sliding at last to the dagger's hilt. "And you couldn't handle that. You turned her choice into a sentence."

The crypt groaned. Stone trembled faintly underfoot, forcing me to adjust my stance, a tremor that whispered of collapse. Dust sifted from above, clinging to my coat, while the sound of iron dragging through unseen water rattled the chamber. I knew I was no match for her, but there was no way I would leave Isabelle to the witch who had already taken so much from her.

As I scanned the room for a better way to get Isabelle out of there, Lenora moved nearer to Isabelle, and I tensed by her side.

"You don't belong here," she whispered, lifting her hand over Isabelle's body.

With her only a few feet away, my coat shifted as I drew the dagger. The blade caught the lantern's glow and shivered with it, fragile against the immensity of her, but steady in my hand nonetheless. Isabelle's father had left it for her to take her life back, so it was the first weapon I went for.

Moving into a crouch, I blocked Isabelle from Lenora's view. "You don't get to decide that."

Her smile unfurled slowly, curling across the air like smoke from damp firewood, spreading but never warming. It touched nothing in her eyes. "You think you're enough to stop me?"

I steadied the dagger, though my grip trembled. "No. But I came anyway."

My body struck the stone with a force that rattled through bone. The impact cracked across the crypt, reverberating not just in the chamber but inside my ribs. Air tore from my lungs in a violent rush, leaving me clawing for breath that refused to come. Pain flared across my side in sharp, merciless spasms. My shoulder hit first, a brutal blow that sent fire lancing through my vision until spots of white burst in the dark.

Lenora did not advance. Instead, she loomed above me, unmoving, her presence carved into the space like a monument the world had never chosen but could not remove. Her expression carried no triumph. It was colder than that. It was evaluative, measuring every flaw in the foundation of some vast cathedral.

"You think you can take her from me?" she said. The words barely rose above silence, yet they carried. Not merely sound, but weight. The stone itself seemed to hum with her voice. She controlled the crypt and its ghosts, and she knew how to use them.

I tried to rise, but pain clamped across my ribs like iron bands, each attempt pulling fire behind my eyes until the crypt swam and the lantern's light wavered. My hand scrabbled for the dagger, but it had skidded into shadow, gleaming faintly just beyond reach.

"She was never yours," I forced out through clenched teeth, my voice shredded by pain. "You buried her before she had the chance to choose."

Her mouth tilted, but it wasn't natural, a gesture borrowed from a life she had once lived. "I preserved her," she spat. "I made her sacred. Eternal."

Copper filled my mouth as I forced myself upright, glancing at Isabelle to make sure she was still there. "You made her vanish."

The air swelled, pressing into my chest and ears, and Lenora's gaze left me, falling toward Isabelle. She lowered herself with unnatural poise, bending like a shadow folding into its own shape. One hand hovered above the pendant that rested on Isabelle's chest, fingers trembling. Her other hand stretched toward Isabelle's ribs, as though she meant to claim what little warmth still lingered there.

"No!" The word ripped from me, scraping against the walls. I dragged myself forward inch by inch, my body screaming in revolt. Skin tore against the stone, grit embedding in my palms as I clawed toward the dagger. My nails split, blood slicking the floor, but the weapon remained just beyond my grasp.

Lenora did not falter. Her voice wove low, almost tender, venom coiled in intimacy. "You could have been loved," she whispered. "And still, you chose to be lost."

The moment her fingers brushed the pendant, the air ruptured.

It was as though the lungs of the world had been torn open. A soundless implosion split the chamber, dragging the shadows inward before hurling them back in a violent rush.

Light blossomed from the pendant, growing stronger in waves rather than appearing suddenly. At first, it flickered, its glow delicate like a candle battling against storm winds. Then it intensified—a brilliant gold igniting and racing up the chain in a blaze that split the darkness like fire catching dry wood. In an instant, the crypt was filled with its light.

Lenora recoiled, her hand snatching back as if seared. She didn't scream, but her composure broke. The hunger drained from her face. For the first time, her breath caught, betraying the fracture.

When my head snapped toward Isabelle, her fingers moved. It was not much, just a tremor, but it was movement. It was defiance. She was coming back to me. My throat tightened, a sob nearly breaking free as heat rose sharply behind my eyes.

As I crawled to the dagger, the pendant glowed around Isabelle's neck like a flare of living warmth. Its threads of gold spilled across the floor, painting the crypt in light that felt less like fire and more like a life restored—not mine, not Lenora's, but Isabelle's.

Lenora staggered back, and her face shifted, stripped of its eternal calm. What emerged was the collapse of a certainty she had guarded for centuries, followed by fear.

It spread across her features like frost racing over glass, the kind of fear born not from the unknown, but from the instant a long-buried certainty forces its way back into the light. For the first time since I had stepped into the crypt, Lenora Thorne looked small.

I woke to your absence,
and the forest swallowed me whole.
It showed me your face,
only to strip it away,
leaving me with silence
and a voice that breaks on you.

CHAPTER 33

The Flower

A brittle voice fractured the chamber, dragging me from where I had tumbled into death.

Another voice followed, faint, broken—Kayden's—but the words blurred together, too far, too drowned in the dark that still clung to me. A reluctant breath scraped raw into my lungs, as if the chamber itself resisted giving me back. My fingers twitched against cold ground until warmth closed around them—his hand, trembling, anchoring me.

The moment I forced my eyes open, her attention shifted to me.

The witch who'd cursed me.

Standing at the far edge of the lantern's glow, Lenora's spine was rigid, her figure cut into the dark like it had been carved there from the beginning. Her presence bent the chamber inward. She owned this place, and it bowed to her will.

"You weren't supposed to wake," she said, her voice clinging to the walls.

I turned my head, pain striking through my chest, and found Kayden beside me. His body lay slumped against the stone, his breath ragged, blood soaking his coat, each shallow rise a thread I was terrified to lose. A cry rose sharply in my throat, half sob, half plea, but there was no time to shape it. Lenora was moving, the air growing colder with every inch she claimed.

The lantern's glow shifted further across the floor, and beside me still lay Cillian. *Her son.* At his throat still rested an antique pendant, the stone silent.

Another pendant burned now against my chest, alive where his lay dead. When I reached up to touch it, heat bled across my wrist, threading up my arm in veins of gold, until the crypt itself seemed to shiver. Symbols carved into the walls stirred faintly, as though the stone roused with me. I felt them answer one another—the weight of his, the blaze of mine—and in that fleeting current, Lenora's certainty faltered.

"You sealed me in with your son." My voice broke as it left me, steadied only by the fire winding through my hand. While her gaze was fixed upon me, Kayden remained safe. "You buried me beside the boy you twisted into a curse."

Her breath slid sharply through her teeth, thin as a knife's edge. Her lips pressed together until her face hardened into something skeletal. "He loved you," she spat, each word clipped, unwilling to soften.

The pendant bit deeper into my skin as I tightened my grip. "I never asked him to," I said, my throat raw, my voice louder than I meant. "That was yours—never mine."

For a heartbeat, her composure cracked. A twitch in her jaw. A flicker in her eyes. Not grief. Not fury. Something rawer, human, buried too long, already fraying before her humanity was gone.

"I gave you eternity," she whispered, one hand rising, as though she could call proof of it from the air. Shadows stirred at her feet, restless, bound to her.

"You gave me silence," I said. The words came unbidden, truer than breath. "A life of loneliness."

The pendant blazed at that word. Its light bled wide, spilling into every corner of the crypt until even the dust drifting down from the ceiling seemed to glow with it.

Her eyes widened, faint but filled with fear. "You shouldn't be able to hold that." Her voice wavered, disbelief fraying its brittle strength.

"I shouldn't have been able to find you either," I said. My chest trembled with fear, but the light steadied me. "But here I am."

Something in her eyes shifted, and she moved, not toward me, but toward Kayden. Hunger bent her hand, fingers curled in a gesture less like reaching than claiming.

I lurched forward before she could touch him, stepping into her path. Pain seared through me, but fear of losing him cut deeper still, driving me upright. The pendant's glow flared, striking her face, deepening the hollows beneath her eyes, illuminating the cracks that lined her mouth.

For the first time, she hesitated.

Confusion rippled across her expression. It was fleeting, but I saw it—the pause of a predator met with prey that did not run.

"You don't understand what it carries," she hissed, her voice stretched thin with desperation.

The weight of a century pressed into me, but I met her gaze without retreat. I realized, at that moment, that the pendant she'd put around my neck to hold me there had given me the strength to fight her. Whether that was due to her son's selfless affection for me, or due to a flaw in her plan, I did not know, but something had wanted me to take my life back. "I do," I said, lifting the pendant higher, the light spilling between us like a blade. "And I will not give it back."

Fear edged her, a tremor pulsed behind her ancient calm, and in the deepening gold between us, I saw her power begin to fracture.

Lenora did not strike, not yet. Her outline wavered, edges unraveling, as though the weight of everything she had stolen was beginning to slip loose, leaking back into the dark that had birthed her. Each shallow breath pulled her frame tighter, her spine drawn like a bowstring, and at her feet, the shadows stirred. They spread slowly, widening across the stone like a tide creeping toward shore, testing the ground before it claimed it.

I forced myself still. Behind me came the scrape of movement, Kayden shifting against the floor, his breath ragged with pain, but I didn't turn. To look away would mean surrendering the fragile hold I had over her. The crypt had sealed us in like a closing jaw, and I had stepped willingly between its teeth.

Her voice reached me, thin with strain but wrapped in the illusion of certainty. "You should never have made it this far."

One hand lifted. Shadows surged with the motion, rising in a swell behind her. They spread broad, vast wings, blotting the chamber, until the very air constricted in my chest. Cold closed around me, choking each breath before I could draw it, pressing into my throat as the room tried to crush me.

"I wasn't meant to survive you either," I answered, the words coming out with force. The pendant burned against my palm, its heat alive, a pulse that did not belong to Lenora. "But I did."

For a heartbeat, her mask slipped. The calm fractured—barely, but enough. Doubt traced her eyes like light leaking through a seam in stone.

Then she moved.

The shadows lunged forward. They didn't strike. They swallowed. The air folded inward on itself, and the chamber dissolved into a churning dark. My instincts screamed to recoil, but I rooted myself where I stood and raised the pendant.

Its glow did not burst. It unfurled. A radiance stirred from its center, climbing my wrist and twining through the air, threads of gold weaving upward until they shimmered like living fire. The shadows collided with the light and faltered, buckling beneath it.

A hiss bled from the dark. The force of it crawled across my skin, but the mass recoiled all the same, peeling back as if branded.

At my feet, a faint glint caught the lantern's tremor. Cillian's pendant lay still and tarnished. Yet as the light of mine unfurled, the chain at his throat shivered, the metal quivering like a tether straining against its own design. It did not blaze, but it resisted. Bound to silence, to death. And in that resistance, I felt it yield like a locked door splintering under its own weight.

Lenora flinched. Her hands dropped an inch, fingers twitching before she mastered them again. Even so, the tremor betrayed her.

When she spoke, her voice had lost its edge. "You don't have the strength."

The pendant blazed wider, light spilling across the chamber until it reached the carved symbols on the walls, dragging them into a restless shimmer. The weight of two chains pressed against me—one burning in my hand, the other breaking upon Cillian's still chest—and for the first time, I felt them tilt, no longer shackles but scales turning.

I tightened my grip, my voice steadier than my body. "I carry what you tried to bury," I said. The words struck harder than the glow itself. "The part of me that endured when the world forgot. The love you could never command, and that has always been stronger than fear."

There was no scream. No ritual's end. Only the hollow collapse of presence, as if the air itself had been holding a body and suddenly let go.

And when Lenora was gone, the crypt did not echo. It absorbed her absence, stone drinking her away and leaving her no more than a shadow on its walls. The silence that followed was absolute, a verdict too long delayed at last delivered.

The ache beneath my ribs unraveled, thread by thread until it dissolved into nothing. The curse no longer pressed on my lungs. It no longer curled around my name. It no longer stole what had always been mine.

It was gone. And still, I remained.

A movement beside me broke the stillness. Kayden's breaths were ragged, uneven, but they came. His hand reached for mine, and when our fingers met, relief struck so sharply it hurt. I clutched him tighter, the thought already rising in me that I had to get him out—out of the stone, out of this place—before it claimed him too.

I sank to my knees beside him, my forehead brushing his temple. Dust clung to us both, the scent of ash heavy in the air, but beneath it was the heat of him, the one tether that had never broken, not even when death tried to divide us.

"It's over," I whispered. The words trembled with exhaustion. I had never thought I would live to say them.

His eyes opened slowly, rimmed with pain. "You're still here."

A sound broke from me, half sob, half laugh, as I pressed his hand to my chest so he could feel it for himself. "I am," I said. And for the first time in eighty years, the truth of it belonged wholly to me.

But the crypt groaned, stone cracking as though it, too, was coming apart now that she was gone. Dust sifted down in a thin veil, and the runes dimmed to nothing. A fracture split the arch by the door, daylight pressing through in a pale beam.

"We have to go," I said. "Now."

Pulling his arm over my shoulder, I braced myself beneath his weight and helped him rise. The air smelled of earth and sun. It was startling after so much darkness. Each step was an act of defiance, carrying us past the altar strewn with ash, past the ruin that had once held me bound.

The fracture widened as we neared the threshold, daylight pouring through in a pale flood. I tightened my hold on Kayden, feeling his breath warm against me as we crossed into it together.

Epilogue

THE FLOWER, NOVEMBER 10

I awakened to sunlight on my skin, and for the first time in a hundred years, it didn't undo me. Instead, it warmed me. Golden and gentle, its rays spilled across the sheets, folding over my arms and trailing across the hollow of my throat before reaching my eyes. I didn't move right away. I lay still, allowing the light to soak into every corner of me that had only known the night. This wasn't borrowed light. It was mine.

Tears slipped down my cheeks before I realized they had fallen. I blinked up at the ceiling, where lavender and ash lingered faintly in the air. Lenora was gone. The curse was broken, and I was breathing.

Beside me, Kayden stirred. He groaned softly as he turned toward me, one hand rising to brush a strand of hair from my cheek. His knuckles grazed my temple with a touch so familiar it undid something deep inside me—the kind of love I once feared I would never feel again.

"You're here," he said, his voice rough with sleep.

 I couldn't suppress the smile that tugged at my lips. "I'm here."

His body moved more slowly than mine. The wounds hadn't healed. His ribs were still bruised, and a bandage wrapped around his head where he had struck it. Every movement was stiff and painful. We had both bled for this, but we were alive.

Pulling me close, he kissed my temple. "I dreamed we made it."

I smiled into the curve of his chest, joy stirring in me like wings taking flight. "We did."

The house around us no longer loomed ominously. It watched gently now, not as a prison but as a presence at peace. Somewhere inside, Kayden's notebook rested on the windowsill. I knew that when he returned to it, he would write about ghosts and gardens, about third-floor windows, and the girl who had once belonged to dusk.

And I would write too. One seed. One breath. One sunrise. At last, all mine.

Epilogue

THE KEEPER, FEBRUARY 12

I wrote the final line just before sunrise.

The words had waited, not only throughout this journey, but through every sleepless night that brought me here. Nights spent pacing in unfamiliar hotel rooms, nights filled with silence I once mistook for peace.

They endured through winter storms and blinking cursors, through half-empty cups of tea and the kind of quiet that felt like vanishing.

But this morning, she was still asleep beside me, and the sun was already rising.

Isabelle murmured something, half-dream, and shifted beneath the quilt we had stitched from old curtains and what suspiciously felt like hope. Her skin caught the light like gold leaf, luminous and tender beneath the touch of a sun that seemed to have only just remembered her.

The kettle hissed in the kitchen, and a breeze stirred the lavender outside, its scent following me in through the window.

I carried my tea to the desk, where the manuscript lay open, the ribbon pressed against the final page. It smelled faintly of ink, salt, and rosemary—our past woven into every line. I touched the edge of the paper, half-afraid it might vanish, needing the weight of my hand to keep it real.

Outside the window, Isabelle stepped barefoot into the garden, her hair tousled from sleep and her skin warmed by the sunlight. She lifted her face to the sun, her eyes closed. This time, the shadows did not claim her. Instead, she bloomed, radiant and unbroken, as the morning wrapped around her, completely hers.

I watched her—not as a man clinging to a miracle, but as one who had stepped out of the grave with her, breathing only because she did. I had followed her into silence, into darkness, into the very mouth of death, and now I would follow her into every morning that was still to come.

Turning my eyes away from the woman who had given me my life back, I clicked my pen and wrote the final line: *She no longer died at sunrise, and neither did I.*

I once mistook silence for peace,
but it was only your absence.
A room without your breath,
a life without your touch.

Now the light falls across your skin,
and the world begins again.

You lift your face to the sun,
and I remember the grave,
I remember the dark,
but neither holds me anymore,
because you are here.

I write your name into the morning.
The page does not vanish.
The ink does not fade.
You no longer die at sunrise,
and neither do I.

The End

Enjoyed Spirit of the Dying Flower?

If Spirit of the Dying Flower stayed with you long
after the last page, I would be so grateful if you left
a review. Your words help more readers discover this
story, and help indie authors like me continue crafting
tender, haunting, and hopeful books about love, loss,
and starting again.

Leave a review at https://www.amazon.com/dp/B0C
WB69TBX

https://www.goodreads.com/book/show/240494475
-spirit-of-the-dying-flower

Thank you from the bottom of my heart for reading.
Your support truly means the world.

Acknowledgements

This book would not exist without the people who carried me when I couldn't carry it alone.

To my amazing Executive Assistant, Jessica, thank you for helping me keep my head on straight. You make it possible for me to keep this thing going.

To my incredible PA, Aly Dust, thank you for being a creative force and a constant source of support.

To my brother, Heath Barker, your thoughtful beta reads, encouragement, and belief in me gave this story new life when I needed it most. Thank you for reminding me to keep going.

To my super supportive Street Team, your enthusiasm, love, and loyalty made all the difference. You were the wind at my back through every draft.

To my husband, children, and family, thank you for your patience, love, and for understanding that writing a book means sometimes living in another world.

To my readers, thank you for returning to the page, for believing in haunted girls and broken curses, and for holding space in your hearts for stories like this.
This book was a labor of love through one of the hardest seasons of my life. Fighting neurological Lyme disease and tick-borne Bartonella made every chapter feel like a mountain, but I didn't climb it alone. Because of all of you, *Spirit of the Dying Flower* is finally blooming.
From the bottom of my heart, thank you.
XOXO, Cherie

Crown of the Phoenix Series

Crown of the Phoenix

Crown of the Exiled

Crown of the Prophecy

Mate of the Phoenix

Shadowed by Prophecy

Shadowed by the Veil (Coming Soon)

My Alien Mate Series

My Alien Protector

My Alien Rescuer (coming soon!)

Other World Series

The Other World

The Other Key

The Other Fate

Hazel Watson Mystery Series

Kindred Spirits: Prequel

The Sapphire Necklace

Justice for the Slain

Whispers from the Swamp

Crossroads of Death

The Spirit Collector

The Darkness that Follows (Coming Soon)

The Cursed Waters Duet

Song of Death

Goddess of Death

Survivor & Savior Duet

Saving Scarlett

Keeping Caroline

Standalones

Second Chance with Santa

When Everly Saved Emerald Hollow (Coming Soon with
A.A. Weaver)

Spirit of the Dying Flower

The Gladiatrix & the Fallen Son (Coming Soon)

Wings of the Forgotten (Coming Soon with J. Paige)

About the author

Born and raised in the heart of Louisiana's Cajun Country, I'm a passionate writer of dark, fantasy, paranormal, and even alien romances—if there's a romance involved, chances are I've written it. My stories are filled with mystery, magic, and intense emotional connections that keep readers on the edge of their seats.

When I'm not writing, you'll find me creating special editions of my books packed with all the bells and whistles—character art, exclusive swag, and more for my readers to treasure. I love connecting with fans, whether it's through my TikTok shop, my website, or in person at events where I can share the stories I pour my heart into.

A proud mother and new grandmother, I've faced many challenges in life, including a battle with chronic Lyme disease, but I've never let it define me. Writing is my escape and my passion, and with the support of my amazing assistant Jessica, my husband Trevor, and my daughters, Arianna and Brianna, I'm living my dream of writing full-time. Even my two youngest sisters pitch in, helping me with various tasks for the business—it's truly a family affair!

At home in the coastal region of Mississippi, surrounded by love, laughter, and inspiration, I'm never without my two Shih Tzus, Charlie and Luna, along with my three mischievous cats—Ramses, Simba, and Cookie. Whether I'm doting on my furry companions, reading, or soaking up family time, every moment is a precious one.

Join me as I continue to create worlds full of romance, adventure, and unforgettable characters that you won't want to put down!